ONE SAVAGE KNIGHT

A DEMON KNIGHTS NOVEL

HOLLY ROBERDS

BOOKS BY HOLLY ROBERDS

Book 5 - End Game

* For recommended reading order, visit www.hollyroberds.com

ONE SAVAGE KNIGHT

Fear pounds through me every time I approach the man in room #526.

But I put on my big girl panties, and deal because I'm a nurse and helping people is all that matters.

I moved across country to a hell mouth with my fiancé who then dumped me. But I found a new job, got a new apartment, and the new me isn't going to be cowed down by some big, scary guy.

Even if he is becoming more monster than man.

Leonidas is chained up in our research hospital for everyone's safety, since he's been infected by a demon.

This man has no last name, no past, but plenty of secrets. He insists he's a Knight of the Light, with powers to fight the forces of darkness, and we are holding him captive.

But I can't let him go, he needs help. The sickness is changing him, turning him into something dark and dangerous.

Then when the demon who infected Leonidas escapes and starts razing a bloody path through the hospital, I have only this knight to rely on if we want to get out alive.

From the world of The Five Orders, comes a series of stand-alones tales featuring the Knights of the Light.

One Savage Knight *can be read as a standalone.*

THANK YOU READER!

When I'm not writing, I'm hanging out with my reader group, Holly's Hellions, on Facebook, posting hilariously inappropriate memes, as well as sharing teasers and sneak peeks of my current WIP.

I'm also active on Instagram and love my IG reader fam.

Enjoy this steamy, action-packed urban fantasy romance!

Dear family and friends. Thank you for your support.
That being said, this book isn't for you.
Seriously, back away. Don't make this weird.
…mother, put the book down.

1

———

BETSY

He's just a man. Nothing to fear. Just like the rest of my patients, I tried to reason with myself.

Sure. He's a man like a shark is just a fish. Like a machete is just a butter knife. Like glitter paint is just "okay."

False. Glitter paint is everything, and the man I was about to see wasn't anything like the others. The rest of my patients didn't require chains.

My footsteps echoed down the long corridor, and I tried to slow my heart to match their rhythm.

"Hiya Nurse Morningstar." The heavyset guard with kind eyes and a Spanish accent greeted me.

"Hello Diego. How are Loretta and the kids?" I was grateful for a quick chat. Maybe I'd get my pulse under control before seeing him.

You are strong. You are fierce. You are a nurse. You are Wonder Woman.

If she was about to wet her scrubs...

"Little Gabriella turns five on Sunday." Diego smiled. "My wife has been searching for the perfect piñata."

Despite our easy banter, my heart pounded in my chest with increasing persistence and a message that would not be ignored.

Turn back. Turn back. Turn back.

I'd only been working at this research hospital for a month, but Dr. Sterling moved me to this wing a week ago. I'd never heard of the Miskatonic Institute for Deeper Insight, but a doctor I bonded with at the last clinic referred me when she found out I needed to leave in a hurry. The new work differed greatly from my experience. I wasn't privy to certain information about the treatments, which made it difficult to know if I was doing my job as well as I could.

And if this morning was any sign, things wouldn't get easier around here.

My stomach soured at the memory of losing a patient only hours ago. A thick patina of sadness and guilt at not being able to save him engulfed my feelings. I should have done more. The way he gripped my arms so tightly, begging me not to give him the sedative. His death wrapped around my neck like a noose.

Not for the first time, I wondered what my life would have been like if I'd stayed in Montana instead of moving to Colorado. To the very place where a hell mouth opened, unleashing all manner of monsters and dark spirits of untold evil onto Earth.

Whatever possessed me to do something so stupid?

Oh right. I'd done it for a man.

My hand tightened around my medical bag. The mere thought of my ex, and the dull ache in my chest I usually ignored expanded.

I wrestled the heartbreak back into the decoupaged box I kept in the depths of my heart. I'd covered it in pictures of the sad orphan animals from those Sarah McLachlan commercials, Billie Eilish lyrics, and broken heart emojis.

Diego handed over the clipboard so I could sign my name and the time. My eyes flicked to the door where my patient waited, and I flip-flopped right back over into anticipation.

I wiped at the sweat gathering on my brow and tried to come back to the present moment. "I'll be sure to bring your daughter a gift."

Diego chuckled, suddenly self-conscious. "You don't need to do that."

"Nonsense. What is she into?" A million ideas swept through my brain, pulling me away from my anxiety about what was behind door number one, or my lingering heartbreak.

I'd love any opportunity to make someone a cake, but Diego and Loretta likely had that under control. I could knit a blanket for his daughter. One with a unicorn on it.

Where a normal person's brain would have shut off, mine continued to race, planning the coming activities.

Knitting a blanket wouldn't fill the upcoming off-days from work, but I had been meaning to try making those epoxy tumbler mugs.

If I was really lucky, I'd get called in for overtime.

God, Bets, it's been a dour enough scene here. Why would you be in such a hurry to come back?

The voice in my head suspiciously sounded like one of my sisters.

"Gabi's into geology." When Diego laughed this time, he removed his security cap to smooth a hand over his shaved scalp. "The number of rocks she's picked up off the ground and brought home is impressive. It won't be long before I'll need to call in to work because I've been a victim to a rockslide."

A genuine smile broke through my apprehension. "Wonderful, sounds like my kind of girl."

I'd swing by a gem store and see if I couldn't fashion a pretty crystal necklace for her. And a bracelet to go with it. Oh, maybe a couple bracelets, and a hair barrette.

Okay, maybe it was time to seek Crafters Anonymous. I might have a problem.

"Last year, her birthday was cancelled. So, we are really aiming to make this one a humdinger." The resignation in his voice spoke to the calamity we'd all been exposed to.

The entire world had changed since hell on Earth arrived on a big red carpet a year ago. Another dimension, called the Stygian, had opened and released monsters onto our plane.

Sure, we all adapted. Learned not to go out after sunset, carried weapons in our purses, and traveled in groups.

Social media circulated several ways to defend oneself against flesh-eating pixies, hellhounds, and the occasional giant demon overlord. But we were all still in an experimental phase, and the human numbers were slowly but steadily dropping.

Which was why the research at this hospital was so important. When I came on board the research hospital, Dr. Sterling explained to me that a fraction of the demonic entities could infect humans. One patient became inexplicably sick after being possessed. Another got sprayed with some kind of demon secretion and suffered wild hallucinations. The Miskatonic Institute for Deeper Insight dedicated itself to understanding these new ailments.

After leaving the last hospital in such a hurry to get away

from my ex, I was grateful to end up in a place that was dedicated to helping those affected by the supernatural.

Diego's expression clouded as he peered over my shoulder. "Where is your escort?"

I looked back too, though I knew no one was coming. "It's just me today." Pulling my badge off my lapel. With a swipe, the card reader beeped and turned green. The heavy metal door's first lock opened with a ker-chunk.

Diego sobered. "Is that wise, Betsy?"

My spine straightened. "He is a patient who requires care. I can certainly handle one patient." A bold confidence filled me. I almost believed it would last.

"Well, I have to guard the door and can't go in with you. It's not my place to say, but—"

"I'm sorry, Diego, but I'm overdue as it is. Could you please open the door?" I hated the chastising tone I took with him, but sometimes it was necessary to be taken seriously.

Diego shrugged and opened the steel door for me, and I gave him a thankful nod as I walked through.

As he closed it behind me, the tiny hairs on my body rose like needles.

A presence filled the room, pressing on me as if he were right next to me, breathing down my neck.

I was a baby goat in a lion's cage. But there was no turning back now.

2

BETSY

The dim ceiling lights added to the oppressive vibe of the room. The bright light of the full moon filtered in through a barred two-by-three-foot window at the top of the far wall.

Cast in shadow, a figure stood at the center of the cell. Long, shaggy hair hung from his downcast head and arms strung up by chains on either side, shackles locked around his ankles. He looked less like a patient and more like a prisoner. It seemed barbaric, but I reminded myself it was for his own safety and mine.

Circular spiderweb cracks marred the concrete walls. I wondered, not for the first time, if they were from the impact of his fists or from the bodies of the many nurses and doctors before me.

Patient #526 was... difficult.

When the infection was at its height, he'd explode into violent episodes that nearly cost some their lives. A doctor almost had both his arms torn off before they subdued the patient. And here I was, with no backup, ready to administer the drugs patient #526 abhorred.

Do you want to get pounded or are you just stupid? Get out of here!

Based on the heat of rising arousal in my body, stupid was definitely the answer.

Readjusting my grip on the bag I held, I swallowed hard over a throat dry as a week-old crumb cake.

"You're late," came the drawl of a low, near growl.

A concrete ledge jutted out of the wall by the door. I set my case down there and went about extracting the necessary vials, along with two syringes. "Yes, well, it's been a busy day." Then I paused. "We lost a patient."

Sweet shitake mushrooms. Was I out of my mind? I shouldn't have told him that. It was a complete breach of professionalism. But he pushed me off balance, and things just slipped out around him like a marble on a Slip 'N Slide covered in jelly.

"An infected patient?" he asked. His tone skated along a dangerous edge.

My movements slowed to control the slight tremor in my hands.

When I turned back, the shaggy head cocked to the side. "Like me?"

"No," I rushed to say. "The doctor believes you'll be better in no time."

Ever so slowly he rose, coming to his full height. "Liar."

The moonlight hit his face. Fierce, masculine features were arranged in his usual scowl. His eyes flashed silver, evidence of his infection.

It was almost a shock to be in the same room with such a virile specimen. Long wild hair, and a powerful build at six foot six, he was more muscle than man. The thick beard only intensified his untamed power.

He wore loose gray pants, and no shirt. It took near

herculean level of effort not to stare at his massive pectorals. Though it was freezing in here, the patient's temperature ran hotter than a normal human's.

Strung up in chains like this, looming over me, it ironically felt like he had all the power.

"I am not a liar, and I take it as a personal offense to be accused as one."

A beat passed before he responded, as if he were assessing me. "You certainly aren't like the other bastards who run the place."

I bristled. "I'll also not tolerate any cursing."

A slow grin pulled at his lips.

"You do that because you know I don't like it," I said flatly.

"Has anyone told you your cheeks turn pink when you're outraged?" Amusement sparked in his eyes.

Before I could stop myself, my hands flew up to touch my hot face. Then I snapped them down to my sides. "I don't get outraged."

"Offended? Riled?" His voice dropped to an octave so low I felt the vibration between my legs. "Excited?"

My mouth opened, then closed.

"You didn't bring an escort this time," he said, looking around the room as if expecting to see guards emerge from the shadows. "Do you think that's wise?" His tone assured me it wasn't.

"As I said, it's been a very busy day. I told them I could handle this myself."

A dark smirk pulled the corners of his lips. That and the deep scar running through his eyebrow gave him a feral appearance. Sometimes he reminded me more of a beast. I could easily see him swinging on vines through the jungle or fighting lions barehanded.

Switching to my professional, nurse voice, I asked, "How are your symptoms today?" I pulled out my work tablet to record his answer.

"Leonidas."

"What?" I looked up at the hanging man.

"How are your symptoms today, Leonidas?" he said as if explaining to a child. "I figure we know each well enough now that you could start using my name."

When they brought him in, Leonidas claimed he didn't have a surname. And there were no fingerprint or dental records to help us out. He was a mystery. One I secretly wanted to know more about.

Stop it, Betsy, you are a professional.

He interrupted my guilty thoughts. "I want to hear you say it. Say my name." Again, his words penetrated my core, leaving a trembling excitement in its wake.

My fingers tightened around the tablet. I licked my lips before I spoke, forcing ice into my tone. "Are you going to make things hard? I thought we had an agreement. I'd continue to administer your treatments, as long as you wouldn't give me trouble."

He leaned forward, and I had to keep myself from backing up.

A scarred eyebrow rose. "I only agreed to not rip you to pieces. I never said I wouldn't be trouble."

There it was again. A dangerous, salacious implication under his words.

For whatever reason, I was the only one he tolerated. The rest of the doctors and nurses, he growled and snapped at.

Despite the new restraints, he still managed to knock back several of them onto their ass or scare them half to death. He even broke someone's nose with a well-timed head butt.

He'd fought them at every turn over the injections... until I came along.

The first time they sent me in, he snarled and lunged at me like everyone else. I simply set the syringes down and patiently waited for him to be done. Though he scared me with his unhinged beastliness, I never let it show for a minute. After twenty minutes, his rage had ebbed enough to ask my name. I told him he could call me, "Nurse-not-putting-up-with-your-malarkey."

The burst of laughter that had come out of him seemed to surprise even him.

When he appeared more settled, I approached him with the syringes. My hands had been slicked with sweat. Sure enough, as soon as I got close, he jerked against the chains as if he meant to hit me.

But I'd heard about him and his outbursts, and I prepared. I pulled out a small spray bottle from my pocket and spritzed him right in the face.

He spasmed and reared back. "What the hell was that?" More stunned than angry.

I innocently blinked at the bottle. "Just water."

When his scarred brows drew dark over his eyes again, I threw up my hands and said, "Well, if you're set on acting like an animal, I'll treat you like one. Now take your medicine like a respectable patient, or next time I'll roll up a newspaper." I had wondered at that moment if I didn't have a death wish. But instead of going ballistic, he'd just raised an eyebrow and let me inject him without another word.

After that, I was the only person allowed to treat him. He swore he'd rip off appendages the next time if they sent anyone else. No one protested. Now, I was solely responsible for his treatment.

Even though he mostly cooperated with me, I could never forget he could turn on me at any moment. And the pure testosterone of his powerful being reminded me of that every second. I was acutely aware in this space that Leonidas was a predator, and I was the prey.

Thinking back on that day, I couldn't keep from asking, "Why me, anyway? The rest of the staff want to help you as much as I do."

His half-smile was as humorless as it was piteous. "I assure you, they do not." Then he studied me with close attention. "Maybe it's because of your eyes."

Before I could ask what was different about them, Leonidas inhaled deeply and shut his eyes. He tugged at the chains, testing them. The rattle of metal ringing into my bones. "Or maybe it's your intoxicating scent. What are you wearing today, legs? Roses and… chocolate?"

I did my best to ignore the nickname he'd given me, though it affected me more than I could say.

"I don't wear perfume," I said, while typing a few notes. "It can aggravate some patients. But I always keep fresh-cut roses in the kitchen, and I may have done a bit of baking last night." I paused. "Brownies."

He inhaled deeply a second time, on a low guttural growl. "Not brownies. Cake. Triple chocolate fudge cake."

A shiver raced down my spine. I clutched the tablet to my chest.

"Looks like your senses are still enhanced." I jotted down a few more quick notes. "Any more episodes today?"

Silence stretched between us, and I suddenly felt on dangerous ground. As if the question was too personal. Or maybe it was because he guessed I already knew the answer.

He was under constant supervision, cameras perched up in the corners of the room for observation. I just needed to keep tabs on his mental acuity, like if he started losing time, or hallucinating.

The longer it took for him to answer, the longer it would take for me to get home to that bubble bath I'd promised myself.

No, no bubble bath tonight. I'd volunteered to help get the blood drive set up early the next morning. And my neighbor, Martin, fed my cat all week while I took this extra shift. I planned on staying up late to make him an apple pie, his favorite.

Provoking Leonidas was a bad idea. The worst idea, in fact, so I simply waited him out. It had been a long day and my heart was heavy from the death I'd witnessed. But when it came to caring for my wards, my patience knew no bounds.

"Three," he finally answered. "Three episodes, as you call them." He ground out the words with extreme prejudice.

I nodded and made one last note before sticking the pad back into my coat. It was important to make sure the patient was cognizant of his symptoms. Leonidas suffered from seizures, violent fits, and abnormal muscular swelling.

"Nurse Morningstar." His lips and tongue wrapped around my name in a way that spoke of danger, or desire. Perhaps a little of both.

Goosebumps raised along my skin as I reached for the syringes. Suddenly, the space between us seemed very short indeed.

"I want to trust you," he said.

"Of course you can trust me," I assured him, while preparing his injections. The first was a sedative to control his episodes, and the other was the experimental drug prescribed by Dr. Sterling. "I'm here to help you."

"What if I told you, you have to let me go?"

I turned toward him. "That's not a good idea... Leonidas." I paused before using his name. Again, I wished I had a formal last name to address him by. "Not only is your quarantine for your own safety, but it's a matter of public safety."

He expelled a discontented huff. "I'm not infected with anything. I was tracking the creature and about to send it back to hell when we were both tranquilized and brought here."

He'd never talked like this to me before. I set down the medicines to face him fully. "I read the report. But it seems you don't remember the demon infecting you. You showed signs of supernatural irregularity. And we are working on getting you back to normal."

"Supernatural irregularity," he echoed. Hot impatience flashed over his features, turning him into a savage creature for a moment. "There's no irregularity. As I've said, I was about to take down the demon when they stopped me. The powers they saw me exhibit are natural to me. You people have only just learned the demonic exists, but I'm one of the few who were chosen at birth to learn to wield the light. A war between light and dark has been raging since the beginning of time. I've been fighting these things my entire life and keeping me locked away isn't doing anyone any good."

"Leonidas... Leo," I said in a softer tone. "Try not to get worked up, or you might trigger another episode." I made sure not to sound patronizing. I'd heard him mention these delusions before, and I feared his infection would make him lose his grip on reality over time.

"I didn't have episodes before being brought to this

place. That's what I'm trying to tell you." Violence still balanced on the edge of his tone, as he shifted his weight to one leg.

Despite his intent to intimidate me, I met his eye and said, "I know. That's why we are helping you. You developed the infection quickly after you were recovered. And we are doing all we can to get you healthy and back to your home."

With more confidence than I felt, I grabbed the first syringe and crossed the distance to Leonidas.

As I drew near, one side of his lips curved up and a scarred eyebrow arched with wicked promise. "I have never been normal, and I don't have a home."

The sense of being exposed struck me, but it had more to do with not being used to a man towering over me. As a tall woman, there were few who did. As I neared Leonidas, his masculine scent washed over me. The spice of virile man and fresh pine trees. The essence did things to my knees— turned them into rubber.

Nonsense, you are a capable nurse and he is a patient.

I flung the impure thoughts from my head like a pro shot-putter and straightened my spine.

As soon as my fingers touched his neck, Leo jerked. He lunged at me with a feral growl. Though my stomach leapt in surprise, I forced myself to calmly take a step back. "Are you quite done now?"

A dark, throaty chuckle filled the room. "This is why they keep sending you to me. You aren't afraid of the big bad man."

My fingers gently probed along the side of his neck, searching for the jugular vein.

Leonidas let out a male hum of approval at my touch. His face so close to mine, fear and excitement raced each other up and down my body. "Why is that?"

"Why is what?" I completely lost track of what he asked me. The heat of him permeated my skin, while that purely masculine scent rolled off him.

"Why aren't you afraid of me?" Those silver eyes flashed.

Meeting his intense gaze, I said, "Because I am more interested in helping you than wasting time on fear."

The air between us thickened. Understanding sparked in his eyes. Taking care of people around me was more important than anything else. His stance relaxed.

I didn't know how I knew, but we were suspended at that moment, joined by some unspoken bond. Everything fell away until it was just him and me. Leonidas saw to the core of me with that piercing gaze.

The sudden intimacy grew unbearable, and I broke eye contact. I did my best to assume my professional demeanor again, but I felt shaken.

"Do we have time for a sponge bath today, legs?" The suggestion in his voice was unmistakable. His fingers reached up to stroke at the chains.

I pierced his vein with the needle. Leonidas gritted his teeth with a hiss as I pushed the plunger. The sedative.

Then I stepped back to retrieve the second syringe. "Not today, I'm afraid." My tone snapped like a cold rubber band.

Patients often made passes at me. Many said they did it because they'd never seen a tall blonde as built as me, but I knew it was sport that kept them entertained in their sickbeds. It was nothing I wasn't used to handling. And I knew how to put them back in their place.

Though this wild man caused my stomach to flip like an acrobat after drinking twenty energy drinks, I was a professional care provider.

As I plunged the medicine into his neck, I accidentally met his eye. They flashed light silver. Evidence of his infection. I'd seen the before pictures. When he'd come in, they were a complex hazel, golden brown at the center, turning into a mossy green at the edges. But now an unnatural metallic sheen had all but swallowed up the warmth of their original color.

"I'm sorry." The words escaped my mouth before I even knew what they meant.

The question of "why" entered his eye before he convulsed. The chains strained and shook as Leonidas jerked. I stumbled back, out of reach as he growled, and the silver sheen fully engulfed the whites of his eyes.

My hand hovered over the door handle, bag already under my arm. There was nothing I could do to ease his pain as he endured the effects of the medicine. It inevitably would trigger one of his episodes. Dr. Sterling assured me the reaction was to be expected.

Yet, I couldn't force myself to leave. Normally, my armed escort would usher me out of the room, but no one was here to make me go.

Instead, I dropped the bag back on the counter and retreated to the corner to watch. Arms folded tightly against my chest, I stayed with Leonidas as he jerked, growled, and frothed at the mouth. The sedative should have lessened the effects, but Leonidas thrashed, seeming in more pain than I'd ever seen before.

His muscles began to bulge, and the metal chains on his wrists and legs groaned.

I'd watched the footage of his reaction to the experimental treatment and his episodes, but seeing it up close was enough to make me question everything I knew about the human body.

Ten minutes later, he sagged against the restraints.

"Do you really think I'm getting better?" he rasped.

I opened my mouth, then closed it.

Doctor Sterling insisted Leonidas was on his way to recovery, but the more I administered the experimental drugs, the more volatile he became. I had to agree with him —it didn't seem his condition was improving at all.

I wasn't even allowed to know what was in his injections, which bothered me a great deal. All the treatments were stocked in a fridge and labelled with each patient's name, but I had no clue to the contents. I was only to administer and observe. Occasionally, I was directed to adjust the dose, but the doctor made those calls.

Whenever I brought up my concerns to Dr. Sterling, she made a point to remind me I was new here, and I needed to respect the delicacy of the situation, dealing with sickness originating from another dimension. And she never failed to bring up she was the one with the medical degree. If I wanted to be part of something important, I needed to follow her lead and do what was asked of me.

Instead of answering, I pulled a fresh cloth from my bag and crossed over to him. I wiped the sweat from his brow and hairline.

Without looking up, he said, "You stayed."

Though he couldn't see me, I shrugged. "Didn't have anywhere to be just now."

Ever so slowly, he lifted his head as if it took all his strength. "I don't belong in here. You need to let me out."

My heart thumped double time at his raw plea.

"Doctor Sterling is doing everything to help you and get you back on your feet," I repeated, trying to reassure myself as much as him.

With a slight shake of his head, his fierce gaze pinned me through the hair hanging in his eyes. "No. She is doing something to me." For once, confidence drained from his voice, replaced with hesitance and fear. "Something unnatural. I can feel it. She's making me sicker."

The door unlocked, then opened to reveal Diego. I jumped back, hiding the cloth behind my back like a child being caught doing something naughty.

The guard frowned. "You okay, Betsy? You've been in here a long time. I got worried."

"Betsy." Leonidas said it in a low growl, as if experimentally rolling my name around in his mouth. He shuffled back into the shadows, taking the word with him.

"I'm fine, Diego. Simply observing my patient."

Diego nodded, but kept a wary eye on Leonidas, who'd dropped his head back down. "Best to get comfortable, Leo. No one will be available to re-situate you for a couple of hours. It's busy around here and we are short-staffed."

I frowned. "You mean, you are going to keep him strung up like this?"

Diego shrugged. "It's a two-man job, nurse."

Before he finished his sentence, I rolled up the sleeves of my lab coat. "Well, I see two people here, don't you?"

Diego shook his head, eyes wide, as if terrified by the prospect. "No offense, Betsy, but you aren't trained for this."

I'd had enough of people telling me about my limitations today. "The sooner we get this done, the sooner you can go home to Loretta and the kids."

Diego eyed Leonidas, then me, as if weighing the danger of the situation.

"The man is clearly exhausted." I swept an arm at Leonidas, who still sagged against the chains. "It's highly unlikely he will undergo another episode in the time it'll take us to get him comfortable."

I saw the moment Diego lost the fight with himself. I did

my best to cover up my smile of satisfaction. Today had been hard. I needed a win.

With a brief tutorial on how the restraints worked, Diego directed me to help him with Leonidas. When we released a cable, Leonidas would be lowered, and we'd need to catch him and move over to the bed. He'd still be restrained by chains, but he could walk around more freely. Not tied up like some sacrificial animal.

As soon as I unlocked the cable on my side, after Diego, the chains slid with a sound rattle, and Leonidas dropped, arms landing on our shoulders. The man weighed a ton, but I was no wilting flower. Despite the chill of the room, his body was surprisingly hot as he leaned against me. Then I realized his eyes were open, trained right on me. Shock jerked through me as he seemed to see through me to my soul. My knees threatened to turn to Jell-O again.

Red lights and blaring sirens went off. For a split second, I'd thought it was my brain reacting to Leonidas's unerring stare and warm touch. But no, the institute had gone on full alert, which meant one of two things. There was either a contaminant or a subject loose. Or worse. Both.

3

―――――

LEONIDAS

A burst of adrenaline shot through my veins at the cacophony of light and sound. But in an instant, it ebbed away. My body, exhausted from whatever Betsy had just given me, sucked the energy up like a greedy child until I was drained again.

Both Betsy and the guard stilled. Diego cursed under his breath. I lolled my head in Betsy's direction. My nose ended up nestled in the blonde strands of her hair and wonderful, tempting smells engulfed me. They inspired a spark in my nether regions.

"What's wrong?" I whispered in her ear. It was as if someone had poured acid down my throat. Lightning seemed to be stuck in my head, continually shocking my brain with white-hot bolts. The need to close my eyes and curl up in a ball was overwhelming. Instead, I embraced the pain, allowing it to become part of my experience. Neither good nor bad, they were simply sensations. The equanimity I gained allowed me a sliver of awareness I didn't have a moment ago.

Under my arm, a shiver vibrated through Betsy's body. Was she afraid of me?

"I— I don't know." Uncertainty laced Betsy's tone. I could smell the fear now emanating from her, and I wanted to hold her closer until she felt safe again.

Diego's voice was as clipped as his movements. "We need to reposition him so I can get out there and see what's going on."

They worked faster, setting me on the bare, thin cot. At least the bedding was like that of the temple.

Both Diego and Betsy kept looking over their shoulders toward the door, as if sensing some danger approaching. They didn't realize it only slowed them down. When performing a task or duty, it was of utmost importance to give it your full attention until completed. Never look back.

Betsy's hair swept across my bare chest as she reached for the cables under the cot, attached to the concrete floor.

She was a distraction. My pain-addled brain rolled with thoughts of all the delicious ways I could replace her fear with other, stronger emotions.

A crash broke through the screaming sirens. All our attentions jerked to the door. This time, human screams joined the alarms. More crashes and gunfire.

Another lightning bolt struck the front of my brain and I cried out. I dug my palm into the burning in my skull. The metal of my chains creaked as I strained them with a pained cry of my own.

A metallic liquid coated my tongue, and hot wet blood covered my hands. No, not hands, talons. My vision turned crimson, and I was no longer in my cell, or hospital room, as they called it. Leathery wings flapped behind me with powerful strokes as I hunted. People screamed and scrambled to get away. With a slash of my claws, red spattered the white lab coats.

The blood lust and urge to kill was overwhelming. They all must die. Hot pellets accompanied an annoying rat-a-tat smashed against my thick hide. Dropping to the ground and whipping around, the spikes on the end of my wings caught the gunman across the throat. With a gurgle, his hands flew up in a futile attempt to staunch the spurting life force.

Satisfaction and horror rioted inside me for dominance as I continued to kill my way through the hallway.

Someone yelled my name, and it hit me with the full force of a slap. My eyes snapped open, and I was back in my hospital cell.

What in the gods' names was that?

Betsy's face hovered over mine, her expression filled with concern and worry. Some of the pain had ebbed, but I was still as weak as a worm. My arms were free now and only my feet were chained to the floor.

The floor shook with vibrations. More blood-curdling screams.

"Stay in here. Don't come out until I get you," Diego directed Betsy. The guard unholstered his gun, but I knew it wasn't enough. I opened my mouth to warn him not to go, but in a moment, he'd swung open the door and shut it behind him with a resounding bang.

Betsy paced the room, a frustrated expression on her face.

"You have to let me out, Betsy. We need to go."

Closing her eyes, she took a deep, even breath. "No, Diego said he would come back for us. We are safe as long as we are in here. Nothing can get through that door."

I rose to my feet, albeit unsteadily, but I got Betsy's attention. She had to turn her head upward to meet my gaze. Her lips parted in awe.

"We aren't safe in here," I said.

Betsy's phone buzzed. She fumbled to pull it out of her pocket. Eyes darted back and forth as she read a message. A strange look overcame her. Like she'd disconnected from reality to spiral inward.

"What is it?"

Betsy's gaze jerked up to meet mine. "They're instructing us to clear the institute."

It was the only solution. Get everyone out. What was coming didn't care about steel doors, or nurses who smelled of chocolate and roses.

"And they're saying to leave the subjects behind," she finished.

My legs gave out on me as another bolt of sizzling pain shot through my head. More blood, more cries of terror, and the stench of death surrounded me.

Then Betsy was there, kneeling before me. She'd guided me to sit back on the cot.

My palm dug into my left eye as I pressed for any modicum of relief. "You need to get away from me."

A smirk pulled at the side of her lips. "I can handle you." The screams were closer this time. Too close. Her smile wiped away as she stood.

A violent smack against the door had us turn to find Diego's face plastered against the small viewing window. The man's wide eyes were sightless. He slid down, a streak of red left in his wake.

Betsy gasped and covered her mouth. "Oh god."

"You have orders. You need to follow them," I urged.

Betsy's brows furrowed. "You want me to leave you here?"

"Orders are orders," I said.

An undecipherable expression crossed her face. "Yes, well, sometimes the orders are wrong." She dropped to her knees, reaching for the chain. Diego had taught her how to wield my constraints, and in almost no time, she had them undone.

Gently pushing her to the side, I moved to the door. I glanced out the window. Bodies slumped along the hall, blood pooled on the ground and smeared across the walls.

Curiosity flooded me, and I realized it wasn't mine. My vision flashed to red, and I was suddenly outside, looking at the door. The bearded face in the door's window sent a riot of emotions through me.

For a moment, I was both staring at the creature and at myself. While everyone else had been prey to this monster, it regarded me as an equal. As it assessed me through the window, something pulsated between us. I didn't like it. The darkness of the Stygian, the pure hatred inside me, grew. I needed to sever the connection, so I pushed back against it until it snapped.

Betsy's hand reached for the knob. I grabbed her wrist and dragged her away from the small window. I drew her into a crouch in the room's corner.

"It's just outside," I whispered.

Betsy's eyes widened, and the smell of her fear intensified. The part of me connected to the beast, reveled in the scent. It was both sour and sweet.

"But it can't get in here." She matched my low tone.

The door was solid steel. It didn't matter. Nothing would keep out the creature. I felt its power as if it were my own. I knew the intensity of its singular focus. In that last second of our connection, it had identified me as another apex predator. An adversary to be destroyed so it could remain at the top.

"We need a different way out," I said.

Betsy's head swiveled, searching the room. "How? Neither of us can fit out that little window, even if we could break the glass." Panic skated along her voice as she neared hysteria.

Perhaps it was the drugs coursing through my veins, or the fact our death waited outside, but I reached forward and pushed her blonde hair back behind her ear. I drew strength from her softness, and knew though I was weak from the sedatives, I had to try.

I got up onto one knee and touched my hands in a triangle. Closing my eyes, I went inward as I chanted.

"What are you doing?" Betsy whispered.

As I chanted, I sensed the approach of the monster just outside. I couldn't afford to stop.

The words continued to fall out of my mouth, but I did not feel the spark.

Something rammed against the door and Betsy yelped.

I scraped the bottom of my internal well and found... nothing.

The words came faster as I forced myself deeper into my trance. I might be weakened, but I reminded myself this is what I'd trained for, since as long as I could remember.

Still, it did not come. I couldn't shake the leaden heaviness around my muscles or mind. The sedatives were potent enough to keep me from seizing, and also strong enough to keep me detached from my power. It was how they'd trapped me here for so long.

Another ram and the metal shrieked in protest. The door wouldn't last long. I had to jolt myself. A needed another wave of adrenaline to fight off the drugs.

I turned and grabbed Betsy, slanting my mouth over her soft lips. Energy exploded inside me as my tongue met hers, and I found she tasted far more delicious than she smelled. All my senses embraced the feel of her breasts pressed against my chest, and the dip of her lower back as I held her to me. Betsy's fingers curled around my arms and my cock hardened. Heat and desire muscled their way past the numbness. My senses were at attention, willing to do anything to sink deeper into the nurse against me.

Then, as quickly as I pulled Betsy to me, I released her. There was no time to focus on those swollen lips and mussed hair that beckoned me back.

Magic sparked at my core, and I went into action. My hands formed a triangle again as words tumbled over each other, gathering, building, stacking on top of each other, making a tidal wave of power.

Steel continued to bend and scream as the beast outside hammered its way through.

There. The spark ignited inside me. Warmth grew between my palms.

"Leonidas," Betsy said in warning behind me.

I focused on the power they had taught me to wield. But it wasn't like before. The light inside me was unsteady.

"Leonidas," Betsy repeated, her voice more insistent this time.

Light surged out of my hands as I opened a portal. Space split in front of me, surrounded by crackling energy. It was too dark to see where it led, but anywhere was likely safer than here. No longer needing to chant, my jaw clenched as I tried to hold onto the power.

"Leo!" Betsy screamed.

My eyes snapped open. The door curled down from the top as if it were a banana peel. Massive black talons bent the metal of the door back, blood dripping off the tips streaking down the door. Red, hate-filled eyes glared from a face of dry flesh stretched taut against bone. An inky blue tongue shot out from a mouth that opened up down the monster's neck, down to his chest, splitting it where the heart should be. Sharp fangs lined the vertical edges of its mouth.

A long, muscled arm swept out as it struck lightning fast.

I grabbed Betsy, pulling her back just as those claws raked across her midriff. She screamed in pain. The monster's enormous leathery wings could not fit through the opening, stopping it short for a moment. I had no time to think. Holding Betsy against me, I barrel-rolled both of us through the portal.

As we went through, the beast smashed down the rest of the door, lunging after us. But I wielded the magic by a thin thread. I let it break and the portal crumpled behind us.

Before I could find out where I'd transported us, I sucked in a lungful of water, and a fresh burst of panic exploded in my mind.

There was no telling what body of water we were in, or how deep I'd sent us. Death may claim us after all.

4

BETSY

I broke the surface with a desperate, choking gasp for air. My vision blurred from oxygen deprivation. The water froze the marrow in my bones.

After I'd coughed and sputtered most of the murky, putrid liquid out of my lungs, I blinked a couple of times. Once I cleared my senses, I inhaled the strong rot of algae and goose feces.

The full moon was out, a bright shining coin against a dark sky. Thankfully, the clouds had parted so I could make out the trees bathed in silver light off to my left. The cuts on my torso stung, while my heart cried at the impossible distance to land.

I knew I needed to keep swimming or the pain and shock of all that just happened would wind around me like serpents and drag me back down.

As I swam, weighed by waterlogged sneakers, I kept my eyes set on my destination. I had tunnel vision until I felt mud under my hands and feet. After clawing my way out of the lake, flattening a patch of reeds, I collapsed. I spent another several minutes coughing and puking my brains out, trying to dispel as much water from my lungs as I could.

Something heavy splatted next to me. Icy mud droplets exploded against my face. I jerked back from the onslaught, my adrenaline managing one last desperate spike. My nerves felt as raw as a lump of bright red ground beef. They settled a fraction when I realized Leonidas was the object who collided to the ground by me.

Mimicking my previous bout of coughing and vomiting, he cleared his lungs. Too cold and tired to move, I remained on my side, watching him.

The last vestiges of summer had given way to autumn weeks ago. While the days were still warm, the nights had chilled the lake. Hypothermia was a very real danger after our plunge in the frigid water.

Familiar sirens wailed in the distance. We were still on property of the Miskatonic Institute. Every day I drove by a sizable lake on my way up the long winding road up a hill where the institute sat atop. We were likely a half mile from the building containing the raging beast.

Leo's eyes found mine, and we shared a silent moment of respite, lying in the mud.

Soon my relief at being alive gave way to the million questions racing through my mind.

"What was that?" I finally spoke, my voice was raspy from vomiting up water.

Leonidas took a couple more clearing breaths before answering. His unerring gaze locked onto me. "It's the creature I was hunting when your doctor had me captured. Surely you knew what they kept in that institute." His tone held biting recrimination.

"I know what that was. There was a picture in your file of the demon who infected you. They kept it contained for research, to help aid in your cure. I'm asking how were we in the building one second, and under water the next?"

"Part of my supernatural irregularity." He grimaced.

When I was about to ask him to explain, a sharp gasp came out instead as a fresh wave of pain stabbed my torso.

My arms instantly pressed against my stomach. I didn't want to pull them away or look. I clenched my eyes shut against the pain. I only opened them again when Leonidas got to his feet.

Was he leaving me here? After all, he viewed me as one of his captors.

"Let me see," he said in a gentle, coaxing voice.

My arms pressed tighter against my stomach. I knew I should assess the severity of my wound, but pure fear replaced my insides. Paralyzed by the prospect of escaping the creature only to find my guts were hanging out, I remained in a tight ball.

Leo laid a large hand on my arm. "Just a quick peek. On the count of three."

He sent me a reassuring look that was far too effective.

"One," he counted with a nod of his head, touching my other arm as well as the first.

"Two." I nodded along with him, my nose stinging with unshed tears.

"Three," he said, and I allowed him to pull my arms away so he could see my gashed stomach.

I sucked in a breath as cool air hit the exposed flesh, and the sting of my cuts turned up the volume on my pain. After a few mere seconds, I pressed my arms back down. Tears leaked out of the corners of my eyes, more from stress and fear.

"Good girl," Leo said, still talking in that calming croon. "It's only a flesh wound. You'll be alright."

The beast who'd been locked in a cell had a soft side, and it positively bewildered me.

A surprised squeak escaped me, as powerful arms lifted me up. No one had held me in their arms like this since I was a child. But in Leonidas' well-muscled arms, I was vulnerable, delicate, and feminine.

Once I'd hit the six-foot marker on my nineteenth birthday, delicate was a word expunged from my vocabulary. I could manage grace, but I was never delicate. But cradled in Leo's arms, I felt revered and cared for like a much-treasured queen.

In this case, a queen shivering like a drowned rat as I endeavored to apply pressure to the cut on my stomach that was likely growing ten different infections.

When our eyes locked, a spark of excitement leapt inside me, along with that same heat he inspired. I swallowed hard. Leo searched my face as if unsure about something. Whatever he was calculating, he resolved it and started toward the line of pine trees.

"What are you doing?" I asked through chattering teeth. The cold of the water bit at me mercilessly, but his body was oh so warm.

"Getting you help."

"What about the creature? The others trapped in the building?"

His face hardened. "It's too late for them."

I couldn't swallow past the lump in my throat. My shivering intensified. The already faint sirens all but disappeared as Leo walked us deeper into the dense woods.

The million questions I had tripped over themselves in my brain until they were tangled in an incoherent mess. Numbness spread throughout me and instead of fighting it, I leaned into Leo and let him carry me. Never in my memory had I so surrendered to anyone else. But I trusted him.

Nonsense. Trust builds over time. You don't know him at all. You are simply too worn out to care.

Despite my imposing logic, I couldn't fight back the pleasant feeling of security growing at the center of my chest as he carried me. Ear pressed against his warm skin, I let my fears drift away on the steady beat of his heart.

At last, we emerged from the tree line next to a main road. I didn't know how long he'd been walking, but I'd finally regained some of my strength.

"You can put me down now." Even as I said it, part of me regretted it.

Okay, all of me was reluctant to be let down.

Leo walked alongside the asphalt, one side of his mouth curving up. "I could, but I'm not going to."

"You really don't have to carry me. I know I'm... big."

The smile faltered as he lifted a brow, as if amused. "You are not big."

"Yes, I am," I protested. "It can't be easy carrying me. Let me down. You need your strength, too." I wiggled to get out of his arms, but he tightened them around me.

"You aren't big," he corrected me again. "You are a tall, gorgeous woman with the longest legs I've ever had the pleasure of ogling, but you are not big. And I have the strength to carry gorgeous leggy women to the ends of the Earth if need be."

Oh my.

If he were anyone else in any other situation, I'd give him a verbal whiplashing for objectifying my long legs, while denying what was certainly a truth about my size. But lord help me. When it came from the savage man who saved me from a creature from hell, I all but purred in response.

Pull it together, Betsy.

Blinding light cut our conversation off. An oversized black truck pulled over a few feet in front of us. Bright yellow words stenciled along the side of the vehicle identified the driver as "Neighborhood Watch."

Since hell spilled onto our plane, communities grew tighter as they worked to protect their own. Neighborhood Watches became forces unto themselves and regularly patrolled their assigned quadrants, ready to lend a hand to anyone in trouble.

Shovels, rope, a first-aid kit the size of a suitcase filled the back of the truck. And, of course, a locked gun rack loaded with several weapons. A sizable barrel labeled 'salt' sat next to the rack. Maybe there was something to the *salt as demon repellent* rumors.

The face of a black man in his mid-forties leaned over toward the open passenger window. "Y'all need help?"

"Yes, the young lady needs medical attention," Leo said without hesitation.

The man jumped out of his car and raced around to get the side door for us. The radio on his hip crackled with chatter. Neighborhood Watch was no joke.

Though by the conspicuous lack of ambulances and cops, no one had gotten word outside the institute that a demon escaped. With my phone back in the building, I couldn't do anything to help either. Hopefully, this man would call someone, or let me use his phone once I explained.

"The name's Montrell. And there's an urgent care not far from here. I can get you there in a jiff."

Leo slid me into the seat with ease, but I still had to bite back the moan of pain as my body shifted. I couldn't bring myself to pull my arms away from my stomach.

The door slammed shut. My gaze jerked up to Leo's in surprise. "Aren't you coming?"

The truck was oversized, and Leo could have fit in the back. He ignored me, shaking Montrell's hand with both of his. "Thank you for your help, friend. I have somewhere to be, but I trust you'll get her there safely."

Then, without another word, Leo turned and walked back into the woods.

I swallowed back my protest. Montrell paused as if he were going to call out to him, but seemed to think better of it.

After all we went through, he just left? My brain could not make sense of it even as Montrell started up the engine and drove off.

Laying my head back against the seat, I wondered why it mattered so much to me that Leonidas left.

My nurse intellect kicked in. What would I tell any other patient?

You've been through an incredibly traumatic event, your workplace turned into a bloodbath and the people you know are likely all dead. And Leonidas is the only one to share your experience. Of course you want to stay near him. It's reasonable psychology.

Not to mention, he still needed help too. Would he be okay on his own? Or would his episodes worsen until...

I tightened my grip against my stomach, trying not to think about it. There was nothing I could do as Montrell drove us away.

5

—

BETSY

Leo was right. My cut wasn't too deep, though it stung like crazy. It wasn't anything some stitches and a bandage couldn't fix. And to my intense relief, my bloodwork came back normal. The fear of incurring a demonic infection chewed me up while I waited for results. But the doctor assured me they would discharge me within hours.

Montrell hung around the lobby until he was sure I'd be alright, but not before leaving a card in case I needed him for anything else. The man was an absolute saint, and I swore I'd find a proper way to thank him. Even if that meant baking him enough cookies to eat from here to the moon.

The pain of my wounds paled in comparison to my discomfort at being on this side of the clipboard. It was always strange receiving medical care. As a nurse myself, I always felt like a bother, and had to suppress the urge to jump up and help.

When the police came and took my statement, I had to cover my face and work through sobs threatening to break me as I explained what happened to Diego. Poor Loretta. I couldn't even think of his girls. Not to mention the rest of my co-workers.

When I asked when the officers would check out the building to help any survivors, the two men exchanged a look.

No. They wouldn't. The police could only take care of so much. After dark, with the situation I described, they weren't equipped to help.

The institute sat on a generous span of land, surrounded only by woods for miles. The most the police would do was put out an alert to any people living or working in the surrounding areas. Doors and windows would be locked up tight tonight.

This was a matter for the supernatural task force. A new, specialized branch of security trained for such situations. But they were new and stretched thin.

The officers advised me to go home and rest. They would follow up with more information as they got it.

When they asked how I got out of the building, something stopped me from telling them the whole truth. Maybe because I worried I was going crazy, but in the bigger scheme, why wouldn't a man be able to open a portal to another place? After all, there were demons running amok.

God, a person could go nuts trying to grasp all the new rules that demolished the old way of living.

It was only a year ago that a dimensional rift opened in Colorado for a short period, unleashing all kinds of hellish beasts before someone closed it back up again. Only the barest details were disclosed via the news. It appeared they knew very little about how all this transpired, adding to the paranoia.

But everyone quickly realized things wouldn't ever go back to normal with so many creatures running free-range, spreading across the globe. But now there were secret, magic-wielding, demon-fighting warriors.

Still, I kept Leonidas's portal power out of the conversation.

The hours passed in a blur, and it felt like I'd lived not one but two lifetimes since that morning. When I finally stepped outside the hospital into the crisp night air, the noise fell away and I could think again.

After jamming my own soggy, ripped attire into a trash bin, I convinced a nurse to lend me a pair of scrubs. We met a few months ago, volunteering at the same soup kitchen in downtown Denver. When I explained that for my sanity, I needed to get in some clothes and get some fresh air, she made magic happen. Note to self: knit her a scarf in her favorite color, purple.

As I stood outside in the dark, waiting for my ride, I shut my eyes and sucked in a big gulp of clean mountain air. The backs of my eyes and nose stung as the chill of being utterly alone wrapped around me.

I longed for my sisters back in Montana, but I didn't want to wake them up for nothing. I also didn't have it in me to hash over what just happened again without a week of sleep and ten gallons of hot chocolate to soothe over my wounded bits, both inside and outside.

Why, god, had I moved to Colorado, away from all my friends and family?

Okay, I knew why. And I pushed away the answer as soon as his face popped up in my mind's eye.

No need to pour salt on my open wounds.

"Are you alright?" A voice came from the darkness somewhere to my right.

Empty of all adrenaline, I didn't even jump. If the creature appeared in front of me, he could slice me to ribbons and I wouldn't even have flinched. I was too dang tired.

Instead of the living nightmare, Leonidas took a step out of the bushes. The hospital light cut across half his face, but he came no closer.

"What are you doing over there?" I asked. My voice sounded far away to my own ears. I was detaching, likely still experiencing shock.

"Are you alright?" he repeated, his words rougher this time. His silver eyes flashed.

"Yes. They stitched me up." My hand drifted to the bandage wrapped around my waist under my shirt.

Leonidas's shoulders dropped a few inches, as if some tension fell off him.

I was about to point out he needed medical attention, too. Without his treatments, he would only worsen. But as the words were about to come out, people exited the hospital behind me, drawing my attention. When I looked back, Leonidas had disappeared.

"Leo," I whispered into the darkness, once the people had gone.

My gaze traveled up, and I noticed a camera. Had he been avoiding it?

Why? How had he gotten us out of the research hospital like he did? With that portal thingy? Was it a side effect of his infection?

No, that couldn't be it. He was so deliberate, the way he dropped to a knee and chanted.

Was he actually a demon? I immediately flicked that idea out the window. Leonidas was all man. If the bone-tingling feminine response I had around him wasn't enough, I certainly had the medical proof to be sure. So who and what was he?

I rubbed my arms, goosebumps rising on them.

A forest-green Subaru drove up. A man in his mid-sixties wearing a pork-pie hat jumped out. "Oh my gosh, Betsy. Are you okay?"

"I'm so sorry to call you, Martin. But there was no one else."

My neighbor waved off the apology. Even though his lips were downturned in a concerned frown, smile lines reassuringly framed his eyes. "Don't give it a second thought. And for heaven's sake, get inside. It's freezing out here."

Ever the gentleman, my neighbor opened the car door for me. It was then I noticed he wore loafers and a coat over his plaid pajamas. He'd wasted no time coming to my rescue. What a dear man.

As I got in the car, I said, "If it's not enough that I ask you to feed my cat when I'm working long hours, now I'm waking you up in the middle of the night."

"Hush now," he said. "I get all the benefits of having a pet without fuzzing up my apartment. And lord knows you supply me with enough pies, knit sweaters, and casseroles to keep me warm through any winter. I don't know how you manage all that between working and the volunteer work you do."

I smiled, but nothing he ever said could assuage my guilt over the late-night pickup, or help with my cat. But I was too selfish to give up the cat I adopted when I moved to Denver.

As we pulled away from the hospital, I searched for Leonidas, but saw nothing.

My fingers touched the cold glass, as Martin switched on a soothing jazz station and expounded on how glad he was that I called him. I'd told him there was an incident at work, but I couldn't tell him much more than that per my nondisclosure agreement with the hospital. But I knew he wouldn't push. He was probably the only one I knew who wouldn't.

A dark figure moved along the roof of the hospital. There was no way that could be Leonidas. He couldn't scale buildings in a matter of minutes.

Could he?

Who knew what he was capable of, infected by the demon who nearly killed us. Leonidas had changed, and no one was there to help him. He needed medicine, care, and...

You? my brain mocked.

I swallowed. I wanted to help him.

Despite assuring myself he'd gone with the wind, one question swirled around me with untamed hope. Would I see him again?

6

LEONIDAS

I watched the older man drive Betsy away with my enhanced vision. My ability to see in darkness and distance far surpassed what I remembered.

The parking lot lights illuminated the pads of her fingers pressed against the glass and something in my stomach jerked inside my gut. I wanted to follow them. Make sure she got home safe.

Just as the urge had pulled me to follow Montrell, feeling instant regret at leaving Betsy with a stranger. Though I meant to return to the institute, my feet had turned in the direction of his taillights. True to his word, the urgent care wasn't far. Still, I couldn't leave until I saw her one more time. Make sure she was fine.

Was it because I owed the nurse a debt for freeing me, defying the orders of her superiors? Or was it because there was something magnetic about her that kept pulling me back in?

I'd been a captive too long. Trapped in that institute, without a reasonable one among the ranks, Betsy stood out. She carried a quality everyone else lacked in that godforsaken place. If there was a word for it, I didn't know it. But she was so very alive, warm, and there was a comfort I felt whenever she was near.

Everyone else seemed disconnected, grayed out, and stuck inside themselves. That is when they weren't pissing themselves in fear at the prospect of approaching me.

If I was to be held against my will, I would do my best to make things... difficult for them.

But the nurse with long legs, who didn't put up with my 'nonsense' as she put it... The nurse whose name I'd only recently learned, turned the world from monochrome to bright color. Her scent, her sharp wit, even the way she chewed on the inside of her cheek, was bewitching.

Something fluttered under my breast every time the door opened, as I anticipated her return. When Betsy stepped inside, new life swept through me, along with many other emotions. A few of them curled and stiffened below my waist.

Though Betsy went about her job with precision and professionalism, the transparency of her emotions moved me. She cared about what she did, and my well-being mattered to her. I could see it in her eyes, in her every touch. To everyone else, I was simply a job to be shot up, studied, and groomed as if I were some animal. To Betsy, she would nurse me back to health, even if it meant she had to bleed herself to do it.

Reason kicked in. Of course I felt the need to make sure she was alright. I was simply returning the courtesy she'd bestowed to me. But our dalliance had ended.

The nurse didn't matter. All that mattered was slaying the creature. Time to return to the Miskatonic Institute to retrieve my weapon. I shouldn't even have taken the time to follow Betsy to make sure she was safe, but I couldn't keep myself from doing so.

I needed to finish my mission before I could return to the temple and report to my master. A knight of the light didn't return until the job was done.

I maneuvered back down the building, avoiding all cameras along the way, making my way toward the woods.

Some of my strength returned as the sedatives wore off and the run through the woods got my blood hot and pumping again.

Directing my sights to the south, I started back toward the institute.

Pain exploded inside of me.

My eyes clenched shut against the sensations wracking me. I found myself on my knees in the dirt, gasping for breath as something roiled under my skin.

Two swords sliced through my back. I arched my back with a cry that resonated in the night. Somewhere in the night, a wolf howled back.

How had I not noticed anyone approach? When I twisted around to catch my killer, there was no one there. But two leathery wings flapped, wet with fresh blood. My blood. My wings.

Bones groaned and shifted inside me. I doubled over; my hands clenched into fists.

My last thought before the pain and darkness engulfed my consciousness was, *What's happening to me?*

7

BETSY

"Leo!" I screamed, bolting upright.

The nightmare released me from its inky tendrils as I realized I'd fallen asleep on my couch, sewing. Fred Astaire and Ginger Rogers were still tap dancing their way into love on the TV, so I hadn't been asleep long.

With a quick glance at the clock, I saw it was four a.m. I dragged my hand over my face, trying to rub away the fatigue and stress. I picked up the half-finished costume. My sister Hallie asked if I'd make Halloween costumes for the twins. And then when I said yes, of course, Rebecca said my nieces would be heartbroken if her aunt didn't make her one too. Though it was still a couple weeks away, it didn't help when my sisters kept calling, telling me their kids changed their minds about what they wanted to dress up as. At this rate, I'd have to pay overnight shipping to get them to my family in time for Halloween.

It wasn't unusual for me to be up in the wee hours of the morning. I rarely got over three or four hours of sleep, but after the night I'd had, it would have been nice if my brain powered down for longer after the traumatizing day.

I considered grabbing one of the precious sleep aid pills I used when I really needed to make sure I recharged, but decided against it. The prospect of picking back up with the nightmares where the monster slashed Leonidas's throat was enough to have me up and running for a caffeine fix.

Meow.

"It's okay, Bubbles. It was just a bad dream," I assured my cat as I set the kettle on the stovetop.

Bubbles perched atop the kitchen island. The white, fluffy ragdoll cat shot me a skeptical look from her one good eye. The other was completely scarred over.

I collapsed on the couch again. My hands lightly touched my stomach. The painkillers dulled the pain, but the mere memory of those sharp, monstrous claws and my breath turned quick and shallow.

Bubbles leapt from the counter and trotted over to the couch before leaping up next to me. She stepped onto my legs before settling down in my lap, forcing me to pay attention to the fluff ball instead of spiraling in my mind. I swore sometimes that my cat was an intuitive healer.

Bubbles rubbed her head against me. Her purrs sent soothing vibrations into my body. With a sigh, I laid my head back and focused on the silken texture of Bubbles' soft fur. Tension slid from my shoulders, but the uneasy feeling in my gut refused to unwind.

Maybe I should tell them I couldn't help at the blood drive this morning?

No, Betsy. You said you would help. And flaking out is not an option.

My tablet vibrated from where it was perched on the coffee table. My phone and purse were still at the institute, and I'd work on getting them tomorrow... or I guess, today. In the meantime, I could get by with email on my tablet and use the emergency credit cards I kept in a lockbox.

It was an email from my sister, Adie. She wasn't much of a sleeper either. Especially since she'd gotten pregnant.

"Can you send me your new address? I have something I need to send to you."

I typed it in and sent it to her. Moving from Colorado Springs to Denver happened in such a brief span of time, even I hadn't adjusted. I'd only been in this apartment a month, but anyone would think I'd been here a couple years the way it exploded with all my craft supplies and book collection.

My ex never appreciated the precarious piles of potential I kept around the apartment. At least now I didn't have to feel guilty about my mess, living alone.

"Have you heard from Jeremy lately?"

My fingers hovered over the keys, unsure what to write back. The uneasy feeling in my gut churned double time. She knew Jeremy and I were over, but she somehow made it seem like it was my fault, and I could just wave a hand and patch things up with him.

The need to explain he broke up with me, for the twentieth time, quickly disappeared.

I understood why she kept hoping for it to magically get better.

Adie had married Jeremy's brother, and the four of us had been friends for as long as I could remember. Both she and her husband were in denial the foursome was broken.

I played the conversation in my mind before it even happened.

If I wrote I hadn't heard from Jeremy, she'd insist that I

reach out to him. I should ask if he needed anything. Since he was so busy at his new job, he could barely feed himself.

If I mentioned I had to transfer hospitals to get away from Jeremy and I had my own thing going on, she would say that men weren't as tough as women. That as soon as I made him another one of my pull-apart cinnamon breads, the wedding would be back on.

As I volleyed the phantom conversation in my mind, the energy sapped from my limbs. This was exactly why I didn't run back to Montana after the breakup. I was still trying to find my footing. Though I filled my days with so much activity, I had yet to put a toe on the ground.

Perhaps I should tell her I was too busy to think of Jeremy. I was too busy escaping a demonic creature with a He-Man type who made my knees Jell-O and my pulse race.

Bubbles jerked up to her feet, head tilted as if listening intently.

"What's wrong, Bubs?" I set the tablet down without responding.

Bubbles' head snapped to look out the window this time. I redoubled my petting to calm her, but she leapt from my lap and raced away to the bedroom, likely to hide under my bed. She wasn't easily spooked, but I knew better than to chase after her.

Bang.

My body slid to the far side of the couch, away from the sound in a blink. Hand pressed over my pounding heart, the slam of something against my window came again. The blinds were down to my patio where the ruckus currently shook the French door.

"Holy schnikes," I breathed.

What were the odds of being attacked twice in one

night? Far too good. Especially with hell beasts running loose.

But when I'd moved into an apartment by myself two months ago, alone for the first time, I'd taken precautions.

Reaching under the couch, I pulled out a rifle. With one last glance in the direction where Bubbles disappeared, I both regretted not adopting a guard dog at the same time I considered hiding under the bed alongside my cat.

But no, I knew how to wield the firearm in my hands. Montana girls knew how to hunt, even if it wasn't their favorite pastime.

A heart-stopping thwack directly landed against the glass door this time. With a big inhale, I grabbed the wand for the blinds and twisted.

As soon as I saw the cause of all the noise, I set the gun down and hurried to open the door. I had to carefully do so as Leonidas was on the ground, slumped against it.

Red-tinged clouds spiraled up through the purple sky as dawn neared. The tea kettle screamed in the kitchen.

Leonidas stared up at me with red-rimmed eyes, desperation shining out of them.

"What did you do to me?" Then he collapsed, out cold.

8

———

LEONIDAS

I woke up to the smell of something baking, something with spices. Before I could place where I was, I rolled over in the soft bed and stuck my nose in the pillow, deeply inhaling a scent more delicious than any spice.

Betsy. I was in Nurse Betsy's bed. My growl of appreciation vibrated into the pillow. An expanse of colorful florals covered the plush comforter wrapped around me. The small bedroom filled with sunshine, intensifying the warmth of the cheerful yellow walls. Across from me a tall bookshelf burst with novels of men without their shirts, along with a number of medical texts. Along the wall, even more books stacked up in precariously tall towers.

In the gap between the bed and the wall, I discovered a staggering number of pillows. They were all colorful, woven, puff balls.

But the closet drew my eye. Something massive, white and puffy was sticking out of it, keeping the door from closing. It appeared to be a dress of some kind, but it was larger than any kind I'd ever seen a woman wear. I'd only seen Betsy in her nurse's uniform.

When I got to my feet, soreness stretched through my body accompanied by fractured memories of last night. The fleeting luxury of waking up in Betsy's bed went up in cinders as reality set in. On instinct, I reached back to feel for any wings but found nothing there.

My pants were tattered at the knee and split in places around the thigh as if I'd nearly broken them off. I'd transformed. Into something else. Something wrong, dark, and monstrous. Revulsion and fear wound their way around me as I tried to make sense of what happened.

I had little to no recollection, and only vaguely recalled finding my way to Betsy before passing out.

Anger and suspicion flared up in me. What had those people done to me? What had Betsy done to me? The leggy nurse with the seductive mouth seemed like an angel, but now I suspected her of devilry.

She claimed they were trying to heal me. No matter how many times I tried to explain my powers were natural and I'd gained mastery of them when I was child. But turning into an actual demon? The nurse with nice legs and sparkling eyes had to know what she was doing. I was a fool to be taken in by her. The lies stopped now.

Making my way down the hallway I found Betsy pulling a pan out of the oven. For a brief moment, all my fears evaporated as I took in the nurse in her natural habitat. Barefoot, humming a tune, with her hair fastened up in a messy bun, the woman did things to me. My blood ran hotter. She wore a white tank top and overalls that were rolled up at her ankles.

The apartment was bursting with color and textures. Yarns, paints, and cooking pans covered all the surfaces. There was so much... life in here, surrounding this one woman, the center of the colorful vortex.

It was the polar opposite of the institute and from the temple where I was raised. I was used to cold, empty stone passageways and spartan rooms. Objects were only present if they were an absolute necessity.

When she turned around, placing the pan on the kitchen island, her eyebrows shot up. "Oh, you're awake." Shucking the oven mitts, she hurried over. "Your vitals were stable last night, and you insisted I not take you to a hospital... not that they'd know what to do with you anyway. Only the institute was equipped for your infection." She pressed her fingers against my neck while consulting her watch.

The vortex of color, comfort, and oh gods, the smell of her skin continued to draw me in.

No matter how inviting Betsy was to my senses, I needed to remember who she worked for. The institute that had captured me and held me prisoner.

I took hold of her wrist, pulling her fingers away from my pulse. "What did you do to me?"

Confusion flashed over her eyes. "What do you mean?"

I tightened my grip on her wrist, grabbing hold of my anger and directing it where it belonged. At her. "The drugs you gave me. They've done something to me, changed the way I am. Last night I changed into... something else."

"Something else?" She didn't understand. I dragged her up against my body as anger shot through me.

"A monster." My words came out low, dangerous. Our faces were inches apart, so I bared my teeth at her. I wanted her to be afraid. People and demons who were afraid made mistakes. If she was hiding something, I'd back her into a corner until her secrets fell out at my feet.

Her eyes turned round. Fear and confusion wafted off her in powerful waves along with something sweeter... darker...

"Do I need to rip this pretty arm off, so you'll tell me what you've done to me?"

Perhaps she'd even known what I was all along, a knight of the light, a warrior chosen to fight the darkness. Master Violetta warned me to never get involved with civilians. They taught us at the temple to only rely on the word of our masters and on ourselves when we were in the field. But everything had gone so wrong.

Betsy attempted to wrench her arm out of my grip, but I only held her tighter against my body. Where I was hard, she was soft, and it inspired all manner of animal instincts inside me. Some violent, and others... As if she could read my thoughts, her eyes first widened in shock, then they narrowed. "I haven't done anything to you, apart from try to help. And what do you mean, you changed into a monster?"

"Maybe I should fucking show you," I growled, my nose running up along the creamy column of her neck.

Not that I knew how to replicate last night's occurrence, but I bet it had something to do with following the instincts pounding through me. Something dark and dangerous lurked in the depths of my being now.

If she didn't comply, I'd use more persuasive tactics. Though between the thick smell of cinnamon emanating from her skin and her damp brow from the hot kitchen, the type of persuasion I wanted to use was unorthodox at best.

Giving into my urge, I snaked out a tongue, for one long lick. Oh gods, she tasted like sweet sin. My core shuddered and I hardened.

Betsy pulled away and the whap of something soft bopping my nose surprised me into letting her go.

"Down boy," Betsy warned, a rolled-up magazine in her raised hand, threatening a second bop.

Like the spray bottle, it more surprised than set me off.

Before I could do or say anything, Betsy's chin lifted as she spoke in a commanding tone. "No, you know what? This is ridiculous. You will not talk to me using that language. I called in sick to the blood drive I promised to help get set up this morning, so I could stay and help *you*. So, here's what is going to happen. First, you will go and get cleaned up. My shower is in there, and then"—she pointed at what used to be a table, now covered in all manner of cooking and crafting items, with three mismatched chairs— "you will come back, sit here and tell me everything. And you won't threaten or menace me while you are in my home, mister. Remember, I'm the one who could have left you behind, chained up and helpless. And then I took you into my home when you collapsed on my doorstep. Show some gratitude."

She was right. This woman had defied direct orders to free me. I was the one who returned to her for help. And I woke up safe, unharmed, and unrestrained.

Stress, confusion, and the darkness inside me were making me erratic. I trusted no one, especially not myself.

Even if she was innocent, Betsy likely knew something about what was happening, even if she didn't realize it. Perhaps the only one left.

"Fine," I groused, then pointed a finger at her. "But when I get back, you are going to tell me everything you know." My eyes slowly scanned the kitchen. "And I get to eat whatever smells like cinnamon."

I could tell from her sassy expression, she was about to spout off something smart.

I stepped into her personal space one more time. "Even if that's you."

Then I turned and went back toward her bedroom to the adjoining bath. A grin curled my lips. I wasn't truly certain if

Betsy was my ally or enemy, but I would enjoy myself in the process of finding out.

In the shower, I suppressed the urge to take my time and smell all the many soaps. When I found the strawberry one, I glopped a healthy amount all over my body. Blood rushed to my nether regions as I inhaled deeply. But there was no time to take my fresh wave of desire in hand, no matter how tempting.

When I emerged, Betsy's signature clean scent clinging to me, I observed she'd already stripped the bed sheets for cleaning. Back in the kitchen, she pulled out yet another pan of whatever delicious thing she'd baked.

The pan dropped to the counter with a surprised yelp. For a moment, I worried she'd burned herself, but her wide, frightened gaze was fastened to me. I looked down to see what alarmed her but found nothing.

"You— You're not wearing any clothes."

"Mine were destroyed past putting them back on," I explained, crossing the room to take a seat at her table. As I walked to the table, Betsy's eyes bounced back and forth from me to various points around the room as if a bird were zooming all around.

She covered her eyes, turned around, then pulled her hair. A racket of metal hitting metal sounded as she ran into a stack of baking pans of various sizes and shapes that all toppled over. Dropping to the floor, she tried to push them back against the wall, but her eyes turned back up toward me. Before she covered her face and moaned, her cheeks turned cherry red. The pans clattered back down again.

"Are you having a fit?" I inquired, while I went to sit at the table. Rolls of fabric and containers of paint and glitter covered half of the surface, but she'd cleared the space in front of two of the chairs where she'd instructed me to sit. I made myself comfortable.

"I am not having a fit. You are… naked."

"Good eye, legs. What shall you point out next? That your place clearly has been overrun by a horde of artful children?"

She snapped to her feet, fire blazing in her eyes. Then she whipped around to face away from me, yet again, with a squeak.

"What? There aren't any kids. I like crafting things." Her tone was indignant and positively adorable. I didn't bother telling her the varied textures and colors in this place comforted me. Just as she did.

Betsy disappeared back to the bathroom, then returned with a purple towel. "You can use this," she said, avoiding looking at me even as she held it out. Bright pink stained her cheeks, and she kept licking her lips.

I stared at it. "For what?"

Her eyes finally met mine as her mouth dropped open. "Okay, it's one thing to deal with patients when they're nude, but you can't just walk around my apartment without any clothes on."

"This is one of those civilian things, isn't it?" I asked, taking the towel.

"What do you mean, civilian things?" she asked, though something else clearly continued to distract her.

"During my missions around the world, hunting demons, I mainly kept off the grid, but sometimes I would have to blend in. That meant learning the eccentricities civilians abide to."

"Yes, I'm super eccentric not wanting a man I hardly know walking around my apartment naked." She waved her hand at me, while keeping her eyes on the ceiling.

I couldn't explain it, but I felt a sense of loss at her referring to me as a near stranger. She wasn't wrong, we'd only been in contact over the course of the last week. But I felt a connection to her that made it seem like our acquaintance had been much longer.

Betsy turned away after I took the towel so I could try to wrap it around my waist. However, the fabric was too small to encompass my hips without my holding it up, so I simply laid it across my lap.

"Alright, you are safe now," I assured her, though I was tempted to do away with the towel and chase her around the apartment.

What was this woman doing to me? First, I wanted to tear her to pieces, then went straight to nuzzling her, and now this. Had I lost my mind in that prison they called a hospital? Or was it Betsy that drove me to distraction?

A plate clinked down in front of me, and all thought fled. My stomach rumbled as the heavenly scents filled my nose. The pastry was nearly the size of my hand. Perfect.

Gooey cream melted off the swirly roll.

"What is it?" I asked, leaning down for another deep inhale of the heady spicy scent.

Betsy sat down next to me with her own plate, but looked up in surprise. "Cinnamon rolls. Haven't you ever had a cinnamon roll before?"

I shook my head, even as I grabbed the sticky bun and shoved half of it in my mouth. It took some doing, but I managed to smash the rest of the glorious, sugar-laden roll into my mouth. "Perhaps I can persuade the monks at home to bake such delicious confections when I return. After I complete my mission and kill the beast, of course."

"The monks?"

"Yes, the monks at my temple. They usually stick to

vegetables and whole grains, but it takes a high caloric menu to keep up my physique." I patted my hard stomach. "They took to making high caloric stews and gruels, but I must confess, I allowed myself to grow used to civilian food on missions. Unlike my brothers, I tended to bend the rules a bit more. Where it doesn't matter, of course."

Betsy's roll remained on her plate, untouched. She stared at me in wonder. "Temples? Monks? Missions? Who are you?"

Once upon a time, it was the most guarded secret. Never reveal the brotherhood, never expose the temple. But since the Stygian opened up, bringing hell on earth, priorities had shifted.

"I am a Chevalier, a knight of the light of the order of Luxis."

"What's the order of Luxis?" She bit her lip as she set her cinnamon roll on my plate.

"Thank you." It was too good to refuse. "One of the five ancient orders dedicated to protecting this earth from the forces of darkness. The Stygian. The order of Luxis is the order of light. We are chosen in the crib and then trained to wield our will to fight."

"Your will..." She trailed off as if trying to comprehend. "Fight back how?" She finally cut into her cinnamon roll with her fork.

"With our power. Only a knight of the light can wield powers unlike any mortal."

"What kind of powers?"

"You witnessed my power when I opened a portal. I am trained to fight and conquer demons of any and all kinds. We can also banish dark spirits back to the Stygian, the hell dimension, from whence they came."

"From whence they came?" she asked, her voice sounding pitchy. "Who talks like this?"

I didn't bother responding, focusing instead on sopping up the remaining icing on the plate with my bit of roll.

"And you have... brothers?" she continued.

I paused before shoving the last bite in my mouth. I didn't like to think about the boys who did not survive the trials to become knights. At the end, there were only five of us standing, and now, even less.

I finally answered. "Yes. My brother knights were also chosen and wield similar abilities. Many of them have died in the good fight, but a few have survived the great battles."

She set her fork down to rub her temples. "Why didn't you tell the doctors any of this?"

"May I have another?" I asked, pointing to the tray.

Twisting around, Betsy frowned. With a wave of her hand, she said, "Oh yes, please do. I always end up making four times what I need. Have as much as you want."

I didn't ask twice. I was up and across the room, towel floating to the floor. I scooped out one and then two more rolls onto my plate. I was about to return to the table, when I scooped out a third roll, so they were preciously balanced on my plate.

"I did tell the doctors. Doctor Sterling kept insisting I showed signs of supernatural activity which meant I'd been infected by a demon."

Betsy observed the towel on the floor, then she looked upward, pinning her gaze to the ceiling. "She didn't believe you?"

The plate hit the table a with a loud clack. Betsy jumped, still keeping her eyes on the ceiling though I was seated again. "No. The damned woman insisted I needed to be locked up for my own safety until they could do some research and help me. And you people have been experimenting on me ever since."

Though I wanted to dive into the rolls and not talk about this anymore, I leveled a stare at Betsy. "I was in there for a full two lunar cycles. The doc did something to me. Last night, I shifted into a monster, like the one I was hunting. The one that attacked you," I said, my eyes lowering to her stomach where I knew she was bandaged. I'd let her get hurt, and the feeling sliced to my core.

Her pupils expanded. As if she were drinking in every word.

This was what was different about her from everyone else at the institute. While I'd grown accustomed to being treated a certain way at the temple, and then again disregarded in my cell, Betsy engaged with me as if I were more than what I was. As if I were important. Someone worth saving.

A pink tongue moistened her lips and I was entranced by the motion. It stirred things in me. Something deep, never touched before.

"Changed how?"

My gaze still caught on her lips, I leaned in. "Large, leathery wings. Violent urges." The words came out just above a whisper, raspy.

"Then perhaps you *were* infected?" Betsy's eyes flicked back and forth from my eyes and lips. Her tone matched mine.

There was a second, unspoken conversation taking place between the two of us. My pulse quickened and suddenly I was starving. Not for more of the cinnamon rolls. No, the hunger grew in the pit of my belly the longer I stared into those crystal blue eyes and soft, pink mouth. Arousal curled through my lower belly.

"No. Whatever has happened to me, it was done to me. And you are going to help me figure out what." A forcefulness returned to my words, but it was only because I needed her to understand that she was stuck with me.

Her hands pressed against her stomach, and she bit her lip, nervousness written in every line of her face. "Can I ask you a question?"

I nodded.

"Why... why did you kiss me? When you were trying to make that portal?"

My fork cut through the roll again. Each bite was better than the last. "I needed a burst of adrenaline to overcome the sedatives and you were close by."

Her face drew down into a frown. Then she was up like a shot, banging around in the kitchen.

"Do you want some coffee?" she asked too loudly. "I need some coffee. How do you take yours? I take mine with lots of cream and sugar. I know I shouldn't, but I don't like the taste of coffee by itself."

Knock knock.

Busy making coffee and talking to herself, Betsy didn't even hear the tap at her door. So I made myself useful. Grabbing the towel again, I crossed the room. I made sure to pinch the towel around my waist so as not to offend, per her instruction.

A man slightly shorter than me stood there. He sported dark facial hair and I could instantly tell the man needed the bit of scruff for respect. He may have been muscular in his younger years, but the remnants of his strength had turned to softened bulk.

A frown darkened his face as he scanned me from head to toe with both disapproval and challenge in his dull green eyes. "Is Betsy home?"

My instincts shot up to high alert. I didn't like this man. I couldn't say why. He certainly wasn't a beast from the Stygian, but he emanated a false confidence in his posture that offended my senses. Not to mention, I didn't know what he wanted with Betsy. A feeling of possessiveness washed over me.

"Uh, hello there." The man waved his hand back and forth. "I asked if Betsy was home."

"Leo, what are you—oh." Betsy peered around me at the man. She stiffened next to me. I smelled fear and sadness waft off her. But she rolled back her shoulders and stared him down.

"Jeremy. What are you doing here?" Betsy asked.

9

———

BETSY

"Betsy, who is this?" Jeremy demanded.

With that, my new reality splintered.

My ex-fiancé seemed... smaller.

Jeremy had no problem charming all the ladies throughout medical school, but he'd made it clear I was his girl.

Until I wasn't.

Maybe it was that my former fiancé had tumbled off the pedestal I'd put him on, or maybe hanging around a stunning, muscled specimen like Leo changed my perspective.

Despite his downgrade in size, the ache under my ribs expanded at the sight of him. Rejection, sadness, and heartbreak warred for dominance. The life we led together and the future we'd planned had turned to ash. I suddenly felt two inches tall, and as vulnerable as if he were about to step on me.

I still remembered every detail when he explained why we needed to see other people next to the stack of wedding invitations. The flowery font suddenly mocked me when he said we'd been together for too long and neither of us knew what we really wanted. My hands were ice cold when he took them in his warm, dry ones. My body understood what was happening before my brain did.

He needed to focus on his fellowship at the hospital, and being tied down in a new city with a new position was distracting.

He called me a distraction, then gave me a week to find a new place and then requested I find a new hospital to work at as well.

The memories sucked me down like sticky molasses, though I faced my ex in the present.

Jeremy gestured to Leo again, expecting an answer.

Right. My eyes turned to the man next to me. Tall, packed in muscle, with a towel loosely hanging around his waist, he resembled a Norse god. His wet hair hung over his sculpted shoulders, and while he appeared relaxed, one hand holding the top of the door, the other still holding my purple bath towel, his sharp silver eyes were trained on Jeremy, surveying him as if deciding the best way to cook him. Over an open spit? Or perhaps broiled.

Waving away the strange fantasy in my mind, I brought my attention back to Jeremy.

"He's none of your business, that's who he is," I said, sounding braver than I felt. "Why are you here, Jeremy?" He should still be in Colorado Springs. There was no reason for him to drive an hour to end up here, on my doorstep.

My ex took his time looking back and forth between Leo and me, then broke out into a chuckle. "This is a joke, right?"

The blood drained from my face while my stomach flipped.

"Who is this?" Leonidas asked me.

The door to the stairwell creaked open. Just what we needed. More people in this messed-up mix.

"Her fiancé," Jeremy said without pause.

"My ex-fiancé," I corrected. He'd also been my high school sweetheart, but now he was someone who'd destroyed a life we spent almost a decade building together.

"Oh hi, Betsy. How are you feeling today?" Martin asked as he joined us in the hallway. My neighbor wore his usual pork-pie hat and was carrying reusable bags full of groceries. He paused when he saw Jeremy and Leo.

"Can we talk in private?" Jeremy asked, sending both Martin and Leo vaguely hostile glances.

"No." I crossed my arms. "Whatever you need to say, you will say right now." I didn't know how much more he could break my heart, but I wasn't willing to be cornered into it again. I didn't want to chance being alone with my feelings. At least with Leo and Martin in view, I could remember to focus on others rather than myself.

Jeremy took a deep breath, as if bracing himself. "Okay. Betsy, I made a mistake. We belong together. I want things to go back to how they used to be; you and me, in Montana."

My jaw dropped.

It was too much. After yesterday, losing a patient, being attacked by a massive demon, all my co-workers killed, and a man with superpowers banging down my door for help. Jeremy tipped me over on the scale of things I was willing to handle.

An evil spirit must have possessed me at that moment. It was the only explanation for what I did next. I said, "This is my boyfriend, Leo." Then I boldly laid a hand against those hot, washboard abs, and gave Jeremy a pointed look. The feel of his hard torso sent heat waves rocketing through my body, but I did my best to focus on the nightmare in progress.

Martin remained in the hallway. I wasn't entirely sure if it was because he wanted to make sure I was okay, or if he wanted to witness the spectacle taking place.

"This guy?" Jeremy hooked a thumb at Leo. He assessed Leo slowly but surely. Then finally he started, "Listen, Bitty—"

"Don't call me that," I snapped. I'd always hated that nickname. I never told him because he loved it so much, but I didn't owe him anything now.

Who are you? You don't talk to Jeremy like this.

I was having an out-of-body experience.

"Betsy," Jeremy said again, trying to reason with me. "We both know you're just trying to make me jealous."

It was clear from his tone and his voice that he didn't believe me. He even shot Leo an apologetic look.

A nearly naked man stood in my apartment, and Jeremy thought I was lying.

No, never mind that I was. He had no reason to believe so.

My cheeks flamed with embarrassment as my confidence waned. My hand slipped off Leo's abdomen, and I considered crawling into one of my kitchen cupboards to hide.

Martin had the decency to focus on rearranging the groceries in his arm and fish for his keys.

So absorbed in my spiral of embarrassment, I didn't notice Leo changed hands on his towel until he wrapped his nearest arm around my body. He tilted me back and pressed his lips against mine. Just like the last time, the chemistry was instant. My hands instinctually came up to his face, pressing against the beard on his cheeks. In contrast to his hot mouth and body pressed against mine, his hair rained cold droplets on my skin and chest. My nipples tightened with an instant, aching need.

When Leo released me, I still needed a second to realize I wasn't floating. As it was, my brain was as fuzzy as a heap of cotton candy.

Martin grinned and stepped forward, pushing Jeremy aside to stick out a hand. "I'm Martin. Pleased to meet you. I live next door."

Leo took my neighbor's hand in his massive paw and gave it a firm shake. "The pleasure is all mine, Martin." He even tilted his head in a gesture of genuine respect.

Meanwhile, Jeremy's face turned a lovely shade of green.

"Well, we have a busy day ahead of us," Leo said, wrapping his arm around my waist and pulling me back into my apartment. "If you'll excuse us."

Then he released the towel so he could close the door with his other hand, flashing both my ex-fiancé and my neighbor. Jeremy's eyes widened as he took in the beast between Leo's legs. Martin's whistle of awe came through the door. Apparently, he'd also been impressed.

My face had gone almost completely numb, and I couldn't think. It was almost as if I'd blacked out the moment he kissed me, and I needed to be caught up on what I'd done.

Panic crept in. Had I looked as shocked and aroused as I felt? Did I look like a dumb guppy? The disconnect between my brain and my face was disturbing. I patted my hands over my face to see if that could inform me.

"What face am I making?" I asked Leonidas.

Not bothering to pick up the towel, "A beautiful one." Despite the compliment, he said it wearing a deep frown. Leonidas almost looked... angry. A dangerous spark lurked in his eye. It was the same one I'd seen when he'd been chained up, on the verge of an episode.

Was he angry at me? For using him? Or because I was supposed to be helping him and not getting caught up with my personal life? That was likely it. He needed to get rid of Jeremy so I could focus on what the institute had done to him.

Did he call me... beautiful?

Breathe, Betsy.

"Thank you. You didn't have to go along with it, and you did. It's just when I saw him, I got so panicked, and you were there being... you." Was I babbling? I was babbling.

I smoothed back my hair, though it did nothing to cure the flaming heat in my cheeks. "Jeremy wasted nine years of my life and threw me away like I was nothing. I was afraid of what I'd do if you weren't there as a buffer."

"And what is that, exactly?" He advanced toward me, like a panther about to pounce.

Arousal and excitement hit my toes and bounced right up my body like a carnival game, resonating through my every atom.

Whoa nelly, *I'm in trouble.*

"Go back to what I've always known," I answered.

"Is that what you want?" The question came out on a near growl.

I wanted a future again, some certainty about where my life was headed. After the life we planned over the last decade went up in a puff of smoke, a barren wasteland of nothingness lay before me. And it scared the ever-loving bejeezus out of me.

If Leonidas and Martin hadn't been there, I was ashamed to say I might have considered Jeremy's offer. Just to get that future back. Just to have that certainty.

While keeping my eyes averted, I grabbed the towel off the floor and held it out to him so he could cover the monster between his legs.

He took the towel but didn't use it as I intended. Instead, he said, "We need to return to the institute. My weapon is there."

I nodded, looking anywhere but at him. "Right, of course. And I need to get your files. Get some answers about why you changed form. But you can't just walk out in the nude. Let me go pick up some clothes for you. There's a store just up the street. I'll be right back. Just sit tight." With that, I grabbed my purse and slammed the door behind me, not even bothering to grab a jacket.

Only once in the hallway did I take a deep breath. Everything was spiraling out of control and nothing made sense, from Diego's death to Jeremy showing up on my door, to the ferocious, near-naked man I'd just left in my apartment.

But trying to figure out why things happened was a waste of time, when there was plenty to do. I marched to the stairs, glad to have a mission.

10

LEONIDAS

The mission had been simple. Kill the creature.

And even after being captured and held prisoner, the mission remained the same. Kill the creature.

So why was I standing around Betsy's apartment, waiting for her to return?

Either I needed her to help me figure out why I'd transformed and how to stop it, or I wanted to make sure Jeremy didn't return. Not only did I instinctually not like him, but the urge to mark Betsy as my own in front of him had been a purely animalistic need.

As I kissed her, the word *mine* tore through my body. I wanted to possess her in every way. My heightened senses had picked up the sour anxiety clouding around her at seeing Jeremy. But when I kissed her, it transformed into a sugary, butter-rich veil that enveloped both of us. Then she'd made a breathy little moan, and her nails dug into me.

The fact I'd not ripped off her clothes and tried to take her right there at her threshold had been a feat of incredible willpower. If she hadn't left the apartment when she did, I might have lunged at her and done it anyway.

While Betsy's very skin sang to me, as well as her beautiful blue eyes, there was a darkness to my urge. I learned last night that there was a demon inside of me. And I could sense it wanted her. I could not allow that to happen.

True to her word, she was back in fifteen minutes with a bag of clothes. With a shrug, she offered the contents to me. "I hope they fit you. Um, I didn't know what kind of underwear you prefer, so I got you boxer-briefs. I hope that's okay."

I pulled on the gray sweatpants, not even opening the package she referred to. "I don't prefer any kind."

The pants stretched sufficiently, but the black shirt was tight against my chest. Betsy looked away as I dressed, but her cheeks had turned pink. Then the way she eyed my chest even after I dressed, she still seemed as uneasy as when I was nude. Her arms crossed over her breasts, and I sensed the move created an invisible barrier between us.

But I didn't have time to pull apart her eccentricities.

"I need my weapon and I need it now," I informed her again as I pulled out a pair of boots from the bag, along with some socks. The boots were only a slightly tight fit, good enough to keep on. "The creature is likely still on the loose, and I need to be armed. I'll be back." I turned to go, when I realized she trailed behind me. She ran into me when I stopped.

"What are you doing?"

"I'm coming with you."

I stepped in toward her, blocking the door. "No, you are not."

Betsy's chin set as she stared me down with a resolute

gaze. "Of course I am. I am still your nurse and therefore still in charge of your well-being."

I shook my head and spread my arms, pressing my hands into the walls of the entryway. "It's too dangerous."

"You're right," she acquiesced, looking away. Then she turned and crossed back to the living room.

I dropped my arms, no longer needing to bar her exit.

Then I watched her pull out a rifle from under her couch before pulling a box of ammo out from a coffee table drawer. She loaded the gun, stuck the rest of the ammo in her purse, and slung the firearm strap over her shoulder. "Okay, I'm ready." The way she stood, and the set of her jaw, warned me she might shoot me if I tried to prevent her from going.

I sighed. "I'm not going to convince you to stay, am I?"

"Nope."

I leered in her direction. "What if I tied you up?"

She cocked the gun with surprising swiftness and authority. "Try it."

While one part of me didn't want her out of my sight, the other part still wanted to chain her up the way she'd done to me. Though in my scenario, she wasn't wearing clothes and was subject to my every whim.

I focused on the spot over her shoulder and attempted to control my urges before they took hold of me.

With a sharp nod of my head, I conceded. "I'll make a portal and we'll be there in moments."

Betsy's eyes widened. "Last time you did that, we ended up underwater."

"I was still under the effects of the sedatives. Now that no one is pumping me full of drugs, and I'm rested, I won't make the same mistake."

I dropped to a knee and began the chant to bridge time and space.

No sooner had I spoken a couple of words than they turned to ash on my tongue. I broke into a coughing fit, now choking on the words as if they were physical objects in my throat. My palms flattened against the floor as my body wracked with violent coughs. The sacred words awakened the demon inside me, and he was angry. It was as if I'd tried to poison half of myself.

Betsy set down her rifle and was at my side, rubbing and patting my back, asking what she could do to help.

"Betsy," I gasped out, still on my hands and knees. "Get away."

She didn't move, continuing to stroke my back. I turned and yelled "Get away" again. Except this time the words came out as an inhuman snarl as my jaw unhinged, fangs elongating, cutting my lower lip.

Betsy stumbled back from where she was on her knees. As her butt hit the floor, the back of her head bounced off the table leg with a loud smack. With a wince, she grabbed the back of her head.

Her pain sobered me. I reeled in the beast fighting to get out. I had to protect Betsy. If I lost consciousness and turned into the thing I'd been hunting... Images of waking up in her apartment to a bloody mess and sightless blue eyes sprang to my mind's eye.

Instead of helping me to control the crack and shift of my bones, the shift came even faster. Pain lanced my back, right at my shoulder blades. My muscles expanded and grew.

I hadn't even registered that Betsy had run off until she returned. She dropped to her knees next to me.

"Quick, sniff this up."

She held a mortar and pestle, and held out the marbled bowl to me. I took it in both hands and shoved my nose into the white powder inside, inhaling deeply.

Another fit of wracking coughs overtook me, this time from the burning and tickling sensation in my nose. Seeing some powder left, I sniffed again. My senses dulled and my blood felt as if it were moving slower.

After giving me the bowl, Betsy backed up, but remained crouched, at eye level. The rifle was by her side.

Good girl.

Whatever she'd given me, the drugs spread out through my limbs, relaxing them. The creaking of my shifting bones stopped and the pain in my shoulders subsided slowly, but surely.

A wave of relief and exhaustion swept through me as I sat back on my heels. Betsy sat there with me for several long minutes, not saying anything, simply just being there with me, and I found it reassuring. Even though the second I started shifting, she should have been out the door.

"What was that?"

"My sleeping pills. I use them sparingly, so I had a good number of them left."

"And I needed to... snort them?"

She shrugged. "You could have swallowed them, but they'd have to cross the lining of your stomach to your bloodstream. It could take as long as thirty minutes. I got the sense we didn't have that kind of time. This way was much faster. How do you feel?"

I shut my eyes. "Slightly dizzy, but better. You stopped the change."

She sighed. "We need sedatives if we're going to keep your transformation under control. I took a major risk giving you that many pills."

I got to my feet, feeling steady enough. It was careless to come into her home. I didn't deserve to be in her apartment. Not before, and especially not now, that the darkness tainted me. I'd denied it emphatically, but now I had to concede Dr. Sterling might have been right.

I was no better than the things I fought now.

"Okay, how about this time we drive?" Betsy volunteered.

11

LEONIDAS

The ride share, as Betsy called it, dropped us off at the gates of the institute. Betsy said we'd drive her car back. It was still in the parking lot where she'd left it.

Bright yellow caution tape covered the massive wrought-iron gates of the institute.

Looking up at the drive, Betsy stuck her hands in the pockets of her sweater. "Do you think they even went inside to check things out? To see if anyone was alive?" Her voice was small. "Or did they just stick up all this tape to keep people out until the supernatural task force could come see?"

"Your law enforcers aren't equipped to handle a supernatural incident like this," I said. "But this is what I do."

As I made my way toward the door, Betsy kept pace. I stopped.

It was strange to have spent so long a time in a building, yet see it for the first time from the outside. My prison.

"You should stay here," I instructed.

Betsy rolled her shoulders back. "Absolutely not."

"It might not be safe for you in there," I insisted, taking a step closer. My height allowed me to tower over her. I found my size was a useful measure in persuading people to do what I asked.

Instead of shrinking back, Betsy stepped in even closer. The warmth of her body and scent of her skin radiated through my shirt. The urge to crush her against me and kiss her again sent fire shooting through my blood.

She narrowed her eyes. "Well then, it's a good thing I have you with me, seeing as this is what you do," she said, parroting my words.

"You'll be a distraction in there," I said, my words low and husky, unwilling to back away, though we practically shared the same breath. My gaze kept falling to that smart mouth. It invited all kinds of exploration. But now was not the time.

Her eyebrows rose with an imperious air. "Do you know where and what sedatives you'll need to get so we can keep your condition under control?" When I didn't answer, she went on in a clipped tone. "Do you know what records to look for to ascertain what's happening to you? No. We may not be in the institute anymore, but I am still a medical professional, and you are still technically my patient. So, if you'd be so kind as to escort me in so I can help the both of us, I'd very much appreciate it."

A half snort, half huff escaped my nose as I failed to come up with a sufficient answer. Irritation mingled with the lust she evoked. She was absolutely right. I needed her if I wanted answers, and a way to keep myself from changing again.

Betsy's lips curved up in a self-satisfied grin as soon as I let out the sharp exhalation, as if she knew she'd won.

Impossible woman. Still, neither of us moved away from each other. It was as if some magnetic field existed between us. The desire was becoming as inconvenient as it was maddening.

Before I knew it, my thumb reached up to brush across her lips. Betsy's smile disappeared under my touch as her eyes turned to dark pools, underlined with fear and need.

Fear of me? Fear of what she felt?

All I knew was I wasn't the only one who felt the pull. My fingers trailed across her jawbone and skimmed down her elegant neck.

"Fine. But you'll do everything I say while we are in there," I said, my fingers now tracing the bit of exposed collarbone.

Betsy sucked in a breath, and I took that to be her agreement. I took one step back, and the air rushed back into the space between us. Wasting no time, Betsy strode past me up to the front doors. I allowed her to take the lead, enjoying the view of her shapely backside with an appreciative hum.

Betsy typed in a pin to unlock the front doors. Without turning around, she asked, "Are you coming? Or are you going to stand there and stare at my ass all day?"

I got moving while suppressing a smile.

My good humor faded as we stepped through the front doors. No more sirens or flashing lights, but a foreboding filled the air. My senses cranked up to high alert as my hand itched for my battle axe that was somewhere in this building.

"We'll need key cards," Betsy said, rounding the front desk and grabbing a card. "This'll do."

"Where would they keep my weapon?"

"Your personal effects?" She looked around, seeming at a

loss. Then she snapped her fingers. "Right, there is a locker room for all that."

Excitement filled me as I anticipated being reunited with my weapon. As my only constant companion through the years, I wondered if someone else might harbor the same feelings about a friend.

It wasn't far from the front desk. She led me inside a room of shelves.

"Ha!" she cried out. "My purse." Keys jangled in her hand as she punched the air in victory. Then she dug out her phone. Her face paled when she viewed the screen.

"Bad news?" I asked.

"I missed a lot of text messages." She looked up, fear stamped in her eyes. "Like a lot. Both from my family and from Jeremy."

"Did they know your safety was compromised?" I asked.

She shook her head. "No, but there are about seventy-five missed messages. Usually, I have my phone on me and promptly respond, so I don't notice how many I get, but..."

"But?"

"But I guess I didn't realize how much I made myself available."

"Do you like being available?" I didn't have a phone. The objects seemed to be a source of both joy and great agony. I wasn't sure what her experience with the small device fell under.

She blinked as if she had never considered the question before.

"Perhaps you should ignore your phone more often until they stop calling on you so much," I suggested.

A strange look crossed her face, and her attention went back to the screen, though she typed nothing. "I couldn't do that."

She seemed to be lost in her own world, so I resumed my search.

Neatly labeled boxes full of clothes, wallets, and personal effects lined the room. My eye caught on a glint from the corner of the room. I crossed over and wrapped my hand around the handle of the battle axe.

Pulling out the weapon, power hummed through it into my hand and up my arm.

"Whoa," Betsy said, taking a step back. "That thing looks to be half my body weight."

Unable to take my eyes off my old companion, I traced the intricate glyphs along the curved double blades. "It was a gift from a Norwegian family after I saved their daughter from possession. It was the weapon of a Viking and now of a Chevalier."

"Chevalier," she repeated.

"A knight of the light," I elaborated, turning back to her and setting the axe over one shoulder.

"Chevalier is just the French word for knight," she pointed out.

I nodded. "Our faction has French origins, though I do not believe the order stayed rooted long in France itself. They don't allow the Chevalier to dig into the history of the order of Luxis. We are to focus on fighting." I examined my weapon again. "Between the age of the weapon and the faith poured into the etchings of the Celtic glyphs, this darling has power of her own."

"Her own?" Betsy raised an eyebrow and set a hand on a hip.

"Betsy, meet Sheila. Sheila meet Betsy. I'm sure you two will make fine friends." I grinned.

Betsy snorted and turned around to head back out of the locker room, but not before I caught her smiling.

Back in the hallways, I insisted on taking the lead while Betsy directed me to where she needed to go. We passed broken windows, rooms littered with debris and upturned desks. Despite the streaks of blood and the metallic stench in the air of human rot, we never crossed a body. Did the creature round back and eat all of his kills? When I'd connected to its psyche, I hadn't felt ravenous hunger. I felt rage.

Thankfully, I didn't sense the creature now.

I immediately scolded myself for finding relief in that. If the creature was here now, I could finish the job and return to my master. Betsy's safety should not overrule my need to finish my duty. The longer that evil thing roamed free, the more people would be hurt. I needed to strike the evil off the face of the earth.

"The lab is just up the hall there," Betsy pointed out with a sigh of relief. "We can get you some proper medications."

I wanted to ask her if she wanted to hold my axe, but all my senses tuned into a very present threat. My entire body reacted to the dark presence despite not knowing where it was. I grabbed Betsy as she tried to pass me. She yelped in protest, but I clamped a hand over her mouth, pulling her back flush against my chest.

"Be still," I breathed into her ear. Her soft hair tickled my nose. I didn't want to release her from against my body, even as my grip tightened on Sheila.

Betsy wrinkled her nose under my palm. Sulfur. All things from the Stygian carried the distinct stench of sulfur.

The flapping and chittering echoed faintly around us. My gaze rose upward, and Betsy's did the same. Thank the gods I still covered Betsy's mouth as I helped her suppress a shriek of fear.

All hanging upside down, leathery bat-like wings

wrapped around their bodies, the crib slept. Their bodies resembled gnarled, ghoulish babies with blue-black skin. Their long spindly arms and legs enabled them to easily pluck their prey off the ground and tear into the intestines midair.

Occasionally, one would flap or stretch their wings, chittering in their sleep.

The crib were nasty flesh-eaters. It explained why we didn't find any bodies. They must have found their way into the institute through the broken windows and feasted until dawn came. Now they were sated and sleeping off their meal.

Betsy trembled against me. She was right to be afraid. There were at least twenty of them hanging from the ceiling. I'd fought a horde of them in battle, but they were vicious, bloodthirsty creatures with fangs as sharp as their long, gnarled claws. I didn't know if I could fight them off and protect Betsy at the same time.

We needed to move quietly if we didn't want to disturb the nest. Betsy stiffened against me at the same time the hairs rose on the back of my neck.

Following her wide, frightened stare, I found one of the crib staring right back at her with dark ghoulish eyes. Anticipation raced along my veins like an electric current. There was no room for fear, only action. Fear was a certain death sentence.

"Run to the lab when I tell you," I whispered into her ear. Her trembling intensified.

"Now."

Without waiting for the crib to attack, I pushed Betsy forward and flung my axe. The crib's head flew through the air before the rest of its body collapsed in a heap on the floor.

Betsy's footsteps echoed as she raced for the lab. Shrieks reverberated against the walls as the rest of the crib awoke. A burst of rancid sulfuric winds accompanied the crib as they exploded from the ceiling.

As they did, the demon inside me awoke with a snarl.

12

BETSY

I told myself not to look back as I ran down the hall to the lab door. Even as I clutched the keycard in my hand, I feared it would slip out and fall to the floor. A cold burst of wind with a rotten egg stench swept my hair forward.

A sonorous war cry drowned out the shrieks of the winged demons. Leonidas.

Sliding to a stop in front of the lab door, I chanced a look back. My breath caught in my chest as I took in the carnage. With his long hair flying, and battle axe swinging, Leonidas in fact looked every bit like a Viking waging war. Black ichor and bits of wings sluiced through the air, slapping against the walls, ceiling, and floor.

Leonidas chopped the head of one of the flying demon babies, black blood striped across his face like war paint. One monster sunk its claws into his arm, and Leonidas cried out in pain. His silver eyes flashed with fury as he grabbed the demon, hurling it to the floor and stomping on its head with a sickening crunch.

I'd never seen pure wrath before. There was a primal

purity to Leo's rage that hit me in the marrow of my bones. Even if I wanted to go back and help him, I knew I wouldn't last two seconds.

Bodies piled at his feet as heads rolled and separated wings fluttered to the ground. A pair of dark, hate-filled eyes locked on me again as one creature targeted me. I swiped the card against the door. The lock turned green with a cheerful bing. I swung the door open and ran inside. As I slammed the door shut, a long spindly arm stuck through, keeping me from shutting it entirely.

I screamed in fury as I threw all my body weight against the door. My rifle was slung across my back, but I hoped it wouldn't come to that. Shooting in such close quarters was not ideal.

The creature was strong, bulldozing against the door. I dug my heels in, sweat covering my body as I fought the creature's brute strength with my will to live. The sole hand grabbed out, too close to my face as I continued to push my shoulder against the metal.

Something knocked into the door, so hard I almost fell.

Not wasting a moment, I redoubled my efforts to shut the door. "Not today, you monkey's behind," I screamed.

Something dripped in my eye. Blood. My head must have knocked on the door hard enough to split it. But I knew head wounds bled profusely. My eyesight hadn't gone blurry, so I was probably fine.

I envisioned pushing so hard the door sliced off the demon's arm. Yet the demon continued its side of pushing against mine, and my strength was giving way.

Eff eff effity eff. I glanced around the room again to spot anything I could bash against the flailing appendage.

My feet slid back a foot as the door parted enough for the demon to wiggle more of its arm through. If the demon got through, nothing would keep it from ripping me to shreds.

I cried out in raw fear and panic, trying to dig up all the strength inside me. The door pushed open another several inches.

My mind raced, knowing I was in the last few seconds of my life. Would my brain replay all the best parts of my life? All the worst? Instead, my mind went blank, as fear chilled me through and through.

My body lurched forward, my head smacking against the door as the resistance from the other side disappeared.

I got back on my feet—tears, sweat, and blood moistening my face. Peeking out the door, I saw Leo's muscular, ichor-spattered figure standing over the dead winged beast. His long hair obscured his face as he looked down at his kill. The screeches and flapping of wings had all but vanished. He'd killed them all.

The gun suddenly felt too heavy, and I couldn't breathe. I pulled the rifle off my back and set it against the wall for a moment. Using the backs of my hands to wipe at my face, I tried to pull it together. "Oh god, I'm so glad you are alright. You saved me." My voice had a tremor, and I desperately wanted to fall into Leo's powerful arms before I collapsed. It was the only place here that might feel safe.

"Betsy." Leo's voice came out strangled, unnatural. "The danger hasn't passed."

Swinging my head in all directions as my heart jumped, I saw nothing. "What is it?"

Leo lifted his head, meeting my gaze. Sheila lay on the floor, forgotten. Silver completely engulfed his eyes, giving his appearance an alien look. His body shook as if he were fighting the change, but fangs elongated in his mouth. "Run," he commanded.

With that, he arched his back and let out an inhuman roar. I nearly fell into a puddle at his feet. The violence struck me with all the certainty I was a cute little bunny rabbit, and he was a raging, hungry predator. Scrambling back, I went to shut the door, but a dark wing smashed into the door, sending me onto my ass.

Oh god. He was right. Dark wings had emerged from his back and his recognition seemed to vanish. The other wing flapped and hit my rifle, sending it careening across the room, far out of reach. And Sheila remained in the hall on the floor.

I was completely screwed.

In that moment, realizing I'd separated myself from my weapon, I felt as dumb as a girl who walks into a haunted house and goes straight to the bathroom to take off all her clothes for a shower.

Leo prowled forward, stomping on the dead demon, crushing its skull as his sights set on me.

"Leonidas," I pleaded, getting to my feet. "It's me. Remember who you are. This isn't you. This is the infection." My hands blindly searched the counters of the lab, trying to locate a weapon of any kind.

His canines elongated into fangs as he released another terrifying roar. Glass beakers shook against each other until they tumbled over the edge of the counters. Bloodlust shone in his silver eyes as he stalked toward me. His body jerked and trembled as if something had jumped into his body, possessing him.

Still, he approached me with singular focus. Whatever I faced now was not the man I knew. Leonidas was right. He had transformed before, and it was happening again, right before my eyes.

Leonidas stumbled as his body contorted, something

rippling under his skin as if he were undergoing a metamorphosis.

I turned and flung open the fridge door. Finding the bottle I needed, I sunk a needle into the liquid, pulling the plunger. Then, before I could let myself think, I ran at Leonidas. His hand jerked out and grabbed me by the throat at the last second. I stabbed his arm with the needle, sending the sedative flowing through his veins.

Leo snarled and growled in my face before licking up the side of my face, tasting the blood there. I trembled from my head to my toes and shut my eyes against what was about to happen. I may have hit him with a big enough dose to take down an elephant, but he could still crush my windpipe in a second.

Then his grasp loosened. Leo stumbled back, the strange roiling of his skin calming. Leo fell down, convulsing in a seizure.

Without even taking a breath, I got to my knees to turn him onto his side so he wouldn't swallow his tongue.

"It's okay, it's okay," I soothed in between coughs, not knowing at all whether it would be okay. I kept glancing at the door, fearful some other fiend would explode through there. Maybe the nightmare from last night. Still, I stroked Leo's hair until he calmed.

Something moved in the hall. My heart jumped up to my throat as I froze.

Oh god, was it more of those creepy bat babies?

I crawled over Leo's body to grab my rifle, then went back to put myself between his body and the open door.

The sound grew closer.

"Leo," I whispered. But he was out cold. Between the fight and seizure, he'd passed out. I was on my own. I tried to swallow down the lump of cold, hard fear.

Whispers bounced off the wall.

I took the safety off my rifle and cocked it.

The hushed tones cut off abruptly.

Crabapples. If the thing in the hall didn't know I was here before, it knew now.

A shadow fell across the door. Whatever was outside seemed to have many limbs and was gigantic. I fought the need to hyperventilate. Maybe if I could get the right shot in, I could take out whatever was coming.

I hoped to god that was true, because it was all I had in me.

The massive, tentacled shadow elongated and grew as the creature neared. Sweat covered my face and chest as I kept the firearm aimed at the door.

Just as the creature rounded the corner, my finger began to squeeze the trigger.

The second I met with not one but two pairs of very human eyes, I let the gun drop, but I'd squeezed off a shot. The bullet connected with the wall next to the door. A lanky man with spiky hair in a Metallica tee stood in the doorway, his green eyes the size of saucer plates. A bag dropped at his side, papers and USB sticks sliding out.

The woman next to him had near black hair, sharp Bettie Paige bangs, and a baseball bat riddled with nails settled over her shoulder. Both were armed to the gills, guns, knives, and spray bottles attached to their backs and utility belts.

The woman's gaze bounced between me, the rifle, and the man she was with. With a low whistle, she said, "Whew, two inches closer, and you'd have another hole to breathe out of, Travis."

People. They were just people. My entire body sagged in

relief as I set the gun down and ran my shaky hands back over my hair again.

The man continued to gaze at me with a mixture of shock and horror. The blood drained from his face, leaving a pale, ghastly pallor. "Whack a Ghoul. Here to clean up all your supernatural messes," he announced with a slight tremor in his voice. Then he went about shuffling all the papers and sticks back in his bag, zipping it up this time.

The woman's gaze landed on Leonidas. Something sparked in her hard, dark eyes. "Holy shit, it's Leonidas."

Could this day get any weirder?

I instantly regretted asking that question.

The two descended on Leonidas like a couple of clucking hens.

"What is he doing here?" the man asked.

"Think she did it?" She shot me a suspicious, dark-eyed look.

"Excuse me," I interrupted their private conversation. "I did not hurt him. I saved him... after he saved me." It was all very complicated, and a headache gathered with the force of a hurricane between my temples.

I'd stomached many medical procedures and emergencies over the years, but the past twenty-four hours had me ready to toss my cookies before sinking into a hot bath and then hiding in bed for at least a month. Or running home to Montana, where gun-toting neighbors did a good job cleaning up the neighborhoods and my biggest job was feeding and helping my family.

"Please move so I can check his vitals. I'm a nurse." I'd hit him with a much larger dose of sedatives than usual, and I needed to make sure he was breathing.

Thankfully, the two of them dutifully moved aside.

I pressed my fingers against his wrist. Thank god, his

pulse still beat strong. Turning him onto his back, I was surprised to see his eyelids fluttering.

"Betsy?" he rasped. "You smell like cinnamon rolls and home." With that, he passed out.

I swept a hand over his cheek as I let the relief sweep over me. Again, tears crowded their way out the sides of my eyes from the stress.

"I guess we know who's responsible for the pack of dead crib in the hallway," the woman said to Travis in a hushed voice.

A hand touched my arm. "Are you okay?" It was the man in the Metallica t-shirt. Strange he asked me that, since I was the one who almost killed him.

I nodded. "Yes, yes, I'm alright." I said the words, but they came from a place somewhere outside of me.

"I'm Travis, and this is Krystan," the man introduced them. "Our business is called Whack a Ghoul, and we were called in to check out and clean up any demonic activity."

At first glance, he seemed like some kind of grunge-rock reject, and she looked like a hard-ass party girl.

On second look, they appeared to still look that way.

I'd peg them to be about my age, in their mid-twenties. Krystan wore fishnets, knee-high stiletto boots, and a miniskirt. Even her top appeared to be a glitter bomb. Bettie Paige slathered on the black eyeliner and red lipstick and had a permanent *eff you* look stamped in her eyes.

While Travis wore an oversized army green coat over the Metallica shirt and looked like he hadn't brushed his hair in days.

"You know...?" I waved a hand toward Leonidas. I'd lost my voice for the moment.

"Leo?" Krystan answered. "For sure. We're buds. Or sort of. But no one's seen him around for a while. We all assumed he was still off on a hunting mission. He's a knight of the light. He's got powers that allow him to hunt the creatures of darkness." She let the question lay bare in her eyes:

Who the hell are you and what are you doing with Leo?

"I... I..." *I was his captor. I helped him escape in the end, though, so I'm not totally bad. And I have an almost desperate desire to jump the man unconscious on the floor as I do to save him.* "I'm helping him on his hunt."

It almost hurt to boil down all the complexities to that phrase. Recrimination ran through my head. I should have believed him then.

I lifted my chin. "Do you think you can help me get him to the car? I have a few things I need to gather, but I can better take care of him at my place."

Krystan shot Travis a grin. "Time to test out how good all that weightlifting is doing you."

"Puhlease," he snorted. "Between all the time I clock at the gym and the time I spend lifting our baby, I'm practically as strong as Calan now."

I didn't know who they were talking about, but I saw the sparks shooting between these two. I could have guessed they were a couple the moment they stepped through the doors... but I'd been too busy preparing to shoot them.

What had my life turned into?

13

───────

LEONIDAS

For the second time, I woke up in Betsy's floral bed. Except this time, an unerring blue eye met me. The other eye was scarred over, giving the fluffy, cream-colored creature on my stomach a dangerous quality. Dark patches colored its ears, around its eyes, and its paws like tiny slippers.

"Betsy," I called out, panic edging my voice. I was careful not to move.

Betsy ran in. "Oh god, are you okay? I was so worried about you."

I eyed the fluff ball on top of me. "This creature means me harm. Could you please remove it?" I'd learned about civilians keeping pets on one of my first few missions. I enjoyed dogs, but this cat clearly had it out for me, according to the gleam in his eye.

"Bubbles?" she asked with a snort, while picking up the cat. "She wouldn't hurt anyone."

I didn't bother telling her I felt the slice of a thousand judgements from that singular eye just now. Not to mention her claws were a little too close to my balls before Betsy extricated her.

"Bubbles was watching over you to make sure you were okay," she said, more to the cat than me, petting her head. "Which is actually weird, because Bubbles usually hides when strangers are around. It even took a while for her to warm up to Martin."

The animal purred under her ministrations. Then Betsy set the cat on the floor. The cat leapt over to a stack of books next to the closet, resuming her watchful eye on me.

Betsy sat down on the bed, her hip against my torso. She leaned over to lay a hand on my forehead. "Are you okay?" she asked in a softer voice. Her hair fell over her ear, sending a waft of her delicious scent over me.

I closed my eyes, reveling in her touch.

"Yes, thanks to you," I said. "How did you get me up here?" I also realized at that point, I was fully undressed and clean. I remembered the blood bath, fighting the crib. Betsy must have bathed me while I was passed out. A rumble of dissatisfaction rolled through me.

As if sensing my thoughts had turned impure, Betsy's eyes danced all over the room, avoiding my heated stare. "You came to enough that you could get to your feet and lean on me to the elevator and then in here."

"Did you undress me?" The thought of her hands pulling off my clothes had me catching a groan in my throat.

Her spine straightened. "Well, I couldn't leave you covered in all that black blood. As your nurse, it's my job to make sure my patient is clean, bandaged, and cared for." It was then I noticed my bicep had a bandage wrapped around it. One of those damned cribs attempted to rip my arm off. There was also a bandage across my chest.

"Sheila?" I asked.

Betsy tried to stifle a laugh. "Yes, I hauled her up here too."

I allowed myself to relax back into the soft bed. Despite feeling rested and cared for, an energy sparked inside me at the sight of Betsy. She was beautiful, kind, and smelled like heaven.

Before I could think about what I was doing, I pulled my nurse over me, into the bed, propping up on an elbow so I could look down at her.

She blinked in surprise. I leaned down and kissed her. Slowly, thoroughly. With women in the past it had been adrenaline-fueled, hormones on overdrive. But with Betsy, I wanted to explore her. The way she liked her lower lip suckled, how her back arched when I slid my hand under her shirt to grasp her hip in my hand.

Betsy's fingers tunneled into my hair, scratching slightly at my scalp, sending my blood south in a hurry.

I trailed kisses down her jawbone, to the long column of her neck, licking and suckling along the way.

"I, uh, I got enough sedatives to make sure you don't shift again. And I downloaded all of Dr. Sterling's files on you. I just haven't had time to go through them yet. I had Martin check in on you while I went to drop off some things at the post office for my niece and nephews."

She was babbling, nerves underlining her words, punctuated by breathy moans and sharp gasps as I continued my way down her collar.

"Mm-hmm," I said, acknowledging her words.

Even as she spoke, her hands ran over my shoulders and down my chest to my abs. "Oh my," she breathed. The tips of her fingers traced the hard ridges of my abdomen before flattening her hands against them altogether, sliding them downward.

A growl emerged from my throat. The sheets wrapped around my waist when I'd rolled her over under me, keeping a barrier between my stiffening member and her body. Her fingers toyed with the edge of the sheet, tickling the trail of my dark hair.

"And this is okay if we do this because we are both adults."

I didn't care what she said, as long as she moved her hands lower. Please, gods, let her hand slip under the sheet. Before I ended up rutting against her thigh, which I was on the verge of doing.

"This can be my rebound. Would you mind terribly being a rebound? Normally, people don't ask, but I've only ever been with Jeremy."

I had zero idea what a rebound was, but I didn't want to hear about the other man and was done waiting. I pushed her dress up, my fingers skimming her smooth expanse of thigh. My mouth watered as I hardened to full mast.

Sliding down the bed, I replaced my hands with my face. The tip of my tongue resumed the trail of my fingers. The scent of her arousal surrounded me. She wanted me too. I laid a kiss against her panty-covered sex and Betsy's hips jerked. I grabbed them, pinning them down so I could explore uninterrupted.

I stiffened my tongue and slowly ran it up and down her cleft. I could taste her through the fabric, and it was more tempting than anything she could conjure in the kitchen.

Her words gave way to incoherent groans. She tried to buck her hips again, but I held her fast. My tongue continued its fiery trail up and down until I'd almost gone mad with desire. Between my mouth and her desire, the thin fabric of her panties was saturated.

I was a selfish bastard. Wanting to take my time

exploring this woman's body, to discover what made her moan and thighs shake. I should have simply entered her and let us both ride things out and be done with this infuriating attraction. But she made me want to draw things out, to take my time and enjoy her reactions as if we were just two people who had all the time in the world.

My fingers curled tighter around her hips. I pushed the fabric aside with my tongue and latched onto the sensitive bud that made her jerk. I sucked and licked that spot with abandon as she cried out. Betsy's groans grew louder as I sucked harder, with more insistence.

I remembered everything. How out of control I'd been at the institute. And I'd almost lost Betsy to the crib, and then I put her in danger. I should leave. Get far away from her so she doesn't get hurt. But the more I told myself I needed to put distance between us, the more vigorously I laved my tongue against her sweet center.

Her cries reached higher pitches, as if she were approaching the edge of some cliff. When the keening moans crested, they became muffled. She'd covered her face with a pillow to stifle the sounds.

Shudders rolled through her body, but I didn't stop. I continued to lap at her until her hips calmed.

When I emerged from under her dress, blood throbbed through my stiff member with an almost violent insistence. Something dark inside me told me to take her right then. Thrust into her mercilessly until I'd broken her.

But I took my time, enjoying the flush in Betsy's cheeks, the way her hair splayed out on the pillow, mussed from her dragging her own fingers through it. She gripped one of those many pillows in one hand. The crocheted pillow was a small black dog with yellow eyes.

I was torn between dropping between her thighs again,

seeing if I could push her over that crest again, and admiring her raw beauty.

"Sweet shiitake mushrooms," she said, covering her eyes as her body shuddered again. "That was... that was..." Removing a hand from her eyes, she met my gaze. "That was an orgasm."

I smiled at her lopsidedly. "I hoped I recognized the signs."

Still running her hand along her forehead, eyes glazed, she said, "Well, I didn't. That was... my first orgasm... I think."

My smile dropped into a hard frown. I spoke slowly. "Are you telling me no man has made sure you finished, legs?"

"Well, like I said, I'd only ever been with Jeremy since high school. And it was always nice, and I thought I'd... but it was never... *that.*"

A dark feeling swelled in me. "A woman deserves plea-sure. You deserve to know it regularly."

Pushing aside the insistence of my arousal, I dragged her panties down and over those perfect long legs.

Then I disappeared under her dress again. I latched onto her sensitive bud, knowing she still hadn't come down from her last orgasm. This time, I slid one finger in between her drenched lips, and then a second.

"No, you don't have to," she protested, almost alarmed.

I only hummed against her. She gasped, and her voice broke as she said, "I probably couldn't even... not twice."

Ignoring her, I slid a finger in, and then a second.

I rhythmically pumped my hand, while attacking her clit with all the hunger I felt for her. Quickly, her words mushed into incoherent groans, raising in pitch as her hips bucked wildly. In minutes, I had her shuddering and crying out again.

Sitting back on my heels, I connected with her gaze, sucking the remnants of her desire off my fingers, loving her taste and the widening of her eyes. A grumble escaped my throat. "Mmm, you taste like honey and sex."

Betsy yanked her dress over her head, revealing more tantalizing skin to my hungry eyes.

White bandages wrapped around her waist, covering the wound from the demon. Something punched me in the gut. Civilians got hurt all the time, but this hit me on an entirely new level. I was... disturbed to see her hurt like this. I couldn't protect her. The mere thought of anything happening to her gutted me.

This was dangerous. Knights of the light did not get attached. Attachments were distractions. Putting myself into the hands of another endangered the mission and could compromise my power.

I forcefully reminded myself we were enjoying a pleasurable tryst, nothing more.

I must have stared for too long, because she covered the bandage and squirmed.

"Are you in pain?" I asked.

She shrugged. "Not really. I took a couple of painkillers, and that seemed to do the trick. And I have to admit, I kind of forgot about it until just now." She awkwardly tried to cover up again with her hands.

I captured them, turning one over to kiss the back of her knuckles. "Well, let's move your focus elsewhere." I leaned over to cup her exposed breasts, letting the soft mounds fill my hands. My thumbs brushed back and forth across her pink nipples.

"Legs, it's not fair for you to look like this." I groaned.

She opened her mouth to say something, but she lost her voice when I tugged and rolled one perfect nipple between my fingers. I suckled the other, discovering a new flavor of Betsy, as delicious as the last.

Betsy pushed me back, then leaned over to pull something out of her bedside table, a small foil packet. Then she clawed the sheet down, freeing my hard length. She wrapped a hand around me, and I groaned.

Efficiently, she opened the packet and slid the protection over me, giving the base of my hardness a squeeze at the end.

The need to sink into her overpowered every other sense. If she didn't know she could orgasm before, I was going to show her every which way I could make her come around me.

I positioned myself at her entrance and threaded my hands into her hair, forcing her head to tilt back. As I sunk into her, inch by agonizing inch, I licked and kissed the sensitive spot on her collarbone. Her hips bucked, but I maintained my slow and steady pace until my pelvis ground against hers.

"Tell me what you want," I whispered into her ear.

She shook her head. Only once had she broken and told me what she wanted, and I aimed to have her voice her needs a second time.

Her hips bucked again, as if she could kick-start me into giving her what she wanted without having to say it. And though it nearly drove me to madness, I resolved not to give in.

My grip on her hair at the base of her skull tightened, and I pulled her head back even further. She whimpered.

In that move, I took away her ability to shy away from my demands. There was nothing I wanted more than for her desires to open themselves up to me, so I could deliver on every one.

"I won't give it to you until you tell me exactly *what you want*." I enunciated the last words with crisp delivery, so she knew I meant it.

"I need... I want... I want you to move," she said, her hips still squirming. I pressed down on them, pinning her.

"What. Do. You. Want?" I growled in her ear. "Say it." The words came out sharp and harsh.

"I want you to fuck me, hard and fast."

Her curse sent a zing of shock through me. She'd been so careful to replace any expletives with some adorable nonsense, but her lapse only heated my blood to combustible temperatures.

I rocked into her, setting a rhythm both hard and fast. But part of me held back. The demon side of me begged to be let off its chains. To claim her completely. It was too dangerous to let go completely. When I did that, she got hurt.

Betsy's back arched, fingernails digging into my arms, her eyes shut tight. "More," she begged.

"I'm afraid to hurt you," I confessed in pants, never breaking our rhythm.

Those bewitching blue eyes snapped open, meeting mine. "I want more," she demanded with the confidence and authority of a woman chasing her own pleasure.

The demon in me cried out in victory as it broke free of the constraints I'd kept it in. My hands lowered to cup her perfect, round ass, lifting it up to the perfect angle. I mindlessly drove harder with everything I was.

All vestiges of gentleness disappeared. I did as she commanded, driving into her hard and fast, imprinting on her body with each thrust.

Any fear she couldn't take it melted away as her cries of pleasure climbed higher. Her nails dug deeper into my flesh, heightening the sensations in my body. All my focus went to holding back my release. Then I felt her internal muscles shudder as she lost control, holding onto me for dear life. She screamed my name, hips jerking wildly, and my control snapped. My release came hard and fast, sending shock waves through me, rocking the foundation of everything I'd ever known.

Betsy's fingers dug into my shoulders with abrupt force. "Did you hear that?"

"Hear what?" The only thing I could hear was her ragged breaths and the pounding of my blood in my own ears. Both covered in sweat, I took in the sight of her. Her hairline was damp and her eyes gleamed.

Finally, a ringing sound cut through the din of our bodies.

"Oh, son of a biscuit, the timer," she said, back to her pseudo curses. I let Betsy push me up. "I left the pie in the oven."

Out of the room like a shot, grabbing her dress along the way. She left me naked, sexually spent, and slightly bewildered.

Meow.

I glared at the cat. "Keep it up. I'll eat you."

The cat merely licked her own paw.

Knock knock.

What was it Betsy had said? Sweet shiitake mushrooms. What now?

14

BETSY

"What now?" I huffed to myself.

After pulling out the apple pie, the rapping sound of knuckles hit my front door.

Maybe if I kept quiet, whoever was at the door would go away. Because between being pleasured beyond my wildest dreams, not once, but thrice, by a sexual god, I was not ready for sense to return to me.

The knock came a second time.

I squeezed my eyes shut. Leonidas was naked in the next room. Even though I'd just experienced the ride of my life, I still wanted to walk back in that bedroom and run my hands and tongue over every muscular ridge of his body, from his carved abs to the magnificent beast between his legs.

Was that too much to ask? To continue a rebound fling with the sexiest man I'd ever seen?

Forget that he was an infected patient, and some kind of knight from a secret order with magic powers. Forget that I was his nurse, and on the rebound from a traumatic breakup.

Knock knock. "Betsy, I can smell the pie. Let us in."

I dropped my head. Apparently, it was too much to ask. I stalked over to the front door and opened it. From the voice, I already surmised who it was. A very pregnant Adelaide waddled into my apartment, followed by her husband, Michael.

"What are you doing here, Adie?" I asked, smoothing back my hair, suddenly conscious of the fact my panties were flung somewhere in my bedroom. My dress was rumpled, but at least on the correct way for having tossed it back on haphazardly.

"Can't a girl check on her sister?" Adie asked, raising her hands in defense. "But since I did come all the way from Montana, could you be so kind as to help me on the couch? This kid has been kicking up a storm since we left."

I jumped too, realizing how rude I was being. "Of course," I said, helping her over to the couch and positioning the pillows in a comfortable position. I'd learned from our other two sisters who had five kids between them how to make a pregnant woman comfortable.

Adie groaned in relief as she lay back into the cushions.

"What are you doing here?" I asked.

Adie shot me a strange look. "Wow, have we been gone so long you forgot how to be a polite host? Are you going to ask if your incredibly pregnant sister wants a drink? Michael is also hungry. Do you have a snack for him?"

Guilt stabbed me. She was right. Those would have been the first things out of my mouth not that long ago. "Sorry, I'm so sorry. I guess living alone the past month has changed me a little."

Rushing over to grab a glass of water, I said, "I haven't had time to go to the store recently. I don't really have any food—"

My brother-in-law pulled a few drawers open before finding a fork. He approached the pie. "That's okay. This will do for now until you can get some stuff to make us lunch."

"Oh, can you make a pot roast?" Adie exclaimed. "I have been craving your home cooking."

I turned off the faucet. "I made that pie for my neighbor, actually," I said, surprised by the irritation that snaked through me. Before, I would have jumped at the mere suggestion of making food for them

Michael's fork sliced through the flaky crust, cutting out a chunk of pie. "That's okay, you can make another. After all, we traveled eight hours to see you."

I hadn't asked them to do that. Something tightened in my chest and my throat. I tried not to analyze it even as I ran the cup over to my sister. She looked into the glass. "Don't you have any juice?"

My world was spinning out of control. I suddenly couldn't keep up with the demands flying at me. Back in Montana, I was excellent at anticipating everyone's needs, but I'd been taking care of only myself the last month, and I felt rusty and overwhelmed.

"Hello there," a deep voice interrupted. Like being wrapped up in a large fluffy blanket, my shoulders dropped a fraction.

"Who's this?" Michael asked with a frown.

Leonidas emerged from my bedroom. But seeing as his blood-soaked clothes were currently in the dryer, he'd wrapped my sheets around him. The most virile, masculine half man, half demon had wrapped my sheets with the tiny yellow flowers around his body.

"I am Leonidas. Who are you?" Leo asked. His question was polite, but there was menace in his eyes. Maybe he was on edge having so many people around who he didn't know.

Or maybe he also wished our time in the bedroom remained uninterrupted.

Though from the way his eyes met mine, I got the sense he was trying to gauge if I was okay.

"We're Betsy's family," Adie announced, derision dripping in her words. "I'm her sister and that's my husband, Michael."

Leo's expression relaxed. He reached out a hand to Michael. "I see. It is a pleasure to meet you."

Michael only regarded Leo's outstretched hand.

"So this is what Jeremy warned us of," Adelaide said under her breath.

"What's wrong with your eyes?" Michael asked Leo, though neither of us answered him.

I turned back to my sister. "You've been talking to Jeremy?"

"Of course we have," she huffed. "You guys may be on the rocks, but Jeremy is still Michael's brother."

In high school, we'd gotten a kick out of being a pair of sisters dating a pair of brothers. It wasn't so fun since Jeremy dumped me, knowing he would be at all future family holiday get-togethers. I hadn't made peace with that yet. Dread filled my insides as I guessed what this impromptu visit was about.

"We are not on the rocks, Adie. Jeremy broke up with me," I corrected my sister. "One month before our wedding."

Michael's fork hit the counter with a tink. "And he realizes now what a huge mistake he's made. He knows coming out here was a bad idea, and he is moving back to Montana, and he wants to move back with you."

"You didn't even give him a chance to make it up to you," Adie said, giving me the big puppy dog eyes that usually melted my heart. "That's so unlike you."

Heat filled my cheeks. Not only were my sister and brother-in-law browbeating me about my humiliating breakup, but they were doing it in front of the guy I was rebounding with not ten minutes ago. They acted like he wasn't even there.

As if hearing my thoughts, Adie's eyes landed on Leo. She regarded him with repressed accusation. "I get it, Bets." She turned her gaze back on me. "You've been having some fun. But now it's time to come back to the real world. With little Mikey on the way"—she rubbed her swollen belly—"all our nieces and nephews driving Rebecca and Hallie to near madness, we don't have any time to take care of ourselves, much less Dad. Have you even called him lately?"

A sour patina covered my tongue. The answer was not for a week. The calls were longsuffering sighs and recriminations about how I should have never left. If Jeremy and I hadn't left for Colorado, we'd be married by now. Not to mention how Rebecca didn't know how to cook like I did, or how he liked his blankets folded. How my sisters were lost without me.

"We miss you, Betsy," she said in a small voice. "We need you. Without Mom, you were all we had. Please don't break our family. Forgive Jeremy, and come home with us, and all will be forgiven."

Leo's expression hardened.

My throat had gone dry. Guilt crushed me until I couldn't breathe.

Forgiveness. It was all I ever wanted, but I'd learned long ago, some things couldn't be forgiven.

"And Betsy, I don't want to put more pressure on you, but... Dad isn't doing well," Adie confessed.

Fear stabbed my heart. "What?"

"Since you left, his health has been declining. Rebecca

and Hallie can hardly keep up with the kids, and I'm obviously indisposed," she said, patting her round belly. "You should come home."

"But Hallie lives two houses away from Dad," I said, trying to create a solution that didn't crush me under the weight of guilt.

"Well, when you left, she'd come to rely on those casseroles you brought over every week, and do you really think she can keep that big house clean by herself?"

"Can't she get a maid service?" I suggested weakly. I did spend a lot of time cooking and delivering foods to make sure everyone ate well. Especially because I knew Hallie hated vegetables and would only eat them if I cooked them in a specific way. It started when she was pregnant, so she could have healthy kids, but she said it helped give her strength to be a better mom.

"What if those kids want to go to college, Betsy?" Michael pointed out. "Should Hallie really be spending their money on a maid service? We are a family, we can take care of our own."

"You live pretty close to Dad," I said, though things felt as if they were spiraling out of control.

Michael and Adie exchanged a look of decided displeasure and surprise, while Leo calmly and quietly watched. Though a line formed between his drawn eyebrows.

"Michael has a job," Adie said, as if the answer were obvious.

"Doesn't Betsy also have a job?" Leonidas interjected.

"I'm sorry, why are you here again?" Adie asked, fire sparking in her eyes. She struggled to get to her feet. I rushed to her side to help her up, but she waved me away with impatience.

"It's okay, Leo," I said.

"Is it?" he asked. "As far as I can tell, these people want you to cook, clean, and care for them like a servant."

"These people?" Adie shrieked. "We are her family, and you don't know anything about our life."

"I know that civilians typically care about their families, and since you've been here, you've done nothing but make demands of her, without even asking her what she needs, or about her well-being," Leo argued.

Adie's glare turned as sharp as a blade's edge. "We have eyes. We can see she is perfectly fine."

Things were spiraling out of control. Adie never backed down when she got wound up, and Leo could shift into a winged, bloodthirsty beast when pushed too far.

"And I know she belongs at home with us, because without her we don't have enough of a support system." Adie shot me a look and it might as well have been a bullet through my heart.

That was my fault. Not because I'd left, but because of what I'd done. If it weren't for me, our mother would still be around.

Leo stepped forward, opening his mouth to say something when he grabbed his forehead, and bent over with a wheeze of pain. "Betsy." My name came out as a desperate rasp. I was by his side in a second.

"What is it?" I murmured so only he could hear me. "Do you need more sedatives?" It had only been a couple hours since his last dose. That seemed too soon, but I'd do it to keep him from shifting.

He shook his head, struggling to get the words out. "No, it's the creature. It's... it's in my head again. Or I'm in its head."

Adie snorted behind me. "Okay, we'll that's a dramatic, cheap move."

I straightened and announced. "I'm afraid I'm going to have to ask you to leave."

Adie's hands protectively flew to her belly. "But we just got here. The bags are in the car downstairs. We were planning to stay with you."

I ushered my sister and Michael out the front door. "That's not possible right now," I said, feeling equal parts guilt and relief. "It's a bad time for me to have anyone else right now. Why don't you go see if Jeremy has any room for you?"

"She wants her sex pad back," Michael said to Adelaide in a not-so-hushed tone. A swell of irritation threatened to crash into me. But I reminded myself he was under stress from the baby coming and taking care of Dad.

And I didn't want to explain Leo was one of my patients, who was infected by a demon who could change any second and be a danger to all of us, including the baby.

"Yes, I need to get back to all the glorious sex, and that's why you need to leave right now," I said in a clipped tone. With that, I shut the door in their shocked faces.

Returning to Leo's side, I joined him on his knees. "What's happening, Leo?" I asked, brushing his hair back.

"I can feel it. The creature from that night. It's reaching out to me. It wants... it wants..." Leo's face turned up to meet mine. Silver flashed from his eyes. "It wants you."

"What?"

Regret crossed over Leo's face right before his eyes rolled up into the back of his head, and he passed out.

WHEN LEO WOKE up on the floor half an hour later, I was across the room at the table, Leo's files in front of me.

Normally I'd be petting Bubbles, who liked to perch in my lap, but I couldn't shoo her off Leonidas. She seemed strangely protective of him.

Before those two strange characters from Whack a Ghoul helped me move him to the car, I'd grabbed a hard copy of Leo's file and had been going over his information for the last thirty minutes. The discovery I made was enough to send bile hovering in my throat.

Leo gently picked up Bubbles and set her to the side. My cat sadly meowed at being displaced. She padded over and jumped into my lap.

Leo pushed back the blankets and pillows I'd surrounded him with. A smile quirked his lips.

"You were too heavy to move," I explained in a quiet voice. "How are you feeling?"

Turning toward me, he said, "I'm feeling like I spend more time around you unconscious than conscious. Should I be worried you were taking advantage of me all those times?" A sly smile curved his lips but disappeared when I didn't return his mirth.

"Your body keeps shutting down every time it gets over-loaded." I gestured to the papers in front of me. "The changes happening inside you… your body is essentially at war with itself. When you won't rest and allow it to try and establish an equilibrium, it forces you to."

"What's wrong, legs?" he asked, standing up.

I licked my lips and rubbed my temple. Stress gathered so tightly in my chest I feared it would explode. "I know why you have a shared connection with the creature. I know—" I hiccupped from the repressed emotion. "I know what Dr. Sterling did."

Leonidas sat in the chair next to me, pulling my leg

between his. He massaged my thigh as if trying to calm me. I couldn't look him in the eye.

"You were right," I confessed. "You weren't infected by a demon."

"I know. They saw me use my powers trying to fight the demon and said it was an irregularity. That I must have been infected to explain my supernatural abilities." He spoke gently, as if I'd bumped my head and forgot everything we'd already discussed. But he didn't understand.

My lips tightened, and I shook my head, almost unable to speak the words. "I infected you."

"What do you mean?" His thumbs still kneaded my flesh.

I should pull away, stop him from touching me. Lord knew he'd never want to touch me again. What I did was unforgivable and soon he'd see it that way, too.

Shutting my eyes tight, I let the words spill out before I lost my courage. "According to this, the so-called medicine I have been injecting you with has actually been gene therapy."

"I don't understand," he said.

Sucking in a deep breath, I explained, "The treatments have been about integrating demonic DNA into your genetic code, and it's why you've only been getting worse. You are expressing demonic qualities, because you are part demon now."

The kneading stopped. Instead of looking at Leo, I focused on the files with all the undeniable data. "They told me it was an experimental drug I was giving you, but it was a protein derived from the monster that came for us that night. You are genetically, and I guess psychically, tied to that... thing."

Slowly, Leonidas pulled away. He stood, then walked to

the center of my apartment as if he needed to put distance between us.

Guilt gnawed at my insides like a rabid dog. Tears stung the backs of my eyes, threatening to force their way out.

"I'm so sorry." I looked down into my lap at Bubbles. She turned her face up at me with an expression full of compassion and understanding. I deserved neither.

"Adie was right. I should never have come out here. I should have convinced Jeremy to stay in Montana and give up that fellowship. Because then we wouldn't have come out here and broken up. I wouldn't have changed hospitals to get away from him, and ended up injecting you with dangerous experimental drugs."

Each domino of guilt was larger than the last, falling in a familiar yet dreaded pattern, until I was nothing but a raw pulp under all of it. This was my fault. I meant to help him, but I'd been using him as a guinea pig in a completely unsafe trial that could and still may end up killing him. Devastated didn't even begin to cover the wash of feeling pounding me.

Feeling the weight of Leo's stare, I forced myself to meet his gaze. I expected to find disgust, anger, and outrage. But instead, he looked as guilty as I felt.

"The creature is coming for you."

It was the last thing he said before passing out, but I had shelved that issue in lieu of going through his medical files.

Leo came toward me with heavy footfalls. "It's coming for you because of me." He stood before me, running his hands through my hair with heartbreaking gentleness. "The beast and I are psychically connected, and I got almost a direct line to its inner workings. It views me as direct competition, which makes sense. As you said, I am now like it. To remain the apex predator, it needs to kill any other alpha, namely me. Even as I gleaned this information, it read me as well. It tapped into... us, and what we did. The demon senses how much I... desire you, so now it wants you too. It views you as my mate, so it set all of its focus on taking you from me."

"Didn't you hear me? I'm the reason you are infected. You should be happy that thing wants to tear me to pieces," I said, words breaking.

Leo framed my face with his large, strong hands. They warmed my cold cheeks. "You aren't responsible for this evil, Betsy."

I pushed away from him, getting up and walking past him. My hands gripped each other at my chest. "Yes, I am. It's my fault. I should never have left my family." My fingers dug into my eyes. "I should go back to Montana."

"And all will be forgiven?" He repeated Adie's words, and they cut me to the core. I curled my arms around my stomach as if it would hurt less. It didn't.

"What did she mean?" he asked. He didn't understand, but I could tell he wanted to.

I didn't answer. The words got stuck in my throat, then curdled my stomach. I hated myself enough right now. I couldn't stand confessing all of my sins.

He finally went on, thumbs rubbing my arms.

"You did as you were told. You believed you were helping, and now we are both in danger." His hands wrapped around my shoulders, forcing me to look him in the eye. But all I saw there was the silver sheen of infection I'd introduced into his body. He had been a captor. The Whack a Ghoul duo confirmed everything about his identity. He was part of an ancient order dedicated to protecting the light. And I'd prevented him from his mission and then poisoned him.

Putting enough chill in my words to freeze water into ice, I said, "We need to go back to the institute. The more information we have on the creature, the more we can help you."

Leo nodded, taking a step back, dropping his arms. My body internally wailed at the loss of his touch, but I stood my ground. Whether he knew it or not, I didn't deserve his forgiveness.

"This has become bigger than both you and me. We need to consult a higher power," he said, his voice all business as well.

"Like... Jesus?" Some days I still hoped the big J would come down here and clean house. Maybe a magic, light-wielding knight had an in with someone like that.

"No, someone else," he said, staring off at the window.

A determined glint in Leo's eye told me we were about to enter his world. I didn't know if I should run screaming, but there was no choice now but to face whatever was coming. It was my fault, and I needed to see this through.

15

LEONIDAS

I gave Betsy the destination, and she assured me she could drive us there. When she asked if I preferred to drive, I told her the truth. "I don't know how."

"You don't know how to drive?" She typed in the address to her phone, which would show her the way.

"It's never been a necessity."

Her nose wrinkled. "How can that be?"

I couldn't help but smile. She was adorable at the most inopportune times. "As you might have gathered, I have other means of travel available to me."

Realization dawned on her face. "The portal thingy you made?"

I nodded. "That is a Chevalier's primary method of transport."

"But now you can't make one," she said, more of a statement of fact.

"It was a miracle I made the one for us to escape, legs. When you administer your drugs, it suppresses the flow of my will and, therefore, my power. Otherwise, I would have escaped from the institute long ago. Now, I believe accessing my powers triggers an adverse reaction from my powers. I can't access the powers meant to fight the darkness if I am darkness myself."

We fell into an awkward silence. Tension grew thick in the small space of her Jeep.

"I need to apologize for what happened earlier," I started, already hating what I was about to say.

"What about earlier?" she asked, a line forming between her brows.

"We should never have engaged in that level of... sexual activity. It is against the code of a knight of the light to do so."

"That was your first time?" she asked, her eyes widening.

I paused. "No, like I said, where my brothers staunchly followed the rules, I've allowed for some bending. But the fact remains, I'm a warrior, a tool for the order of Luxis to wield. I go where they direct me, when they deem to do so. My life is not my own."

She shot me a quick look. "Explain this sexual... bending, you've done."

"Well," I started slowly. "Years ago, there was a girl I'd saved from being mauled in an alleyway by a shapeshifter. She insisted on thanking me, and things got intimate."

Betsy kept her gaze intent on the road. I went on. "But when I went to leave after it was over, she became overwrought. She insisted it was destiny that brought us together, and we belonged together. I tried my best to let her down easily, but she wouldn't hear it. She cried and clawed at me not to go, but I explained I belonged to a larger purpose and should have never given into the flesh the way we had. I was not my own person. I belonged to the Luxis and other people needed my protection."

The image of leaving Jenny in her apartment, crying

hysterically, burned in my brain. Everything I did was meant to help people and causing someone pain like that felt like a sword running through my chest.

"So, while I found I couldn't completely resist the appeal of civilian food and other civilian vices, I learned if I were to get involved with a woman, I needed to be clear about there being no attachments." I'd still found plenty of willing women, but I hadn't warned Betsy. Then again, she knew what I was, both the knight and the monster, and she'd fallen into bed with me anyway. Or rather, I'd dragged her into it with me. If I caused her the same despair as I did that poor girl when I was younger, I would never forgive myself.

She nodded, licking her lips. The desire to kiss her surged through me again. "This actually works perfectly. I am on the rebound, and I've never been with anyone other than Jeremy, so I shouldn't take this seriously. It's best we don't do that again while we figure out what is going on with you." A hand smoothed her hair back as she let out a breath. "And for crying out loud, I'm your nurse. I shouldn't be taking advantage of you, either. Yes. Let's agree to just be on friendly terms."

Despite our agreement that getting entangled was decidedly a mistake, I disliked her quick agreement. It was the right thing to do, but disappointment rocked me. I never resented my destiny with the order until this moment. In this moment, I wished to be my own man. I wished that the duties of protection belonged to someone else, but no matter where I went, it was mine to shoulder.

No matter how Betsy sparked feelings inside me I'd never felt before.

"So, where are we going?" Betsy asked, changing the subject.

"To find out what this creature is."

Twenty minutes later, we pulled up to a stone church in downtown Denver.

"Wow," Betsy said as we got out of the car. "Wait, isn't this a dance club? I've heard about it. It used to be a church, but someone renovated it into a club. Some other nurses invited me to go once, but it's not really my scene."

"Indeed. Unfortunately, the large scene drew a vast number of dark spirits that began possessing people. They turned on each other and the place erupted in a mass of violence. I was the one to show up and to exorcise the attendants. I saved many, but even then, the body count was staggering. The establishment lost its license, and the building went up for sale. When I told my master of it, she decided it would make an excellent spot for the order of Luxis to post up in."

"How many posts does your order have?"

I sighed. "We used to span the world. Our order devotees were in every major city and many on the outskirts. But one of the other orders, the order of Tenebrae, who'd we'd not seen in many years, systematically went about destroying our temples. Before we realized what was happening, we'd lost most of our order. A spirit from the Stygian aided the order of the Tenebrae. They unearthed powerful objects that helped them in their designs to return to power. In fact, the Luxis was almost wiped out and would have been if it weren't for my brother knight, Calan."

"Is that who we're here to see?" she asked.

I shook my head. "No, he is in Europe with his pregnant wife." I ascended the stone steps leading up to the door.

"Then who are we here to see?" she asked.

I knocked on the front door. "My master."

A look of concern passed over her face. "Master. It makes you sound like some kind of slave."

I didn't have time to answer. A panel in the door slid open and a set of eyes peered out. Recognition sparked in them when the person saw me, but they slid to Betsy.

"Who is the girl?" the man asked.

"She's with me," I said gruffly. I was in no mood to jump through any hoops. "We're here to see Master Violetta."

The man paused.

"Now," I ground out.

The jangle of locks and chains quickly followed until the door opened. I gave Betsy a nod before stepping inside. She followed into the stone entryway. The hooded monk held the door open, bowing before shutting it, then hurried in front of me to guide the way.

"Whoa," she breathed. Light filtered in through the massive stain glass windows, illuminating the open floor. Once, people danced here, but all I saw were the piles of bodies and pools of blood as people ripped each other apart.

"The Luxis believes in tradition and the old ways. Time strengthens anything that survives," I explained. "Especially objects and places of faith."

The memory of the bloodbath unsettled me, but this was now a temple of Luxis. The temples weren't exactly my home. A home was a place where one relaxed, lived, and gathered with loved ones. They were always an austere refuge between missions for systematic rest and training. Gathering with the monks wasn't permitted. The knights weren't allowed to fraternize with others beyond their masters. My brother knights and I would only gather for training, both our physical and metaphysical powers. But outside that, we were to dine alone in our spartan rooms, and only come when called, and go where assigned.

The monk led us to the woman under the stain glass windows. When in range, he swept an arm, bowing again.

I approached my master. Master Violetta wore her deep purple robes and read from an old tomb atop a podium. Gray and white streaked the hair pulled back into a tight bun. Lines of age and discipline etched around her eyes and lips. My master had gotten on in years, but the sharpness in her eyes had never dulled. Her long, aged fingers hovered over the book as she read, though she was careful not to touch. The oil from her fingers would damage the pages.

Violetta had always been the records keeper of the order. She wasn't simply reading; she was memorizing. She could call up any prophecy, history, or classification of dark being simply by memory.

We waited in silence until she came to a stopping point.

Finally, she looked up. "Is it done?" she asked, her voice echoing throughout.

Dropping to a knee, I bowed deeply before my master. "It is not, my master. The mission has grown complicated beyond my wisdom, so I seek yours."

When my master did not speak, I dared to look up. She stared at Betsy with a confused, if not suspicious, expression.

"Who is this?"

"Someone who is aiding me on the hunt."

Violetta waved me up with a short, impatient gesture, indicating I should stand. "This woman is helping you? She is not of the order. You are not to involve civilians in the hunt. It is too dangerous, both for the civilian and your mission."

Betsy looked at a complete loss. Her fingers wove in and out of each other as if she didn't know what to do with them, or herself. I touched her arm with what I hoped was reassurance.

"Without her help, I would not have survived. I was captured and taken prisoner."

"Hi, I'm Betsy." She waved her hand at Violetta.

My master scanned Betsy from head to toe, assessing.

Violetta walked over to a rope hanging from the ceiling. I heard no sound, but moments later, a monk scurried in. "Please bring us tea," she directed. Though I could tell the interruption vexed her, or perhaps it was because of Betsy's presence, she invited us to sit over a collection of tufted chairs surrounding a table. "You'd best tell me everything."

Soon, a monk reappeared with a tray of green tea and small clay teacups set out.

I explained how I'd tracked the creature she'd sent me to kill when we'd both been captured. Then I shared how the institute held me captive while administering treatments to help me, but they were changing me. I left out that Betsy had been the one to administer most of them. She focused on the tea when I got to that part.

"When the creature broke out, murdering everyone in sight, I had a vision."

Violetta had patiently listened, but now she straightened. "A vision? What do you mean, you had a vision?"

"It was as if I were seeing through the monster's eyes. I could feel the bloodlust and rage, especially toward me. It views me as a competing alpha, but there can only be one apex predator. It is searching for me and hiding somewhere. Somewhere close by." I closed my eyes. "It hunts at night."

I saw the faces of the terrified victims right before it killed them, as if I had done it myself. He takes them back to his lair and feeds upon their flesh. Then it searches for my scent as it soars through the night sky. Though it could not find me, I sensed it was getting closer and closer. "And now it knows of Betsy as well, and it is tracking her. Wishing to do her harm."

Betsy's cheeks flushed pink. Again, I left out the creature had set its sights on Betsy after we'd committed the intimate act.

I described the creature. How its ribcage split, jutting out from its body. The massive clawed wings and fanged mouth that opened along its throat before meeting the split of its ribs. Until one couldn't tell where fangs ended and ribs began. There was also the part where it was bulletproof.

"What creature is this? It reminds me of so many I have fought from the Stygian, but I am unfamiliar with this one in particular. And why would it have psychic abilities, able to connect to me? I refer to your wisdom, master, and that of our order."

Violetta's lips thinned, a sign she was deep in thought. "This being you speak of; I cannot recollect any such presence in our records. But as the Stygian is an entire separate plane brimming with demons and spirits, it is not unlikely that there are far more beasts than we can fathom who have yet to cross over onto our plane." She raised one long finger. "It does, however, remind me of one we call the tombscream. However, the tombscream does not possess wings as you speak of, nor do they have any such psychic abilities. They are meat eaters and are superb trackers. They cannot live in packs because they are so territorial. This development of psychic abilities in such a breed would be terribly disturbing." Her hard stare landed on Betsy, though she spoke to me. "But regardless of the creature's manifestation, you are to complete your mission. Hunt the beast down and kill the thing."

"If you don't know what it is, how did you know to send Leonidas after it?" Betsy asked.

I bowed my head. Chevalier were not to ask such questions of the order.

Violetta grasped the arms of her chair, and for a moment I could not read her. Perhaps it was a mistake to bring Betsy here.

"The light guides our order, so the darkness does not escape our notice."

Betsy tilted her head. "Even though there are tons of dark beings roaming the earth now? You can tell where all of them are?"

"Betsy," I said, in a low warning tone.

The two women's eyes locked, neither willing to give way. Finally Violetta said, "I will try to sum it up enough for your simple understanding. As one does not eat an entire meal in a moment, we must take events one bite at a time."

Her answer was typical.

Sitting back in her chair, Betsy sighed. "I guess I was wondering if you sensed the connection to Leonidas beforehand. Maybe that was why you sent him after the tombscream."

Violetta shook her head.

Betsy went on, seeming to go inward with thought. "But then again, perhaps it is the genetics that tie your minds somehow."

Violetta frowned. "What is she speaking of?"

"After we escaped the institute, I experienced a transformation. I turned into something similar to the tombscream. I sprouted wings; my hands transformed into long claws. I recall little, but perhaps Betsy is correct…"

"You have the darkness inside you?" Violetta asked, her tone snapping like a rubber band. She reared back as if I were infectious. Her recoil sent a stab of pain through my chest.

"Not exactly," Betsy went on to explain. "The institute..." She swallowed hard. "I administered genetic materials into Leonidas and now he is expressing similar qualities of the demon. Which explains his transformation, but also maybe their psychic connection is a result of that as well."

I didn't get to finish before Violetta was up and out of her seat. She pulled the hanging rope twice.

"What is it, master?" I stood as well.

The hardness drained from her eyes, and in its place stood regret and pain.

Alarm raced through me. Something must be terribly wrong for her to emote so.

"I had hoped when this day came, it would be long after our time, Leonidas," Violetta said.

"What are you talking about?"

"The prophecy," she said calmly, though her eyes flashed with fear.

"What prophecy?"

Betsy went rigid in the seat next to me, listening intently.

My master closed her eyes, tilted her head back and raised a hand, a sign she was about to speak the word of the light. "Ye shall see the sign and know by the light warrior's dark winged form. One by one, the light warriors will turn. From light, there shall be darkness, and it will herald the end of those who created them. Like the pillars of a temple trembling in the earthquake in humanity, when one falls, the rest shall also fall." She opened her eyes. The hardness returned to them. "The factions of five shall be no more."

"Leo, what is she talking about?" Betsy asked behind me.

The door opened, and twenty monks filed in, surrounding us. Next to me, Betsy slowly rose from her seat.

"I have no intention of bringing down the orders, and the rest of the knights would never turn dark," I said, sounding calmer than I felt. "And as long as Betsy is near, I can remain in control."

"You say you've transformed into a dark one?" Violetta asked, folding her hands into her robes.

"Yes, Betsy is helping me manage the condition for now."

My master shook her head. "A knight of the light, infected and changed by the darkness, Leonidas. There can be no cure. You have taken shape of the damned. Your purity has been compromised."

"Purity?" Betsy repeated, disgust in her voice.

"The mission is still viable," I said, all my senses heightening past what I once knew. I could feel the coil of the muscles in the followers surrounding us. They were preparing for a fight.

"I am so very sorry. You have been my ward for twenty-seven years, but this is where your path ends. If the darkness were to gain control of your power, it could be the end of us all."

"How so?" Betsy asked. "I don't understand. Leonidas is a good man."

"You would renounce me?" My voice came out low and gravelly. It sounded like a threat, but it was emotion pulling on my words.

My master did not speak. I had my answer.

"I am the last knight of the light under the command of this order," I said. "The only other two living Chevalier have abandoned you when they learned of your lies, but I did not. I stayed. I continued to dedicate my strength and will to this order, to your judgement to help fight the darkness."

"And you have served the light well," she answered. "But darkness cannot fight darkness."

I knew that tone. Her words were final and damning.

The pain slicing through me might as well have been from a knife. I knew the pains of battle, felt loss and grief when my Chevalier brothers perished in battle, but until this moment, I never knew devastation.

"Okay, this is pure malarkey," Betsy interrupted, taking a step toward Violetta. "Leonidas is not 'dark,' as you put it. He has saved me many times and is dedicated to protecting people. You can't just throw him away because he's not pure enough for you. You haven't even tried to help him."

"That's enough, Betsy," I said, setting a hand on her shoulder to pull her back. "My master is following the code of our order and will not divert." Then, feeling as if my affliction were indeed contagious as Violetta made it seem, I let her go, not wanting to subject her to my touch. "She must do what she believes is right." Meeting Violetta's gaze, I left her in no uncertain terms what would come next. "And so must I."

The monks crouched around us, readying themselves. Things were about to get bloody.

"Promise me the girl will go free," I said to my master. No matter what happened, Betsy had no part in this.

Betsy reared around to face me. "What?"

She didn't understand what was about to happen. They couldn't let me leave here. The Luxis expunged the darkness, and I was the enemy now.

But I could not let them do it. If they killed me, Betsy would still be hunted by the tombscream. I needed to complete my mission, no matter what.

Violetta nodded and opened her hand. "Of course, we

do not hurt civilians. But first, we will make her useful in drawing out the creature."

A chill ran through me. My master intended to let Betsy go free after they used her as bait. The idea of deliberately putting Betsy in danger offended me.

No. It enraged me.

Heat raced through my veins and the darkness at my center churned, making itself known.

"Whoa." Betsy put her palms in the air, a futile effort to slow things down. Two monks stepped forward and grabbed her shoulders and ushered her out of the room.

"No, no, Leo don't let them do this," Betsy cried out. "You are good. Hey, get your hands off me, you creeps."

Her distress reverberated through my bones along with the rejection of my master.

As soon as she was removed, taking off through a doorway to the left, Violetta made her exit as well. The monks removed weapons from their robes and rushed me from all sides. I ducked the slice of sword and sunk a punch into a monk's gut. Throwing out a kick behind me, one monk flew back, knocking down the two behind him.

I'd not bothered to bring Sheila. It was my flesh against their steel, an unfair fight made even more so by the fact I still had sedatives coursing through my veins. At least, my heightened senses allowed me an edge in anticipating their moves.

Reverting to my training, I fell into the flow of violence. Jab, punch, kick, dodge, dive.

The demon was taking over. Anger, grief, and resentment flowed through me. I'd done everything asked of me, and they still planned to burn me.

I grabbed a sword from one of my attackers, throwing it up in time to stop a blade from sinking into my skull. My adrenaline spiked, and I moved with the speed of my prior self.

And they would hurt Betsy. The pain of that pounded through me over and over, shockwaves shaking my core.

My skin roiled and shifted. For once, I didn't fight it. I leaned into the demonic part of myself, bringing the transformation on faster than ever before.

The monks pressed in around me, but with a forceful push, I sent them all reeling. Two swords sunk into my back, and I cried out, feeling blood trickle down from the wounds. Yet none of the monks were near me.

Clawed wings unfolded behind me. I stretched them out as my vision turned red. Fear and awe flashed over the faces of the surrounding monks.

The fight was already over, whether or not they knew it.

Their eyes drank me in, mouth slack with horror.

My consciousness receded, and the primitive side of me awoke with a snarl. The primitive side and I constantly fought for dominance, but we'd finally come to our first agreement. We were aligned in that would both protect Betsy at any cost.

16

BETSY

I banged on the door. The monks had locked me in a small bedroom that reminded me all too much of Leo's room at the institute.

"Let me out, or I'll... you'll be really sorry!" I didn't know what they'd be sorry about. I had no way of getting out and helping Leonidas. But that didn't stop me from trying to break the door down.

My shoulder rammed the door with a loud smack. "Owie," I whimpered, rubbing my arm and hissing between my teeth. It hurt like the dickens, but the door was still wood. A couple more solid knocks, and I bet I could get the sucker to crack.

So what if I had a bruised side? Leo was dead if I didn't get out there and help him.

Crossing to the far edge of the room, I gave myself as much of a running start as I could. Burgeoning myself, I let out a war cry as I flew at the door like a banshee from hell.

Suddenly, I went flying forward as the door opened. Then I slammed into something solid, yet warm.

I looked up into Leonidas's face. Except it wasn't him. His silver eyes flashed with an alien fury. His fingers had elongated into claws and his muscle expanded until the clothes on his body ripped. Before, he still had a head over me, but now he must be seven feet tall. Black leather wings protruded from his back.

A low growl emitted from his throat.

I gulped hard, fear quaking at my core.

Apart from the wings and the overall impressive size, he looked nothing like the tombscream.

"Leo," I said, but the word came out in a whisper.

He growled again, and I stumbled back. Those silver orbs tracked my movement as he took a menacing step toward me. Leonidas was pure predator now. No recognition shone in his eyes. It was like being faced to face with a hungry tiger.

Cold sweat beads popped out on my back, the tiny hairs on my neck standing straight up. My pounding heart screamed at me to run, but he blocked my exit.

This was it. I'd fled the loving safety of my family and Montana to get mauled by a man I'd turned into a monster. Why the hell had I allowed Jeremy to talk me into leaving, I asked myself for the billionth time.

"Leo," I said in as calm a tone as I could manage. "It's me, it's Betsy. I need you to calm down."

He opened his fanged mouth wide and roared at me so loud I feared my eardrums would bleed. The urge to cover my ears and cower overwhelmed me. I reached down to the bottom of my strength and gathered it all up, forcing myself to stand still.

No one came. No one was likely to come. Had he killed everyone already? Blood spattered his clothes, and it didn't look like his.

Don't flinch. If you flinch, you're dead, Betsy.

Knowing I was seconds away from being torn to shreds anyway, I picked the only course of action that might bring Leonidas back to his senses. The crazy one.

"Hey," I barked back. "Don't give me that attitude. I'm the one trying to help you. Don't make me get the spray bottle again."

Half-expecting he'd lunge forward and rip out my throat, I clenched my fists, preparing for the worst. Then he surprised me by cocking his head to the side.

I'd penetrated his consciousness. Just a little, but I'd take it.

Then I smiled. "Or maybe you'd prefer a rolled magazine again?" I took a step toward him this time.

A warning rumble began in his throat.

I reached out a shaking hand and touched the side of his face. My common sense screamed at me.

You are going to lose a hand this way. He's going to turn and bite it right off. Haven't you seen any horror movies ever?

He may have turned into a monster, but he was still Leonidas. His skin was warmer than usual, and I skimmed my hands up into his hairline, gently scratching with my nails.

The rumble in his throat continued, his eyes fixed on me. For all that he'd turned into a terrifying beast, it amazed me how his underlying beauty remained. I'd never think to call a demon attractive, but in a way, Leo still was.

"There," I said, continuing to stroke the side of his face. "I see you in there, Leonidas. You can control this, and I'm right here to help you."

Then I did the stupidest thing of all. I leaned forward and pressed a kiss to his cheek, still petting him.

Unlike the tombscream, or the crib, Leonidas didn't

stink of sulfur. I closed my eyes and still recognized the scent of him. The masculine essence that drove me wild. I continued to stroke and croon to him, soothing reassurances, until I felt two large arms surrounding me.

When Leonidas took a shuddering breath, I opened my eyes in time to see the last bits of his wings recede back into his body. Once they'd finished their disappearing act, he slumped against me. Too heavy for me to hold, I directed him into a nearby chair. I crouched down, facing a now-human Leonidas again. A blank, almost bewildered expression on his face, I worried he hadn't come back to his wits.

"Are they dead?" I finally asked, my throat suddenly dry as the Sahara. As much as I hated the robed A double S's, I didn't want anyone dead.

After a long moment, he shook his head as if remembering himself. "No. But we need to go before they come." Then he stood and took me by the arm to lead us out.

After quickly finding a back door, we hustled back to the car and peeled out with a screech. The sky turned a violent orange, spiraling clouds tinged with purple as the sun set.

"Are you okay?" I asked, chancing a glance at Leonidas. He seemed completely closed off since those first few moments when he'd turned human again.

He didn't respond.

I remembered the flash of raw pain and betrayal when his master essentially shunned him and sentenced him to death. Of course he wasn't alright.

My mind raced for a way to help. It wasn't in my nature to let things lie. There was always a way to make things better.

We went to his master for help and information, but we'd only made another enemy. Now we needed to tread more carefully than ever. We still needed information if we wanted to track down the tombscream.

"Your master won't help? Well, we will get our own intel," I said, knowing exactly where to head next.

17

LEONIDAS

etsy drove us back to the institute, the second time today. Night had fallen, and this morning felt like a million years ago and the pleasure we found in her bed seemed like even longer. We rode in silence. Cold settled in the air around us, either from the chilly autumn night or because of what cooled between us.

She had to be terrified of me. I almost killed her, for gods' sake. I'd completely given over to the demon side of myself. Only when Betsy snapped at me in that sassy way she had when we first met in the hospital did I recognize her. Then her touch, her gentle kiss, the familiar scent of cinnamon and comfort I'd come to associate with her penetrated my consciousness, calming both me and the beast inside.

But it didn't change the fact I'd come too close to mauling her. Maybe Violetta was right. Perhaps I was too dangerous.

My master was the closest thing to a mother I'd ever had. The Luxis might not be a home, but the order was where I belonged, and that had always been a comfort.

Being cast out felt as though someone had cleaved through my ribs with an axe.

As she neared the institute, activity caught my attention.

"Pull over," I directed Betsy. "Behind those bushes and turn off the lights."

She did as I asked.

"What's going on up there?" she whispered, though no one would hear us several hundred feet away from the commotion.

Eight black SUVs and about twenty people in suits milled about. Their headlights illuminated the front of the institute.

"I don't know," I whispered back. We leaned in close so we could see through the gap in the brush, our heads inches apart.

I did my best to focus on the activity on the lawn and not the delicious smell of honey and cinnamon from the woman next to me. The urge to find solace and home in her lips pulled at me, but I pushed it away.

First one, then two, then four suited people exited the building carrying boxes and computer parts. They loaded up the SUVs before going back inside to retrieve more.

"Crap, they're taking all the records I was hoping we could use," Betsy whispered again. She paused, then said, "I don't want to sound like a conspiracy theorist, but considering I just found out we used you as an experiment, this looks like a cover-up to me."

Betsy grabbed my hand even as I reached for the door handle. "What are you doing?" she asked, her voice sharp with fear.

"I'm going to get those records."

"If you haven't noticed, there are twenty of them, maybe more inside."

My arm retracted so I could lean in closer to her. "Do you really think that's going to stop me?"

She squared her shoulders off toward me and said in a firm tone, "They're armed."

I had also noticed the guns strapped under their suit coats.

"And so am I," I said, nodding to the axe in the back of her car.

Horror and disbelief laced her words. "You are not going to kill a bunch of people simply because they have something we want."

"I'm not going to kill anyone," I assured her. "I'll simply explain I need those documents and if they say no, I'll swing my axe around until they see it my way."

The line between her brows deepened as she frowned. Though it resembled more of an adorable pout, and I had to resist the urge to kiss her to see how that pout tasted. "You are going to stroll in there and either get somebody killed or trigger another episode where you might or might not shift into a demonic creature."

I opened my mouth, then clicked it shut. Not willing to concede she had a point, I turned back to watch the suits. We watched for some time, then restlessness got to me. I couldn't sit here and do nothing. Betsy was right. I didn't want to risk transforming again, so I'd have to sit tight. But I needed a distraction.

"So, you left Montana for your... Jeremy?" I asked.

Betsy sighed. "Do we have to talk about this?"

Without turning to look at her, I said, "I could stick with my plan and take Sheila for a stroll."

"Fine," she said, her voice tight. "We dated since we were sixteen and he proposed when we graduated high school. But then there was med school for him, and nursing school for me. We worked at the same hospital in Montana and when he got a fellowship in Denver a couple of months ago, he insisted the opportunity was too good, so we left. And I got a job nursing at the same hospital."

Betsy absentmindedly rubbed her ring finger. She likely missed her engagement ring the way I missed Sheila when she wasn't near. That thought created a painful pressure in my chest.

"Then what happened?" The suits were standing around talking now, perhaps doing a last sweep of the place inside, but they shut the trunks.

She shrugged, staring at the cars, but I sensed she was looking through them rather than at them. "A month ago, he broke it off. Said he needed to be free to thrive, and he couldn't do that while taking care of me at the same time."

Something bubbled in the pit of my stomach. At first I couldn't identify the emotion, then I recognized it. Anger.

"He took care of you?" The sentence felt wrong coming out of my mouth. "From what I know of you, all you do is take care of others."

It was true. She took care of me and went far and above any care I'd known before. My comfort seemed to be her sole purpose, whether it was keeping me safe in her bed, ushering me into the shower, or feeding me cinnamon rolls. And now she'd helped me control the inner monster, not running away screaming like she should have.

It wasn't just me, either. Betsy treated everyone as if they needed a helping hand. I was no stranger to a life of service, but I surmised she may have saved more people than me.

She shrugged again. "I liked more affection than he had the bandwidth to give. And when he came home from the hospital, he either crashed or went out for drinks with his new co-workers. When I expressed my need to spend more time together and I didn't love how much he was drinking, he explained the right kinds of relationships in the hospital were a top priority. I had to be okay with being second priority. He let me plan our wedding, though. We would have married..." She stopped to mentally calculate. "God," she breathed. "Tomorrow. Tomorrow would have been our wedding day." She ran a hand over her eyes with a despondent sigh.

The fluffy white dress in her closet stuck out in my mind. Women often wore such dresses on their wedding day, and I suspected that had been hers. Conflicting feelings of wanting her to have what she desired and being grateful they didn't go through with the wedding rioted through me with more force than I wanted.

She interrupted my thoughts. "What are you going to do about the Luxis?"

"I don't know."

"Are they going to continue to hunt you?"

"It's likely."

"How could she do that?" Indignance slipped into her voice. "I've known you for a week, and I know you are worth fighting to save. Violetta said she's raised you for twenty-seven years, and she's ready to throw you away. I can't imagine."

"Why? Because your family has practically hunted you down to drag you back to Montana?"

The sharp look I got told me I'd crossed a line.

After thinking a moment, I said, "I will try to find a way to reverse what's been done to me. And if that isn't an option, I need to prove that I can still be of use to my master."

"Even though she burned you?" Betsy asked in disbelief.

"Though bitterness fills me at being cast out, I am still a

knight of the light. I am a tool of the Luxis, and they created me. Without them, I would have no purpose."

"Hmm, I guess we have that in common. Our need to be useful."

"Our need to save others?" I added.

She let out a dry laugh. Then she said, "Why not start a new life? I'm sure you could dodge the Luxis if you really wanted to."

"Because being a knight of the light is my destiny. My body may be changing, but my purpose has not. As long as I can reverse or control the demon inside."

She swallowed hard next to me. "Leo... I'm not sure this is something that can be reversed."

I fell into thoughtful silence.

"Would you really want to go back to having a master tell you what to do?"

"She has guided me, my whole life."

"Sure, but because she wanted something from you."

I didn't bring up the irony of her statement. From what I gathered, Betsy's family was clamoring for her to return because they had a list of to-dos they wished her to complete. Instead, I said, "We both want the same thing. To protect the innocent, to fight the darkness. She is attached to the old ways and does not see the benefit of being flexible. I've had the benefit of fieldwork to understand that flexibility is tantamount to fighting the darkness."

"She's kind of like a mother to you."

My head snapped toward her. "What makes you say that?"

Betsy shrugged. "The way you talk about her. Something in your voice. It sounds like it's more than just a mission. You sound like you miss her. Like how I miss my mom. Before my horrid teen years, she had this way of making me feel like I belonged. If I had a problem or needed guidance, I went to her. And I miss that every day." Betsy looked into her hands as her voice tightened with emotion.

Her words pulled at my gut in more ways than one. The Luxis was an order, not a family. But the way Betsy spoke of her mom, I couldn't deny that my master evoked similar feelings. Even when it hurt the most, I still understood her dedication to duty when she burned me.

I needed to turn away from wherever this was headed. "So your sister and the pie thief want you to marry the imbecile, even after he left you?"

"He's not an imbecile," she said, almost as if it were a reflex.

"He absolutely is," I said. "Whatever man would make you second priority is a disgrace to mankind. You deserve to be lavished with attention like a queen."

"As you mentioned, you haven't been among civilians that much, but that gets exhausting after a while. I need to learn to lower my expectations."

I reached for her chin, gently directing her face toward me. There was such sadness in those eyes. A deep yearning to always do more, and yet never getting there.

"If I were my own man, I would wake you every morning with my mouth between your legs, carry you when you were tired, and bring you everything your heart desires."

Our faces had grown close enough that I could taste her sweet breath.

"But you're not your own man," she said hesitantly. Her eyes flitted back and forth from my eyes to my mouth.

Things had changed. I wasn't beholden to the order of Luxis anymore. But that didn't mean I was free.

Pain lanced through my heart. "No, I am not. I was a

weapon, but now I'm something worse. I'm a danger to you, like Violetta said."

Still staring at my mouth, Betsy licked her own lips. I groaned at the sight of that pink tongue, remembering the feel of her mouth and needing another taste.

"So, commitment is out of the question," she said, more than asked.

"Absolutely." Our words had grown husky with twin need.

"Then maybe we can focus on having no-strings sex."

My heart raced, my skin ached to touch her as if she'd pushed a lever on all my senses up to eleven. The shock of her suggestion must have shown on my face, because she rushed to explain.

"I mean, since the creature already thinks you've claimed me, and I need to figure out what I've done to you, maybe we can use the pauses for hot meaningless sex."

Despite all that had happened today, a wicked grin curled up my lips.

Car doors slammed shut, startling us apart. Engines started up with a rumble. The suits were moving out. Pressing my hands against the dashboard, I struggled to keep myself back, though every ounce of my being commanded I go after them before it was too late.

"It's our last chance, legs. I can still get those files."

A soft hand fell on my forearm. "No, let them go. I have another idea."

18

―――――――

LEONIDAS

"I'm not sure if this is the right address," Betsy said, peering over the steering wheel at the house she pulled in front of. In a line of close-set houses in downtown Denver, we pulled in front of one painted deep purple.

"This is the correct house," I affirmed, unbuckling my seatbelt, already out of the car.

I pressed the doorbell, and it lit up with a blue circle. A wail came from inside, breaking the silence of the night.

Minutes later, the porch light turned on and the door swung open. "Are you kidding me? We just got him to sleep —" Krystan answered the door wearing sweatpants and a sports bra. Her jet-black hair was tied up in a messy ponytail. She smelled like soap, but with my heightened senses, I could also smell carrots, peas, and milk underneath.

"Hello, Krystan."

The woman in front of me was rail thin, and stretch marks crawled up her stomach like tiger stripes, making her all the more ferocious. Anyone who underestimated this woman, for even a second, would be making a huge mistake.

She half-scowled, half-smirked. "Glad to see you back on your feet, you big oaf." With that, she held her arms out. I gathered her in a hug, pulling her off her feet. Krystan didn't care for affection, which made it all the more fun to force it upon her.

Behind her, Travis came down the stairs with a boy a little over six months old in his arms. Like Krystan, Travis had dark bags under his eyes and his hair stuck out in absolute chaos.

Stepping back, I introduced Betsy. "This is Betsy."

"We've met," Krystan said, regarding Betsy with a wary but not altogether unfriendly gaze. "Come inside."

"So, how do you know each other, exactly?" Betsy asked, as we followed Krystan past the pink floral sitting room to the dining room with a marred wooden table that could seat twelve. The house smelled of mothballs and vanilla. This used to be Krystan's grandmother's house until she passed.

"We saved the world together," Travis said, following behind us, bouncing the baby on his hip.

"Couple of times," Krystan shot back over her shoulder. "Coffee? Tea?"

"Cocoa?" I asked.

Krystan smiled. "With the little marshmallows, I remember." She turned her gaze on Betsy.

"Oh no," she waved a hand before pulling them back against her body. "I'm just fine." She seemed nervous to not be the one in control. Normally, she would be the one offering drinks, trying to make someone comfortable. I got the sense she wasn't often on the receiving end.

"She'll have cocoa too. Extra marshmallows," I instructed. Krystan raised an eyebrow, her dark eyes darting back and forth between us. I shot her a warning glance. She stifled a devilish smile before disappearing into the kitchen.

Then we sat at the table while Travis continued to stand, gently bouncing the baby.

"So what can we do for—" The baby interrupted Travis, letting out another shrill wail. "Sorry guys, he doesn't go down easily."

Betsy stood back up and held her hands out. "May I?"

Travis instantly handed over the crying babe. Betsy cradled the baby in her arms with a soft cooing sound. She paced, softly telling the baby he was alright. In moments, the baby calmed.

Travis dropped into the seat next to me. "What the heck? I was doing the exact same thing. Does my baby hate me?"

I slapped Travis's back in encouragement. He buckled under my touch. It always amazed me how such a skinny guy survived so many apocalypses. I would have bet he'd be the first to go.

Betsy sent him a commiserating smile. "Your baby doesn't hate you. Don't take it personally. My sisters call me the baby whisperer. I have the same effect on all my nieces and nephews. It's just a talent I have. What's the little guy's name?"

"Tristan," Travis said.

"Tristan..." Betsy repeated.

"Yeah, it's our celebrity couple name," Travis explained.

She cocked an eyebrow, while I simply leaned back in my chair, having heard this before.

"You know, like how back in the day when Brad Pitt and Angelina Jolie were together, the public referred to them as Brangelina?"

"Travis and Krystan," Betsy started, but Travis finished for her.

"Yeah, makes Tristan."

She stared at him as if he were crazy. I never got why

everyone had such varying degrees of response to their baby's name. It was clearly a civilian thing.

"Snarpsss wantsss a twinkiesss," a scratchy voice interrupted. It came from the African gray parrot standing on the cage by the table.

"Not now, you dumb bird," Travis scolded.

"Then Snarpss will eat your gutssss," the bird retorted.

"Wow, you taught him to say all that?" Betsy asked.

"Snarpsss will eat the ladysssss," the bird threatened.

Travis got up and walked over to the cage, explaining as he went. "No, Snarp is a demon trapped inside a bird's body with an addiction to snack cakes."

"A... a demon?" Betsy's eyes darted back and forth between all of us in the room, holding the baby a little tighter to her.

"Don't threaten Betsy," I growled at the bird.

The parrot's head cocked to the side before jumping to the side to avoid Travis's grasp. "The big onesss like me now."

I didn't like his association. I bared my teeth at him, leaning forward. Snarp flapped his way into his cage. Travis quickly locked the cage and drew a blanket down over it before taking a seat again.

"Sorry, he's not exactly house trained, and he talks a big talk, but the truth is he is super good with Tristan. It's like having a guard dog who can talk."

Krystan came back in with a tray of mugs. Her eyes widened with surprise at seeing Betsy with the baby before narrowing in suspicion. "So, I leave you with the baby for one minute and you hand him over to the first stranger you see?" she asked Travis in a biting tone.

A flash of alarm went through Betsy's face and her

shoulders tensed. Her discomfort affected me more than it should have.

Before I could do or say anything, Travis dropped an elbow on the arm and spoke to Betsy in a kind tone. "Don't take it personally. Krystan doesn't trust easily." Then he turned to his partner. "Check it out, Krys, our boy has finally relaxed. Isn't that a good thing?"

Krystan set the tray down on the table, eyes still narrowed, but some of the animosity drained from her gaze.

Betsy approached Krystan. "I'm sorry. I didn't mean to overstep. Here you go," she said, ready to hand the kid back to his mother.

Krystan looked between her son and Betsy for a long moment. "I guess he could use some rest, if you don't mind holding him a little longer." I knew it just about killed her to say that.

Betsy smiled and nodded her head. Krystan dropped into the chair at the head of the table while Travis distributed the cocoas. It was difficult to tear my eyes away from Betsy as she rocked the babe. There was simply something about the woman that effervesced warmth and softness, with an underlying strength.

Not to mention seeing her rock the baby, an intense primal sensation hit me in the gut though I couldn't name what it was. All I knew was seeing her like that felt right. The soft, unguarded smile on her face communicated she was in her element. We all had our own talents and magic, and she was clearly weaving her best spell. Both the baby and I were bewitched.

"So, what are we dealing with?" Krystan asked with a scowl, a chocolate and whipped cream mustache now covering her top lip. "The end of the world again?"

Betsy's head jerked up. "You really have done this a couple of times."

"No, nothing like that," I said to Krystan. "I need your help. Betsy said you were at the institute."

"Yeah, we were called in to do a cleanup," Krystan said, looking into her mug. Travis shot her a look.

Betsy answered this time. "We went back to retrieve any other records the institute had, but when we got there, a bunch of people in suits were clearing out the place. They took everything, file cabinets, computers, even some of the medical supplies. But I remembered you dropping your bag, and you had all those files and drives…"

"Why would we take files from a place we were one hundred percent hired to clean up?" Travis asked, followed by a nervous laugh. The forced laughter continued on for far too long and dropped into an awkward silence.

Krystan rubbed her brow. "God, Travis, you are the worst liar in history. Even if I hadn't turned into a supernatural lie detector, I'd know you were lying."

His cheeks turned bright red.

"Okay, so no one hired us," Krystan answered him. "We heard what happened on the police scanners and wanted to check it out. We've been hearing rumors about that place for a while."

"What rumors?" I asked. I felt more than saw Betsy stiffen. The baby had fallen asleep in her arms.

This time Travis spoke. "Nothing concrete, but it's a privately funded hospital and we've heard they have been experimenting on specimens. Then we heard they got a government contract, something to do with the military."

"What do you think it means?" I asked, my throat drying up.

Travis and Krystan exchanged another look. "We've

been hearing talk of our government trying to militarize the creatures from the Stygian. Find ways to control those forces." Krystan shrugged. "Could be total crap, though. How could anyone control one of those monsters or harness the energy of an evil spirit?"

"But"—Travis lifted a finger—"it's not out of the question. Hitler often tried occult methods to gain power. Our own government funded a project in the seventies to see if we could get people to astral project to help us spy on other governments. If you ask me, I think that's exactly what our government and all the others would do. This worldwide infestation of demons has united us. But every day we are reaching a level of new normal. At some point, we are going to fight over resources and power again, and if you had a pack of demon dogs at your beck and call, you'd lose a hell of a lot fewer soldiers. If you could get a ghost to spy on your enemies across the country... I'm just saying."

Travis's eyes lit up as he spoke of conspiracy theories. My stomach churned. They didn't know they were talking about the fate the institute had intended for me. No matter where or what I was, people considered me a weapon to be wielded. They would have likely discarded me like Violetta had, if I'd outgrown my usefulness.

Pain twisted inside me again. My master's expression of regret and deep sadness imprinted on me. It confirmed she'd cared for me the way I'd grown to care for her, like we were our own little family. But she'd instantly proven we were anything but, when she sentenced me to death.

When I met Betsy's eyes, her face paled.

"Travis, could you take Tristan?" I asked, sensing she was at the end of her rope.

Travis jumped up and retrieved the calm baby before

setting him in a nearby bassinet. The kid curled his arms up but remained asleep.

I directed Betsy to a chair and took her hand in mine. A tremor went through her fingers. "What is it?"

She licked her lips and took a deep, shaky breath, as if bracing herself. "Remember, I told you of the patient I lost the morning of the attack?"

"The what? You worked at the institute?" Krystan asked, suddenly alarmed. I ignored her and urged Betsy on.

"A dark spirit had infected him. We were treating him for levitation and mild possession. He talked. He talked all the time. He would describe Niagara Falls, and how the water tasted, saying he'd visited that morning. He spoke of the patients in the other rooms like he'd seen them. They kept the patient under constant surveillance, someone always recording what he said. When we administered his treatments, we tried to lead him through specific meditation protocols to relax him. We would tell him to envision flying across China through lush fields and bustling cities. Then we had a couple of Chinese words we would say. The doctor insisted it was related to hypnotherapy to calm the patient. The day... the day he died..." She closed her eyes. "He grabbed me before I administered his treatment. He said he didn't want to go back there. If I forced him to go that far again, he would die. His soul wouldn't come back this time. I assured him to relax into what I was saying. I held his hand and led him through the meditation. I'll... I'll never forget the way tears leaked out of the corners of his eyes as I felt his life leave him."

Betsy wiped angrily at the tears on her face. "Do you think... do you think I killed him? Instead of a meditation, I was directing him to astrally project, and it cut the ties between his soul and his body?"

No one spoke. A grandfather clock ticked, stretching the time. I didn't know what to tell her.

"Oh god." She pushed away from the table and left the room. She rounded the corner, and she closed a door, presumably to the bathroom.

I started to get up when Krystan stopped me with a shake of her head. "Leave her be a minute," she said softly.

"Christ," Travis said, rubbing both hands on his face. "Who knows what else they've been doing in that place?"

Fear and emotion rolled through me. I was their project as well. They were giving me something that changed me in the hopes they could control and use me.

"Leonidas?" Krystan asked, "What is it?"

"I was hunting a creature. Like nothing I'd ever seen or heard of before. Just as I was about to kill it, we were ambushed. Subdued by tranquilizers. When I woke up, I was chained up in a research hospital where I was informed I'd been exhibiting supernatural abilities and, therefore, must have been infected by a demon. Through treatments, they could heal me. They also kept the creature in their institute."

Krystan covered Travis's hand as her mouth dropped in horror. "Oh god, when was this?"

"I was there for a couple months. Then the creature escaped, killing everyone. Except Betsy and I got away."

"You trust her? Even though she worked for the institute?" Krystan asked.

I looked in the direction where she'd disappeared. "With my life," I said without a single doubt in my mind or body. "She defied direct orders to get me out of there. And she is helping me. They did things to me. They changed me. I'm part demon now, and Violetta has renounced me."

"Well, shit," Travis breathed.

Betsy emerged, eyes red-rimmed, but with a new resolve in her demeanor. "Did you take confidential records from the institute?"

"Yes," Krystan said, meeting her intent gaze.

"I would like to see them now."

With that, Travis stood. "Of course. Come with me. They're upstairs." He led her away, leaving Krystan and me.

The weight of an intent stare drew my attention. There was a sparkle in those hard dark eyes. "I like her."

I did too. Far more than I should. Still, I said nothing.

"You like her too," she said.

"I can't be with her, Krystan. I'm a monster now."

Her eyes softened. "That's fucking bull, Leo."

"My master—" I stopped to correct myself. "Violetta said my... change is the beginning of a prophecy. The darkness would taint the knights of the light and bring down the five orders."

"You know as well as I do all the orders are full of shit. They used to have you believe you had no soul, and that's why you were indebted to fight demons for them."

It was true, but it never mattered to me why I fought the demons. I knew it was the right thing to do at my core.

"Maybe so," I answered, "but you know as well as I that their prophecies may come in pieces, but they are never wrong."

"No, they aren't," she said slowly, "but we've seen those incomplete prophecies misinterpreted plenty of times. You aren't some doomsday device. Don't let Vi make you feel that way."

"She gave orders to eliminate me," I said in a low voice.

"Are you fucking kidding me?" Krystan's hands slammed on the table and the baby awoke with a wail. She rushed over to Tristan. "Dammit, sorry, sorry buddy. I didn't mean it." She rocked him in her arms, and he quieted.

She turned to face me. "After everything we've done, they are still pulling this?" With a sound somewhere between a frustrated sigh and a snort, she said, "Well, you know what? Calan left their asses and is happy with Emma now. Maybe it was time you quit the Luxis anyway and strike out on your own. Hook up with tall and beautiful upstairs."

Calan had a different relationship with his master than I had. Violetta and I had been the closest of all the masters and their wards. I'd come to think we were different. It was why I could bend the rules, as long as I didn't break them.

"I can't. I'm a danger to her, Krystan. She deserves... normal."

She shrugged. "Is normal a thing anymore?"

I couldn't respond. I'd never known normal in my life. But I knew it lived somewhere in the bliss between Betsy's legs, her colorful, busy apartment, and a cat with one eye.

19

BETSY

It was the middle of the night when we returned to my apartment with copies of the files. Before we left the purple house, Krystan, who frankly scared the bejeezus out of me, approached me. She shocked me when she threw her arms around me and said she bowed down to the baby whisperer. Travis also gave me his thanks.

But during the drive home, I felt anything but worthy of gratitude. Not only had I gotten mixed up in a morally reprehensible work environment, but I'd also been responsible for the death of at least one of my patients. And what I'd done to Leonidas... I understood he was an old-fashioned sacred hero, and I'd been part of destroying that. I helped destroy his life, his mission, and his home with the order.

The black tar pit at my center sucked me down into the familiar pain of guilt. Once sucked in, there was no getting out. I wanted to run to the retirement home and pick up some volunteer shifts, but this late at night, I'd have to settle for some other activity.

Crocheting wasn't enough to ease my mind. No, I'd have

to pick out a complicated recipe to bake, since Michael ate half the apple pie intended for my neighbor. I could take a shot at one of those ganache Earl Grey pies instead.

The longer I went without thanking Martin for picking me up from the hospital, the faster I sank into that tar pit. And oh god, I hadn't even begun on the care package I owed Montrell for taking me to the hospital. Then, with my sister and brother-in-law in town, I'd blown them off. One by one, I piled more sins onto the mountain that already felt like it was breaking my back. But I deserved it.

I was such an utter and complete rat.

"What are you thinking over there?" Leo asked in a low rumble. I realized I hadn't even been polite enough to put on the radio to fill the silence.

"I'm thinking about making a ganache Earl Grey pie when we get home," I half-lied.

"Aren't you tired?" he asked.

"No. I don't sleep a lot. Especially when I've got a lot on my mind."

"You need to rest. Your body needs to recuperate from the stress."

"Recuperate? How can I recuperate? I just found out I've been torturing and experimenting on unsuspecting people. I killed one of my patients." My voice hit an unnatural pitch.

Just when I thought Leo was going to leave me to my thoughts, he said, "You would never knowingly hurt anyone."

A sob caught in my chest. It was an old sob, one I never allowed to release. It was so old, that particular bubble of emotion was covered in cobwebs and dust from being trapped in my body. I spoke past the pressure that threatened to disintegrate my heart. "It doesn't matter. Even if you accidentally hurt someone, it's just as bad."

Street lights flashed over Leo's face and I caught sight of the fierce expression on his face. As if he were trying to pull out the secrets of my soul and I was giving him a fight.

He wanted the little tattered confetti pieces? I'd give them to him. "It's not the first time I killed someone."

I focused on the white stripes of the road. Then I pulled out the horrible truth, knowing he'd never look at me the same way. But I deserved nothing less. "I killed my mother when I was fourteen."

Leo said nothing, and I didn't look at him in case I lost my nerve. "I wasn't a great kid. I sassed my parents a lot and had a rebellious streak. When I was fourteen, I started hanging out with a bad crowd. We'd steal bottles of liquor and go out to one of our friends' barns and party. Well, one time, someone called the cops on us. They wanted to scare us good, so they took us all to the sheriff's station to the drunk tank. I called my mom to pick me up."

The pressure on my heart intensified so I could barely breathe, remembering the disappointment in her voice the last time we spoke. "She had to come get me in the middle of the night because she told the sheriff she wanted to take care of punishment at home. But she never showed up."

I waited for the tears to come, but I'd long cried my eyes out over what happened. I went on. "Someone in a moving van fell asleep at the wheel and swerved into the oncoming lane and hit my mom. She died because of me."

The night had likely been like it was tonight. Clear, with few cars on the road. But as we drove back to my apartment, my vigilance was on high alert. I was all too aware of how someone could swerve out of nowhere and bash into me.

"Accidents happen," Leo said.

"My stupidity wasn't an accident. If I hadn't been a selfish brat for no other reason than boredom, I wouldn't have killed her. My little sisters would have grown up with a mom. Maybe my dad wouldn't have had a stroke at forty. Maybe my mom could have met all her grandbabies. I've done everything I could to fill her shoes, but no matter how much I try, there is no making up for it. And then the second time I try to be selfish, running away to Colorado with my fiancé, I end up killing someone inadvertently again. Not to mention what I've done to you." A harsh bark of a laugh escaped me. "Adie is right. I should go home with Jeremy and take care of my family. Then maybe I won't cause any more harm if I keep all my focus on helping. God only knows how normal and safe it is back there."

His silence spoke volumes. Leonidas, a knight of the light who lives by a selfless code of helping to protect others, could see the ugliness in my selfish heart. How my nature was to hurt others when I wasn't actively trying to help. I knew he sat beside me in utter disgust, and I welcomed the judgement. Maybe I'd learn this time.

"You're wrong," he finally said. "There are so many things wrong with what you said, I can barely fathom how you've been able to function under the weight of all that you carry. As someone who is dedicated to protecting others, I can tell you as a fact that not everyone will live. Sometimes I am too late to help those in need and sometimes they die in the crossfire. If I carried the burden of their souls, I could not get up and go out and try again. For everyone I lose, I save five more. It's not about saving everyone. It's not about making sure every blow of my axe hits its mark. It's about moving forward, doing as best you can. And if you think following your partner to Colorado to support him is what makes you selfish, I'm not sure what to say about that."

My next words came out quietly. "I wanted to leave. I would have never done it on my own, but Jeremy helped me leave my family. I spent so much of my time taking care of them that I couldn't think straight. I thought coming out here might be good for me, too."

I'd never said it out loud, and it felt as horrible as I thought it would. My guilt notched up to a sledgehammer that hit me so hard, no part of me felt safe anymore.

"Your desire to make a new life did not kill that man," he said.

"How can you say that?"

"The institute is responsible for what's happened. But you act like your need to take care of yourself is what caused all this. Did you know, as a knight of the light, one of the most important aspects to us is recovery? In between fights, I must eat well, I must rest well, and keep my mind clear. If I cannot do those things, I cannot help anyone. Violetta taught me that. When the other masters sought to send me on another mission as soon as I came home battered and broken, she would wedge herself in between us. She'd insist they give me the time to mend, or I could help no one. You want to help everyone, legs, but act like it's a sin to help yourself."

I pulled into the parking spot at my apartment building, ending our conversation. My soul felt as ragged around the edges as a torn-up piece of paper. I didn't know if I wanted to internalize what he was saying or not, so I let the words float outside my being.

As soon as we got inside, I turned on the lamp, casting the warm glow onto my cheery apartment. My apartment usually made me feel better, but right now I only felt wretched.

The door shut behind me, and I felt the solid mass of Leonidas behind me. Slowly, he turned me around to face him. He tilted my chin up so he could stare through me with those silver eyes.

"It's after midnight," he said.

"Yes," I responded, not sure of the importance.

Then he leaned over and kissed me. For a man built of savage power and strength, his kiss was achingly tender. The warmth of his kiss flowed into the cold, barren places of my soul. I kissed him back, emotion sloshing inside me. A messy torrent.

He opened his mouth, and I met his tongue in perfect rhythm. The unique masculine taste of him drove me wild. There was something earthy about him that reminded me of the massive trees on the West Coast. Trees so massive you couldn't wrap your arms around them, but they were ancient and steady.

In his kiss, I found my grounding. The longer our tongues teased and tasted, the more my roots grew into the earth. Leaning into the feeling, I pushed his shirt up so I could lay my hands against his incredible cut abs, up to his strong, broad chest. He let me pull his shirt off, revealing his packed muscle and sculpted shoulders.

I should have been afraid of him. I knew what he could transform into. He was both man and monster, and as much as I feared that, I needed him near.

Even in the silver sheen of his eyes, I caught endless depths of compassion. I could fall there forever and never hit the ground. I continued to run my hands over his chest and abs until he caught my mouth in another kiss. The ache in my heart spread lower until the need to be filled over-whelmed me.

Leonidas pulled my shirt off over my head, then pulled me up onto his hips. My legs naturally wrapped around his waist. A moment of panic overwhelmed my senses. I was too big to be held. I'd drag him to the floor with my stature. As if to prove me wrong, Leo's hands massaged my rear, expertly pressing my center against the hardness under his jeans. He rocked me against him until I threw my head back, gasping.

The black tar that had nearly pulled me under receded, as all my senses could comprehend only one feeling. More.

I needed more of him.

"God, do you know how you make me feel, legs?" he rumbled. Then he reached up to grab my breast. He squeezed it experimentally, sending shock waves down my body. Again, I feared he would drop me, or fall, but he easily held me up while fondling my breast.

His thumb grazed the tip of my breast until my nipple was straining for more through the padded bra that was all too thick now. Again, the need for more pulsated through me with insistence.

"Bedroom," I said before biting his lip. Hand grabbing onto those rock-hard shoulders, I traced the shell of his ear before sucking on the lobe.

Leo shuddered underneath. "Dear gods, woman. You must be a witch to make me feel these things."

Then he did as directed and took us to the bedroom. He laid me back on the bed. Unfortunately, thirty of my hand-made pillows covered the bed. We worked to smack them off to the space between the bed and the wall. Leonidas let out a low throat chuckle that warmed my heart.

After we cleared the bed, he quickly worked the zipper and button on my jeans. He shucked them down my legs, his mouth following in a fiery trail. With one hand, I reached back and unsnapped my bra, flinging it off into the abyss of pillows. Leo set a knee on the bed so he could lean over and capture one of my nipples between his lips.

My back arched off the bed as my body begged for more.

He covered the other breast, warming it from the cool air of the room, while he continued to tongue and nibble around the aching peak of my other breast. Molten liquid surged between my legs as I suffered between the unbearable ache at my center and the need for more of his mouth on my breast. The friction of his tongue against my nipple was like a match striking flint, causing fire to burst into existence in an instant.

Then he stood to kick off his own boots and pants, standing bare before me. With only the light behind him filtering from the front hall, and the moonlight seeping in through the window, he was a glorious vision.

I blinked twice, feeling out of time and space. Never in my dreams could I have imagined meeting someone like him, let alone have him standing naked in my bedroom. He reached down and grasped his hard, rigid length, standing up at attention.

"I want you inside me," I whispered.

"I love when you do that," he grumbled.

I blinked. "When I do what?"

"Lick your lips. You do it when you are concentrating, nervous, or turned on." I could see the outline of a smirk in the moonlight. "The way your lips plump and shimmer after you've licked them is enough to drive a man or monster to madness."

Before I could respond, he covered me with his body. His hardness slid along my soft center without penetrating. The sensation was so good I had the urge to curse. Then his hand found its way between us, dipping an experimental finger inside me. I squirmed and gasped. I wanted all of him. My insides trembled and clamped down in antic-ipation.

"I love how ready you are." He kissed my lips. "So ripe, so sweet."

We both groaned as he slid in, inch by inch. Heat and pressure drowned out all sound and thought. I raked my nails along his back as I threw my head back.

The way Leonidas fought was savage and merciless, but as he entered me, he met my gaze, letting me know he was there. It was as if at that moment, he didn't want to be alone either. I reached up to the surprisingly soft hair on his face.

He kept filling me, stretching me to my limits until my breaths turned ragged. It was just as good as last time. No, it was better, somehow. I didn't think that could have been possible.

He touched places inside of me I hadn't known existed, putting me on the edge right there. To encourage him, I rocked my hips against him.

The sparks from the friction could have started a forest fire. A growl vibrated from his chest into mine.

He thrust into me, finding secret spots of pleasure I hadn't known existed. The world fell away, and my body surged and rocked against the waves of sensation overtaking me.

The first time we'd come together, we explored pleasure. But this time, it was so much more. It was solace and understanding in ways I never knew could be shared with another. It was as if at that moment I never realized how lonely I had been for my whole life until right now.

I never wanted to stop, even as my center tightened, approaching that same cliff's edge Leo had taken me to earlier this morning. I gasped, like a guppy needing air, where there suddenly was none.

"That's it, baby, let go," he said, as if knowing I was close. How did he know me better than I knew myself?

The tightness inside my body snapped as I dissolved into shudders so intense, a bit of fear accompanied my release. I grabbed onto his shoulders, riding out the pleasure.

Leonidas kept rocking into me, murmuring encouragement. Spent, I collapsed in a boneless heap. Leo pushed back up to his knees, but never left my body. I could see the sheen of perspiration on Leonidas's body and our scent filled my bedroom. His lips curved in a wicked half smile.

"Do you have any idea how sexy that is?"

Blood rushed to my cheeks. "I completely lost control. I doubt that looked sexy."

He shook his head, while his hips rocked again slowly. "It's the most erotic thing I've ever seen. You are so responsive, so open and emotive. It's like I know everything you are experiencing because you let me read it on your face."

If my cheeks weren't bright flaming red before, they were now. But the gentle rocking of his hips rekindled my need.

Leonidas reached a hand down between us as he sped up his rhythm while watching me.

Even as the pressure started again in my lower belly, I blurted out, "I can't."

"Oh, you can," he said, then threw his head back, pausing his hips a moment as if trying to regain control. When he dropped his head, meeting my gaze again, I lost my breath from the intensity of his expression. "And all you have to do is lie back and enjoy the ride. I intend to bring you to orgasm again and again until you can't see or walk straight."

I still couldn't catch my breath. Despite his insane claim, I believed every word he said. Leonidas was not a man who made promises or claims lightly.

The third time I crested my orgasm, sweat covered me, and my voice turned hoarse. On the fourth, Leonidas dropped his body, so it was flush against mine again. His fingers wound in my hair as his hot breath fanned against my ear. "Today is the day you told me you were supposed to be married to that fool. But now you are going to remember this day as the one where I brought you to orgasm more times than you believed possible."

Even through my sex-drenched brain, I realized this was why he made a point about it being past midnight earlier.

He continued. "Today is the day you'll remember being a sexual goddess who deserves worship and pleasure above all else. How you brought a beast to his knees for you. Now do it one more time for me. Can you give me one more of those pretty screams, legs?"

I was already well on my way, climbing back up, and his husky words in my ear shot straight down to my center. My legs tightened around his waist as my inner muscles clenched and pulsated. My brain turned up to eleven, so I couldn't hear or think anything.

As I came yet again, Leonidas's hips surged against mine with a feral, possessive growl. Then he collapsed against me. When he tried to roll off me, I wrapped my legs tighter to make sure he didn't move.

"Just a few more minutes," I asked.

He nearly crushed me, but his weight was more reassuring. A comfort I would never get used to.

"Anything you want," he whispered, laying soft kisses on my neck. Somewhere between trying to remember what I was supposed to be doing, and tracing the lines of his back muscles, I drifted into a hard, dreamless sleep.

20

———

BETSY

As soon as I woke, my hand reached for Leonidas but it met with cold, empty bed sheets. I curled in on myself, wishing for his warmth. I stayed there for several long minutes, observing my room.

Normally, I never dallied in bed. The second my eyes opened, I was up and at 'em. But for the first time in what I could remember, I lingered, enjoying the feel of the soft bed sheets and the glorious satiation in my body. With a glance at the clock, I was shocked to see it was almost nine thirty. I rarely slept in past six when I wasn't working. I'd never gotten so much sleep, but Leonidas had worn me out.

All month, I'd been dreading waking up this day, knowing it should have been my wedding day. But never in a million years would I have anticipated waking up feeling sexually spent and satisfied by a man like Leonidas.

It made it hard to decide if my life was a living dream or a nightmare right now. On one hand, a demon was hunting us, specifically me, because Leonidas 'claimed' me, but the larger part of me refused to be sorry about what we were doing right now.

The sound of soft voices roused my curiosity. I got up and grabbed a pair of pink sweatpants, a bra, and a gray T-shirt I'd gotten from the blood drive I'd helped run last year. It was the softest shirt I owned. A soreness pulsated through my center, but I welcomed it. It only brought the scorching hot memories of early morning to the forefront.

As soon as I opened the door, the smell of coffee and bacon invaded my senses. I headed out to the kitchen and was surprised by a number of things. First and foremost, Martin sat at the kitchen counter with a mug in hand. He wore a soft blue cashmere sweater, and had left his pork-pie hat at home, revealing snow-white hair. Next to him was a frighteningly high stack of pancakes and an equally terrifying pile of bacon and scrambled eggs.

But the most shocking sight was of Leonidas cooking in my kitchen, bare chest, with my cat wrapped over his shoulders as if Bubbles were posing as a feather boa.

Leo heaped yet more bacon onto the already impressive pile. Then those silver eyes looked up at me under his scarred eyebrow. Though the gesture was entirely innocent, there was an inherently dangerous air about him. He pinned me with his gaze, and a shiver of excitement ran through me as I remembered the impossible chaos he'd created in my body last night.

Then the most beautiful thing happened. That dark, dangerous man's face split into a smile, and I nearly dropped to the floor in a dead-away faint.

"Well, good morning, sleepy pants," Martin said with a smile, following Leo's gaze. "I hope you don't mind my intrusion, but Leo here invited me in for breakfast."

"It's the least I can do after you taught me how to use the coffee pot," Leo responded.

Martin waggled his eyebrows at me. "I really did a lot by pushing that button."

The deep, throaty laugh that emerged from Leonidas made my toes curl.

Snapping to, I walked over to the side of the island, where Leonidas was reaching for some dirty dishes. Guilt crashed over me. I was the hostess, and I'd slept in. Leo was hungry and had been forced to fend for himself. Panic shot up to my throat, closing it off. It was like promising to throw a party, but then showing up hours late to the shindig I planned nothing for. It was akin to the nightmare of showing up at school and finding out there was a test I didn't prepare for.

"What are you doing?" Leo asked.

I tried to wave him off. "I can take over from here. You should sit and eat. I'll finish up breakfast and clean."

His hand covered mine, forcing me to put down a pan. "You are going to sit down and relax." He gently set Bubbles down on the floor.

"No, I couldn't possib—"

My protest cut off as Leo scooped me up, throwing me over his shoulder. A surprised squeak escaped my throat as I found myself upside down, facing the muscular curve of his lower back.

Then he walked around the island to where Martin sipped his coffee. Despite the rough handling, he gently set me on the stool next to my neighbor.

"You will sit here. You will relax, enjoy some food, and let me take care of this." Warning laced his words. He meant business. "Now would you like tea or coffee?"

I opened my mouth to tempt fate and protest again, but he silenced me with a look.

"Tea," I said weakly. Then I rushed to say, "But you made coffee. I can have that."

Leo reached over, touching his knuckles under my chin, gently forcing my mouth to close. "Martin said you drink Earl Grey in the morning, so I made both." Then he walked over to my rose tea pot and poured steaming amber liquid into my mug shaped like an enormous ball of yarn.

Leo rounded the island, set the tea in front of me, and dropped a scalding kiss on my neck. Martin blushed into his own mug, averting his eyes.

"I don't know where you found this one, Betsy, but he's a good one," Martin said, after Leo returned to the other side of the kitchen. Bubbles jumped to the counter and then onto Leo's shoulder again, as if she couldn't stand to be away from him.

Same, Bubbles. Same.

Again, I wondered if I'd stepped into an alternate dimension. Or maybe a dream. A heavenly dream I never hoped to wake from.

"I hope you don't mind," Leo said. "I helped myself to the sustenance in your fridge for supplies."

Martin set an elbow on the table. "Yeah, why do you have three pounds of bacon just sitting in your fridge? You stock food like you were preparing for the apocalypse."

Judging by the spread on the island, Leo used up all the bacon and eggs.

"You know I like to bake a lot," I said, my voice sounding strange and airy to my own ears. "I had planned to make some quiche for the Denver Rescue Mission."

A plate full of food appeared in front of me, along with syrup.

"You buttered my pancakes," I said, again in the absent faraway voice.

I felt both Leo's and Martin's eyes on me, pausing their movements.

"Was that wrong?" Leo asked, confusion in his voice.

"Yes, no, I mean... no one has ever buttered my pancakes. No one has made me breakfast before. Not since my mom, anyway..."

The pats of butter slid down the pancake stack, and my heart melted right along with them.

Martin's hand wrapped around my wrist, giving me a reassuring squeeze, but kept his gaze averted, allowing me some modicum of privacy while I processed.

When I finally lifted my head, Leo's head tilted to the side, one hand stroking my cat's head. What I saw in his eyes only continued to send me reeling. Reverence. Devotion. All underlined by the ferocity of his character.

"Leo, maybe you can take me to the gym with you sometime," Martin said. "I bet you could help me whip up some guns in no time." He squeezed one of his skinny biceps.

The two men started eating as they broke into a conversation about fitness while I silently lost my mind.

This wasn't me. The early morning hours had been a completely transformative experience, and now I was suddenly dropped into a new life. The intensity of my emotions, the guilt, the pain of yesterday had all but melted away into this present moment, and I never wanted it to end.

The heavenly smells of breakfast, the feel of the cool counter under my arms, the luxury of fluffy, buttery pancakes and crisp bacon bites in my mouth. The sounds of Martin and Leo casually chatting like old friends, and the sight of Bubbles' tail contentedly flicking from his spot on Leo's shoulder.

As long as I stayed in this moment, nothing could ever get me.

Leo's body jerked. He almost doubled over, but not before he gently removed Bubbles from his shoulder to set my cat on the floor again. Bubbles' mewl was half disappointment, half concern.

Martin straightened in alarm. "Leo, are you okay?"

Leonidas shot me a look. Another episode was coming on. I needed to get him sedated, and I needed Martin out of here now.

"Martin, Leo has been having some… health problems. I'm so sorry, but I need to take care of him."

"Of course, I'll get my wrinkly butt out of here. I hope you feel better, Leo. With Betsy by your side, I'm sure you'll be right as rain in no time."

To Martin's credit, he left straightaway.

Before the door even shut, I ran to the case with the sedatives I'd taken from the institute. I shoved aside the pile of yarn to grab a syringe. Leo groaned louder as he fell to his knees, grasping at his torso. His skin roiled. He was losing control.

An eternity seemed to pass as I loaded the syringe. Hurrying back to Leo's side, he was now on all fours; I injected the needle, but before I could push the plunger in, he stopped me. "Wait."

I obeyed, though my thumb itched to stop his pain and transformation.

His head shot up, and those eerie silver eyes stared at the far end of my apartment. "It's looking for us. It's looking for you."

The tombscream. Leo said it wanted to claim me ever since it recognized me as Leo's mate.

"It returned to the institute, then it tried to follow us to Denver."

As he spoke, his fingers morphed into black claws and his veins turned black, protruding from his skin.

I couldn't wait any longer. I needed to sedate him now.

"Do you trust me?" he asked, suddenly closing a hand around my wrist.

"Of course I do," I said, feeling each second tick by with lightning speed.

"Then wait." While his body still roiled, his skin darkening, on the verge of transforming, his eyes held his lucid plea. "Help ground me. I need you, Betsy."

My stomach dropped like I took that first terrifying plunge on a rollercoaster. I removed the needle from his neck, dropping it next to me. I ran a hand through his hair, willing him to stay with me. Trusting him not to turn into a bloodthirsty monster and rip me apart took every bit of faith I possessed. "I've got you." And I meant it.

Bubbles rubbed back and forth against his arms, meowing.

Leo's eyes went out of focus again. He was both right there with me, and far away.

"Can you tell me what you see?"

"It's been nesting. It looks like an abandoned house. But mostly it's been hunting. Trying to find us using the visions through my eyes. It's flying right now. Trying to get closer to us."

My fingernails skimmed his scalp. "Can it tell what you are seeing now?"

"Yes, it knows I am here with you. I can sense how... hungry it is for you."

Goosebumps popped out all over my skin.

Leo jerked, sightless eyes widening. "It's found the purple house."

"Where Krystan and Travis are?" I asked, my alarm spiking.

"I need to go." Leo shot to his feet with inhuman speed. His body ceased transforming, and he was wholly human.

Grabbing my keys, I followed him. "I'm coming with you."

Leo whirled around. "You are not coming."

"The heck I'm not. Besides, how are you going to get there? You can't drive."

"Get me one of those car shares."

"Ride shares," I corrected. "And what happens if you shift and lose all control?"

Suddenly, mere inches separated us. "Do you think I'm going to eat people? Become the monster my master thinks I am?"

"I think you need someone who has your back," I shot back. "And I'm the only one who can help you. So, deal with it, mister. In the car, now."

The knight might be a big scary monster, but I was still responsible for his well-being. And I gave him a look that let him know exactly what would happen if he got in my way.

He wasn't the only one who had a savage side.

With a sigh of resignation, he took a step back. And I nodded in satisfaction.

"Dang right," I muttered to myself, as I opened the door to go.

21

LEONIDAS

The closer we drew to the purple house, the stronger my connection to the tombscream became.

Betsy turned onto the road where Krystan and Travis lived, and it turned into a war zone.

People ran around, screaming in sheer panic. A terrifying winged monster flapped overhead, while Travis did his best to keep it at bay. Spurts of fire streamed from the flame thrower he held.

Krystan stood on the front porch, armed with guns, grenade belts, and gods knew what else. The new mother was ready to defend her home and her child if the creature got past Travis.

The monster artfully dodged another belch of fire. And where Travis might think he was winning at driving the creature off, I knew it was toying with him.

It didn't care about Travis; it knew I was coming with Betsy. He wanted me dead and her for his mate. The demon inside me lusted for violence. I'd sensed the tombscream viewed me as a threat. There could only be one of us. Now I felt it too. There was no room for both of us to exist. Only one, and the dark animal side of me knew the woman went to the victor.

I was out of the car before it fully stopped. With Sheila in hand, I charged the monster with a booming war cry.

Both Travis and the monster turned toward me.

For a moment, my vision flickered red to the creature's perspective. Its attention started on me, but eventually scanned upward until it found Betsy. She'd gotten out of the car to help usher strangers out of the way.

A fierce, violent wave of possessiveness shot through the creature. It wanted Betsy. As soon as it took my mate, it would take its place as alpha.

An eardrum-piercing shriek tore through the air before it dove for her.

Rage, that it thought it could do such a thing, boiled my blood. I would not let it take her.

With my running start, I leapt into the air. As I did, two hot blades jabbed through my back. The pain of sprouting wings was becoming more familiar to me. I flapped my wings, launching upward to collide midair with the tombscream.

Claws tore at my flesh, and hot wet blood fell across my body before cooling in the air. The sharp bones sticking out of its open ribcage dug into me, puncturing flesh. Intense pain flooded my system as quickly as it ebbed away. Logic fled my senses as the primal side took over and only two things mattered. Kill or be killed. Protect my mate.

I grabbed its face, digging into its eyes with my thumbs.

The creature kicked off from me, and we separated midair. Instead of rushing me again, it dove in Betsy's direction a second time. The vile things the creature wanted to do to her flashed through me. Violent, carnal things that would break her body and spirit.

I crashed into the creature's side this time. We hit the ground, sliding along the asphalt. While the beast took the brunt of it, the road chewed up my exposed arms. Before it could get up, I threw a punch into the side of its head. And another. The crack of its skull against the ground would have signaled the kill of any human. But the creature bucked me off with tremendous force. Those curled fangs sunk into my shoulder, and I let out my own bloodcurdling scream.

I grabbed at a wing and pulled hard, in efforts to rip it right off. The jaw released me, and the creature rolled to get out of my grasp. It flapped its wings until it hovered over me.

"Leonidas," a voice cried out.

I turned to see Betsy holding exactly what I needed. Sheila.

Unfortunately, the tombscream spotted her too. He shot off toward her with impossible speed.

But the demon inside me cried out with bone-shaking force. I appeared between them at the last moment. I grabbed the creature's arms, keeping its talons at bay while its fangs and ribs rippled with what seemed to be hunger.

My vision turned red. Excruciating pain raced through my fingers as they crackled, elongating into talons. My body was finishing the transformation, going all the way. The rational, human part of my brain receded into the background.

I released the tombscream long enough to tear my sharp nails through its wings. I disappeared into the fight, barely noting the sting of my wounds, or when its teeth or claws found me. The clang of metal surrounded us, along with the distant sound of sirens.

I lost track of time and space as we battled. Nothing mattered but tearing the other alpha to bits.

"Leonidas," a voice yelled.

I ignored the small voice, but it came again and again, insistent I pay it some mind. When I finally came out of my internal state, I managed to connect that Travis stood there, holding the key. Sheila.

The weapon sailed through the air, and right into my talons where it belonged. Whipping around, Sheila connected with the creature's side just as it was about to rip my throat out.

Glass exploded from house, and cars as the tombscream shrieked in pain. With some wriggling on both our parts, the axe emerged from the creature's side. But as I wound up for a second blow, the tombscream shot up into the sky like a rocket. Then it veered left, flying out of sight, like a bat out of hell.

"Travis," I heard Krystan's panicked voice call.

When I turned around, the ground seemed to fall out from under me. The human side of me muscled forward for control.

Betsy lay on the ground next to a flipped car, her face covered in dirt and blood. Travis rushed to Krystan's side, but when the woman's dark eyes flicked up to mine, she confirmed what I'd already feared. I'd done this to her. I'd hurt Betsy during the fight.

22

—————

BETSY

"I'm fine," I said for the hundredth time.

"You are not fine. You have a concussion," Martin scolded, handing me a cup of tea. He'd been coming home from the gym when Leo brought me home from the hospital. Without a second thought, he'd followed us in.

"What happened?"

Leo remained in the kitchen, palms flat against the kitchen island, his face dark yet unreadable.

Bubbles curled up on my lap, as if sensing I needed some extra love and attention.

"It's a complicated story, but seriously, Martin. I'm fine. I just need rest."

Martin wagged a finger in my face. "Rest, but no sleep. At least not for twenty-four hours."

"Some nurses would argue that sleep is a great remedy. And it was mild. I probably only need to stay awake for a couple more hours, and that's if I'm being extra careful."

"Twenty-four hours," he insisted. "Do I need to stay to make sure it happens?"

The headache throbbing between my temples doubled

at the thought. I was the nurse here, but Martin wanted to feel like he helped. The least I could do was humor him until he left. "That is very kind, Martin, but I think that would be a bit too much stimulation for me. I hardly sleep anyway, so I'll be fine."

Martin walked over to Leo instead of answering. "Make sure she stays awake. She may be the nurse, but she is terrible at taking care of herself. I'd do it myself, but I have promised my grandkids I'd visit them this weekend. My bags are all packed. But if you can't care for her, let me know and I'll cancel everything."

Panic shot up, worsening my headache. "Please, Martin, I'd feel terrible if I inconvenienced you."

"Promise me you'll take care of her for twenty-four hours," he said to Leo, still ignoring me.

The larger man nodded with a solemn expression. Martin patted his arm. "Good man. I trust she is in good hands."

With several more promises that we could handle things, Martin eventually left. But as he left, someone else shouldered their way into the apartment.

"Betsy, oh my god, you're alright." Jeremy's hands closed around my shoulders as he anxiously searched my face.

A low growl emanated from the kitchen. I quickly, but gently, extracted myself from my ex-fiancé's hold. "I'm fine. What makes you think I wouldn't be?" I set down the half-empty tea mug on the coffee table.

"I saw it on the news. There was coverage of a demonic incident and you were in the background, being loaded into an ambulance. Your sister saw it too. She said she's been calling and texting, but you never picked up."

Jeremy then finally locked eyes with Leo. Though they said nothing, the air tightened.

"Oh crud," I said, grabbing my purse from where I dropped it on the floor. "I didn't charge my phone last night." Sure enough, when I pulled it out, I found it dead as a doornail. I got up, Bubbles leaping off me with a discontented meow. I plugged the phone into the charger next to my dining table and the screen glowed to life. Anticipation welled in me, fearful of what was to come.

Then it came. The barrage of dings signaling missed text messages, voicemails, not just from Adie, but from all three of my sisters.

"You need to call them back," Jeremy said, concern lacing his voice. "They are all really worried about you. With Adie about to pop, I told her I'd come over and check on you." Then he reached out to lay a hand on my shoulder, like he used to. "Why don't we get on the couch, and we can bring up the laptop and start planning our move. What was the name of the company that moved us out here again? You took care of the move so seamlessly, I don't even know how we are going to get back. No one knows how to take care of things like you do, Betsy. And when you are feeling a little better, maybe you can make that spicy sausage soup you like so much."

"She needs to rest," Leo interrupted.

I almost shot back he needed to rest. He was a bloody mess after fighting the tombscream, but his wounds had healed over in record speed. Showered and in fresh clothes, no one would ever suspect he nearly got torn apart by a demon.

"What she needs," Jeremy stressed the word, turning to Leo, "is for someone to take care of her."

"I've got that covered," Leo insisted.

The two men walked toward each other until they were

standing off. The tension in the room doubled down on my headache, making me nauseous.

"Really?" Jeremy shot back. "Because if I'd been here with Betsy, this would have never happened. Where were you when she was being attacked by demons in the street? You look like a big guy who could handle things, but when it came down to it, you didn't protect her, did you?"

He didn't recognize Leonidas as one of the monsters battling on television. Thank the lord.

Leo's face visibly soured, as if Jeremy's words affected him. But that was ridiculous. He'd been fighting a big scary demon and the fact that I landed properly, dodging out of the way of that car they'd sent tumbling, wasn't his fault. I'd deliberately jumped in the way to push a man out of the way, then smacked my head into the pavement as a ton of steel had flown over me.

The crack of my skull on the ground had knocked me clean out, and I'd woken up in an ambulance with a worried Krystan hovering over me. They had cleared me with a mild concussion, and they even sent me home. Things could have been so much worse. No one else had been hurt. The wounds on Leonidas even healed up with superhuman speed.

The two men stared each other down with a fierce expression, as if on the verge of a fistfight. But I'd had enough battle for today.

"Jeremy," I started, my voice strained. Then I felt the blood drain from my face before a dizzy spell hit me. The next thing I knew, Leo was there. He sat me on the couch, then stood. I grasped my forehead, wanting the punk rock drummer to stop playing in my head.

"She needs to rest, which means you need to go now," Leo said to Jeremy.

"I'm a doctor. My expertise matters more than some hunk of meat she picked up off the streets."

Another spark and the room would explode.

"Please Jeremy," I begged. "I just need to rest. Please tell Adie I'm fine and I'll call her later."

At first, he seemed unsure whether he should dig his heels in and try to stay. In the end, he walked over to me and dropped a kiss on my forehead. "Sure thing, Bets. I'll check in on you later. Feel better."

When he kissed my forehead, I caught a flash of rage on Leo's face before it wiped away as if it had never been there. He walked over to the window, looking outside, as if needing a moment to gather himself.

Meow.

Bubbles jumped onto Leo's shoulder from a window ledge. His hand went to pet her, but stopped inches from her. Fingers curled into his palm as he dropped his arm, ignoring the pleading meows from Bubbles.

Jeremy slowly made his way toward the door, still going on about how I should take care of myself in his absence. But I wasn't paying attention. Something about Leo had shifted, and I didn't like it. It left me feeling uneasy and adrift.

Leo met my eyes, surprised that I was staring at him. Again, the warmth in his eyes was stamped out, deliberately. He was closing up, and I didn't like it.

I did my best to hurry Jeremy along, placating him I'd do as he said. The pounding in my brain taking precedence over everything.

When I finally got my ex to leave, I leaned back, holding my forehead. "Poor Krystan and Travis. I can't believe they need to leave their home until this thing gets figured out. Taking care of a baby is hard enough."

No answer.

My hand dropped, and I found Leo still poised over the island.

"What's wrong?"

He didn't meet my eyes. "How can you ask that?"

"It's just a concussion," I reasoned.

"It's not just that," he said, his words becoming harsher. "I completely lost control. In my efforts to protect you, I nearly killed you in the battle for dominance. Violetta is right. As the darkness inside me grows stronger, the more at risk everyone is."

"Leo," I said, softly. "This isn't your fault."

Dark, stormy eyes met mine. The anger and guilt swirling there were so intense, it took my breath away.

"Don't. Don't tell me it's not my fault. You are not safe with me." There was more to what he was saying. A secondary meaning.

"So, you are going to leave?" I asked, surprised at how small my voice sounded to my ears.

He shook his head, shaggy hair flowing. "No. I promised Martin I would stay. Twenty-four hours to make sure you are alright. But after that, I'm leaving."

"But—"

"No," he said, sharply. "I've hurt you, and there is no guarantee I won't do it again. The longer I remain around you, the more in danger you are."

His words fell as heavy as his axe. I was surprised I didn't find one of my limbs rolling at my feet. Because the thought of him leaving felt like losing a piece of myself.

"Twenty-four hours?" I repeated.

"Yes, then I'm gone," he reiterated. "I will hunt down the tombscream, and this will all be over."

I hadn't expected to go through with Martin's plan, but it was the only way Leo would stay longer.

If I was the old Betsy, I would tell him to go. Because he clearly wanted out of here as soon as possible. But selfishly, I couldn't do it.

I pulled one of the many blankets up around my chin, nodding as if I was in complete agreement. Though the sudden sharp pain in my heart far surpassed the throbbing in my head.

I reminded myself this could never have lasted. We'd agreed this was a short-term thing. He'd made no promises or commitments, and I could never ask for that. We were from two different worlds. I'd spend the next twenty-four hours coming to terms with that.

A voice in my head, or maybe my heart, whispered... *liar*.

23

BETSY

Eventually, I got Leo to agree to sit on the couch next to me. My feet ended up in his lap for no other reason than the couch was small. Bubbles, the traitor, sat over on Leo's side.

"What do you want to watch?" I asked, picking up the remote.

"On the television set?"

I paused. "Yes, the television set." Most of the time, he blended in, but moments like this reminded me how much of a 'civilian' he wasn't.

"I don't know. I don't watch it."

"But do you like comedy? Action? Romance?"

He scratched an eyebrow. "I don't know."

Anxiety mounted in me. It was silly I felt pressure to put on the "right thing," but other people's comfort was my comfort. If I didn't know how to make him comfortable, I'd sit next to him, stressing out if I put on something he didn't enjoy.

Betsy, get it together. He's a grown man. You don't need to pick the perfect thing to watch.

Despite the pep talk I tried to give myself, my throat still closed up. Not that the one program would dictate whether he would stay or go, but my irrational side insisted he'd walk right out the door if I picked the wrong thing.

Not that it mattered. He was leaving no matter what. And that was for the best.

But maybe if I had a few more days of his presence, I'd adjust better.

The headache doubled down, and nausea crawled up my throat as my thoughts circled down the drain to nowhere.

Leo's brows furrowed, as if he were in deep contemplation. "I like food."

Now this I could work with. "Me too." My lips pursed to keep from smiling. The painful fog still pressed down on my brain, but the tightness in my throat loosened.

In moments, we were watching *The Great British Baking Show*. My head still pounded and my vision was blurry, but the lilting accents were soothing.

A rough shake on my leg had me snap up in a panic. "What is it?"

"You fell asleep," he informed me.

"Right, sorry," I said. I hadn't even noticed I'd nodded off. "Martin is being overprotective. I promise I'll be fine. In fact, rest would likely help me."

Leo laid an arm along the back of the couch to look at me. "If you plan on staying awake, we might need to do something other than watch this show. Even I am becoming drowsy."

I nodded. Pain whipped through my brain. My hands grabbed my skull. "Oof," I groaned. "That hurt. But yes, I think you are right. Maybe I should bake or crochet something," I said, casting an eye about the living room. There was no lack of projects around my apartment. Usually the sight of all the yarns, cookbooks, and patterns filled me with a manic energy, but right now, looking at all of it made me even more tired.

Leo moved closer to me until my legs were entirely on his lap. One of his hands found its way under my shirt until he was toying with the edge of my pants. "I don't think you should do anything so strenuous, but you need to be alert."

Warm fingers slid under the hem of my pants, and I stilled. Magically, the pounding in my head receded as the heat grew between my thighs in response to his touch.

Bubbles had the decency to leap off the couch and slunk off into the bedroom, affording us some privacy.

A finger skated down my already wet center. I bit my lip to cover a moan. I sure as shooting was awake now. "What are you doing?" I managed to get out.

"Like I said." His silver eyes had turned to dark pools. "I need to keep you alert and responsive."

Oh, I was responding alright. Mewls emerged out of my throat as he continued to stroke. My hips bucked. I wanted more. I needed deeper.

With a low, throaty chuckle, he said, "You may be a nurse, but I am the one in charge here. You are going to do exactly what I say."

My eyes snapped up to meet his.

"That's right, legs. I am in charge of taking care of you. Even if I only have you for twenty-three more hours, so you'll do what I say when I say it. Understand?"

The commanding tone should have put me off, but anticipation rippled through me with surprising intensity. The tense air hadn't dissipated between us since he'd declared he was planning to leave tomorrow. It had simply morphed into the steel edge he now wielded against me. As if he were concentrating all that frustration into a sexual power trip.

I swallowed hard and nodded.

As a finger came dangerously close to where I wanted it most, my hips bucked.

"No." His words were cold, controlled. "You are to stay perfectly still."

My stomach tightened as I bore down against the need swelling inside me. He continued the long torturous strokes, never penetrating, going no deeper.

"Please," I finally gasped, my hips rocking.

Leo removed his hand, taking all my relief with it. When he licked his fingers, staring me straight in the eye, a strangled sound escaped my throat.

"I thought you said you'd be good." The smile he gave me was positively wicked.

"I can be good," I confirmed, breathily. My thigh muscles shook as parts of me screamed for his touch to return.

Again, his fingers made the journey back under my clothes. The need to groan and buck and beg for more was overwhelming as his digits resumed sliding back and forth.

"Don't move," he warned. "But tell me what you want."

"I-in," I stuttered, riding the edge of a tightrope. "Put them in, please."

With Jeremy, I would have never said any such thing, but Leo's total dominance helped me lose any self-consciousness. There was only him and my molten desire, both driving me to madness.

"I will," he promised. "But first." He ripped back the blanket and pulled my pajama pants down, along with my panties. I reached for the blanket.

"What did I say?" he asked in a tone that stopped me.

"Don't move," I repeated his earlier command. But the self-consciousness crept back in. "But I'm only half naked and you're fully dressed."

An eyebrow arched before he grabbed the hem of his shirt and pulled it off, throwing it onto the floor. Watching him stretch his arms overhead made my mouth water, and I had the intense urge to lick him everywhere. But I said I'd stay still.

"Is that better?" he asked.

"Yes," I whispered.

All the golden, broad muscle was enough eye candy to give a girl diabetes. The way his hair fell around his shoulders sent electric shocks down between my thighs, and I felt a rush of wetness.

"Now let's get back to what you wanted me to do." His hand covered my mound. "You wanted this?" With that, he slid his fingers between my lower lips, but he didn't press them into me. Again, he stroked up and down, but this time he caressed my sensitive bud. I almost jerked up, instead I closed my eyes as my breathing grew labored.

"How is your head feeling?" he asked.

My head? Oh, right. Concussion. Headache. I faintly noticed the pain, but other sensations were rioting for attention.

"It's fine."

Then he did it. A finger slid inside, and I half-gasped, half-sobbed as he filled me with one, then two digits.

Almost as soon as I got what I wanted, my greed for more swelled. Friction, thrusting, pumping. I wanted it all now. I opened my eyes and bit my lip, keeping my hips still.

Leo smirked at me, as if knowing how tortured I felt. He knew exactly what he was doing to me.

"Are you feeling sleepy?" he asked.

"No," I ground out. My hairline had grown damp, and sleep was the last thing I wanted right now.

Gasping, I shot him a pleading look when he didn't do more than gently circle his fingers inside me. "Leo... I need more. Please. I need more." On one hand, I was entirely at his whim, but the other part of me felt free from controlling every little thing. A thousand scenarios weren't running through my mind. There was only this, and what he told me to do.

"Legs, you've been a very good girl. And good girls get what they want." With that, he started pumping his hand. The wave of pleasure from the friction smashed into me so hard, my eyes rolled up. Satisfaction and a deeper well of hunger warred with each other as his fingers sped up, his thumb rubbing against my clit in a perfect tandem of motion.

"That's it, baby, I want to hear you moan," he said.

The louder I got, the more the pain at the back of my head ebbed away.

Then I was perched on the edge of that cliff as he hit the perfect speed and angle. I gasped, feeling something coming. As if sensing I was close, he sped up again.

Unable to stop myself, I bucked against his hand now, blindly pushing toward release.

"Don't move," he growled. I stilled, scared he would stop. He couldn't stop now.

I pitched over my edge, my body crashing and shaking into orgasm. He didn't even slow the pace, elongating my pleasure.

When my body sagged from the intense relief, I opened my eyes.

I almost couldn't believe someone like him existed. Those dark eyes held danger, but I didn't need to fear him.

No, I needed to fear my own expectations. I wanted too much. Leonidas made me want to reach for more. Where before, I'd always made myself content with as little as possible.

"Are you alright?" he asked. Hesitance wound around him.

"Am I... am I alright?" I asked, incredulous. "The hottest, most virile man I've ever laid eyes on is in my living room, pleasuring me. I'd say I'm doing pretty well."

That wicked grin returned. "Are you still feeling sleepy?"

I shook my head. "No, I'm actually quite awake, and," I sat up, sliding a hand into his lap, "still wanting more."

I kissed him. The depth of the kiss surprised me. There was something so achingly passionate in it. As scorching as it was, I could feel him holding back.

When our lips parted, he looked deeply into my eyes. "Good." Then he moved my legs off him, got up, and walked over to the kitchen.

"Wh-what are you doing?" I asked. The distance stretched between us. It might have been the concussion, but it felt like I missed something.

"I'm making tea."

"But I thought we were going to..."

"You said you're feeling more awake, right?" he reiterated.

"Yes, my head feels better, too." I wasn't dropping hints. I was dropping bombs, yet he continued to go about pulling out mugs and rifling through my tea choices.

"Good. Wouldn't want to do anything to tire you out."

Oh.

"Oh."

So, he intended to make me alert, and that's why he...

Shame and something else swept over me. He'd pushed me to voice what I wanted, and now he wasn't even going to give it to me. The desire I voiced hung out there like a dangling hunk of meat, and he didn't plan on taking a single bite. Suddenly, that meat seemed rancid and rotten. I felt dirty and exposed for having asked for what I wanted.

Disappointment came first, but something surprising followed it. Anger.

I couldn't sort out if I was impressed by his tactics, or offended by his clinical manner. Feeling exposed, I wrapped an afghan around my waist and got up. I'd almost reached my bedroom when he said, "What kind of tea do you want?"

"Oh, you've already put yourself out. I couldn't possibly inconvenience you any further."

With that, I slammed the door shut behind me. I rubbed my face as I set my back against the door. To say I was confused was an understatement. My body was still revved up, and wanting more, but he'd thrown a bucket of cold water on me.

Knock knock. "Betsy? I need to keep an eye on you to make sure you don't fall asleep."

I'd thought having him for twenty-four hours would be good, but confusion and embarrassment rioted in me.

Another knock. "Betsy?"

"I'm fine," was all I could think to respond.

"Betsy let me in."

I already had. In ways I never knew I could. I thought I'd loved Jeremy, but the intensity of feelings Leo inspired were so beyond anything I'd ever known and it had rocked my entire world.

And suddenly I wished I'd never left Montana and that I'd never met Leonidas.

Adie was right. I belonged in Montana with my family. Since coming to ground zero, I'd done more harm than good. I neglected the people who really needed me. As soon as this monster business was resolved, I would go back.

I could be the girl I used to be and forget any of this happened.

24

LEONIDAS

"Betsy." I knocked again. "Let me in. You shouldn't be alone."

"I can take care of myself," her voice shot back. The pain I heard underlying her tone chewed me up. I'd done that.

I'd told myself I was helping by playing and arousing her to keep her alert. But now I realized I was only justifying what I truly wanted. Her. I wanted her to fall apart in my hands. Shake, tremble, scream and beg for me.

Make her feel a modicum of the desire I felt for her. Every part of me, the man, the knight, to the dark demonic corners of my soul, I wanted her.

But after I'd brought her to orgasm on the couch and she'd asked for more, I couldn't allow myself to cross that line again. If I gave into the pleasure of her body, I feared I'd never leave even though I promised to do just that, an hour ago.

"No, you can't," I insisted. "You take care of everyone else, but who takes care of you?"

The door swung back open. She wore pants again, her hair a delicious mess from squirming on the couch.

"Is that what you call that?" She waved a hand back toward the living room. "Taking care of me?" She was angry. Why did it feel so good to see her angry?

"Yes. You need to stay awake. Or perhaps you would prefer if Jeremy were here?" I allowed myself to sink into anger as well. The thoughts simmering at the back of my mind were suddenly falling off my tongue.

"Maybe I should have let Jeremy stay and told you to leave."

Her taunting agreement caused a burst of heat to flood me. "He can't care for you. Not the way I can."

She crossed her arms over her chest. "Oh really? Because I feel pretty exposed and vulnerable, and I know he wouldn't have done that."

I pointed at the door. "He wouldn't have done that because you would be too busy taking care of him, even though you are the one who is injured."

She dropped her arms and stomped into the kitchen. The cabinet slammed shut after she grabbed a glass. Then filled it with water, as if needing something to do. "Don't act like you know my life. You think I'm the one being used? What about you? This order treats you like a tool."

I splayed my hands on the island across from her as she took large gulps. "That's different. It is my destiny. It is the closest thing to a home I've ever had. I belong with the Luxis."

The cup clacked against the counter, her fingers turning bloodless around it. "She's not your mother. No matter how much you want her to be."

A cold calm washed over me as I stepped back. My words

came out detached and even. "Yes, I know. I have no family. Thank you for making sure I remember. But I'd rather not have any family than have yours. You talk of needing to go back, to take care of them. But after your beau left you, did you ever wonder why you didn't return to Montana?"

Sharp pain crossed her face, like I'd cut her with a straight razor. I instantly regretted the words, but I couldn't take them back.

Still, she needed to hear it, even if she didn't want to. Part of her wanted to be free of her family, and I knew exactly why. She wasn't meant to serve their whims. She was meant to follow her own path.

When she gathered herself, the words came out hard and biting. "I have to let you off the hook for saying something so awful, because you have been on your own, in isolation like some ninja warrior, but here is a little lesson. I may be able to talk bad about my family, but no one else is allowed to."

"Betsy," I said. "I am sorry. I should not have said that. But you deserve so much more, and every time your family or Jeremy come up, you become anxious, on edge. As if you owe them your every breath. And you don't. You are more magnificent than you understand, and you don't constantly have to prove your worth."

"Same, bucko."

The silence settled around us, like the quiet fall of ash after an explosion. I didn't know what else to say. We'd gone for each other's jugular, and the ironic part being we'd done it because we wanted better for each other.

I wanted to blame the demon inside, but I knew the insistence pounding through me had nothing to do with my new abilities. It had everything to do with my investment in Betsy.

Betsy returned to her bedroom, but left her door open. Bubbles followed her to the threshold, then looked up at me, then at Betsy with her one good eye. Then she slunk into the bedroom to comfort Betsy.

Twenty-three more hours, and then I would disappear from her life forever. I'd hunt down the tombscream and after that... I didn't know. I couldn't go back to the Luxis and hunt the way I used to. If Violetta hadn't already sent hunters after me, she soon would.

SNOW FELL THAT NIGHT. Large fluffy flakes filled the skies. Though the temperature the previous day was in the seventies, the weather chilled, like our dispositions.

In the morning, Betsy insisted we go out to breakfast as she fed Bubbles. Indeed, I also felt the smallness of the apartment close in around us as I did my best to stay out of the way. Betsy did not fall asleep. I made sure to pass her door periodically to keep an eye on her. Her gaze remained fixed on her laptop, earphones in.

This morning, she sported purple bruises under her eyes. She'd pulled her hair up in a ponytail and donned an oversized cream sweater that stretched out from the neckline to expose one perfect shoulder that made my mouth water. The way her black leggings clung to her made me want to pull her up onto me so they'd wrap around my hips before I took her back to the bed.

There was a fragileness about her. Though she tried to pull a tough exterior over it, her defenses couldn't hide the truth. I wasn't sure if it was the physical toll of the previous few days or if it was my words and actions that cut her so deeply.

I was grateful we were getting out. Since last night, our words hung in the air, a sour mist I couldn't escape.

When I cautioned her against driving in her current state, she replied we would walk to a breakfast place nearby. Her eyes never met mine as she spoke, wrapping a colorful handmade scarf around her neck. She'd bundled up and pulled on big brown boots.

Before we left the apartment, Betsy's hand hovered over the door handle. Then she abruptly returned to the closet to pull out a bright blue knitted scarf. Still careful to avoid my gaze, she looped it around my neck. My hands fisted at my sides as she adjusted the scarf. The overwhelming need to touch her, to close the distance, both physically and emotionally, nearly pulled me off my feet. But I remained still.

She'd gotten me a dark trench coat when she'd gone shopping, and it brushed against my boots. With that, we set out into three feet of snow. We crossed to a shoveled sidewalk alongside the road. All the while, I focused on the plan. Fifteen more hours and then I'd go straight for the tombscream. If there was a way we could connect telepathically, then maybe there was a way I could open up my consciousness to draw it out. And things would end one way or another.

Betsy flailed, slipping on a patch of ice. Her body tilted back as she fell. In less than a heartbeat, I caught her in my arms. She was still tilted back, our faces mere inches apart. I could almost taste her sweet breath.

Pain and longing zinged through me as I slowly righted us. The way she had to drag her gaze from my lips up to my eyes caused my blood to heat. But I forced myself to release her, and we began walking again.

"Thank you," she said, breaking the silence.

"You're welcome."

She opened her mouth, then closed it.

"What is it?"

"I keep feeling like I should apologize." Her jaw tightened. "But I'm not the one who should apologize. I did nothing wrong."

"You didn't," I agreed.

"Good, I'm glad we agree," she said, as if she were still trying to convince herself she was in the right. She took a deep breath and then said, "I managed to look at the copied files we got from Travis and Krystan. I mean, my brain feels like a bunch of loose marbles are rolling around right now, but I did my best to sift through some of the information. There were a lot of references to a subject with similar symptoms to you, patient #232. Maybe he's where they got this horrible idea to purposefully change you. I'll look at it more in-depth today, but I think there may be a possibility of treating your condition." She shot me a wry smile.

Betsy was still trying to help me. Even after what I'd done last night. I'd told myself I was keeping her awake and alert, and nothing more. Instead, I'd made her feel used.

But I couldn't bring myself to apologize. Because the fact remained, I could not stay with her. It was better she harbored ill feelings toward me. It would make things easier for both of us when I left.

The wretched feelings rioting through me would pass with time, and knowledge I'd done it for her own good.

Betsy led me to a blue-roofed restaurant called IHOP. We were soon seated in a booth, my hands wrapped around a mug of coffee and hers around a mug of tea.

When the food came, she shot me a wry smile. "It's not as good as the breakfast you made, but it's hot and there is plenty of it. I'm grateful this is within walking distance." We dug in. I slathered the stack of pancakes in butter while she filled her waffle with syrup.

"So, when you go... what do you plan on doing?" she asked.

"I plan on finding the tombscream and killing it."

She paused. "And then what?"

"I don't know," I confessed. "I can't go back to the Luxis. If my mast— If Violetta has not already set hunters out to dispose of me, she soon will."

Betsy looked down into her tea with a pained expression.

"And what about you?" I asked. "When the tombscream is destroyed, you cannot go back to work at the institute."

"Knowing what they've done, I wouldn't want to, even if I could. I have a little money saved up but—"

"There you are," a voice cut in.

Betsy looked up, her face scrunching up in confusion. She stood up from the booth to hug her sister. Michael and Jeremy stood behind Adelaide.

"What are you doing here?" Betsy asked.

"We left you alone last night to rest, but I had to see you. So, I used my friend finder app and saw you were here this morning. We decided to join you. I needed to make sure my big sister was okay."

Everyone shuffled into the booth. This time Betsy slid in next to me so she could face Michael and Adelaide. Jeremy attempted to sit next to Betsy, but seeing as I took up a lot of room, Betsy practically ended up in my lap, trying to make space. My hands went to her waist, and an electric zing shot through my body at the feel of her. My fingers tightened of their own accord, and I heard Betsy gasp. That little sound made me want to drag her onto my lap and see if I could make her repeat it.

Instead, I let go and tried to think of anything but the intoxicating scent of her.

Jeremy had to submit and switched sides. He cast me a dark look as he sandwiched Adelaide in.

"Betsy, tell me what happened yesterday?" her sister asked, extending her hands across the table so Betsy would hold them.

When the waiter came over, the conversation was paused so the three of them could order. Then Betsy slowly but surely began to explain. I wasn't sure what she would tell them when she got to the part about my changing into a demon.

I looked out the window.

My blood froze over, then heat exploded from my center. Thunder boomed. There was a crash of glass and I found myself outside the restaurant on the snow-covered ground, standing before a familiar face.

The reaction had been instant and unconscious. I'd burst through the window with such force, it had exploded outward from the restaurant. Shattered glass pieces littered the snowy ground.

"Dr. Sterling," I ground out. "What a disappointment to find you escaped the carnage unharmed."

25

LEONIDAS

The five-foot Asian woman regarded me with cold eyes under her razor-straight bangs. A puffy blue jacket protected her from the falling flakes, but it would do nothing against my claws that had already stretched into form.

The crunch of glass behind me pulled my attention as Betsy gingerly stepped out of the booth and over the broken window, careful not to cut herself.

The rest of the restaurant stared on in horror. My explosion through the window had happened so quickly and unexpectedly, everyone seemed to be glued in place. Including Betsy's sister and brother-in-law. Adelaide's jaw might need to be picked up off the ground later, but for some reason, Jeremy seemed less surprised than the rest.

"Oh my god, Dr. Sterling, you're alive?" Betsy said in shocked disbelief as she hurried over, making her way through the snow. "I thought the tombscream had killed you."

Instead of returning any concern, Dr. Sterling's voice snapped with evident displeasure. "You took the subject home with you?" Though she wasn't much older than Betsy, the woman commanded attention like a general. There was a ruthlessness in her I'd sensed the very first time we met. I'd been around long enough to know not all evil was spawned in hell, and there was a coldness in this doctor's heart that made her susceptible to the dark.

Betsy and I traded a glance. "Everyone was dead," she started, though there was hesitance in her voice. "He needed help. Help to understand what we... what you did to him." Anger filled her voice the longer she spoke.

It was the first time Betsy deferred blame from herself.

Yet I couldn't enjoy her shift. This was all wrong. Why was the doctor here? Uneasiness skittered under my skin like a swarm of bugs. The demon in me also sensed something was off.

"Yes, well, despite the utter catastrophe at the institute, I'm working to pick up the pieces of this mess. While you fraternize with a monster."

Betsy reared back as though she'd been slapped. "Excuse me?"

Dr. Sterling's eyes turned back to me and narrowed. "I didn't want to believe it." Then, as she'd done before, she barked orders at Betsy. "We are going to escort him back."

Betsy stepped forward as if she were shielding me from this imperious doctor, whose energy did not match her physical stature.

"The institute was destroyed. Take him back where?" Betsy asked.

"There is another location where we can continue our work. We can't allow him to walk the streets free."

"You want me to go back with you so you can continue to shape me into a weapon," I growled.

Dr. Sterling's eyebrow lifted in warning. "You are dangerous. You should not be allowed to walk free. You are a danger to everyone here."

"If you're so worried about the safety of the people, what are you doing to find the tombscream?" Betsy shot back finally. "Leonidas has done nothing but protect everyone around him."

Even though I'd hurt Betsy, physically and emotionally, I knew she meant every word.

"We are working to find the asset. And don't be fooled by subject #526. Soon he'll be no different than subject #232."

"Subject #232?" Betsy asked.

"The tombscream as you called him? He was once like this one," Sterling said, cutting her eyes at me pointedly.

"What are you saying?" Betsy's voice came just above a whisper. "That the tombscream was human once?"

"That's exactly what I'm saying." A small, vicious smile pulled at the corners of the doctor's mouth.

It felt as though a truck slammed into me, though I remained standing.

Travis and Krystan had caught on that the institute was weaponizing the demonic entities, but I doubt they knew the institute had turned a regular human into a full-blown demon.

"Tom lost his family when a hellhound broke into his house and murdered them. The poor man's mind broke under the stress. When he came to us, he'd stopped eating, stopped speaking, stopped living. We gave him new life, new purpose."

Betsy's eyes glittered with unshed tears as snowflakes continued to land on her head like a halo. "But Leonidas found him in the woods. If you created him..."

"Yes, he has a special knack for escaping. When we took both him and this one"—she gestured to me— "we took extra precautions to secure him. But Tom found a way," Dr. Sterling finished bitterly.

"If he hadn't broken out and destroyed the institute that robbed him of his humanity, I'd still be back there," I said. Despite the intense opposition I felt to the mutated human, I technically owed him my life.

"And you still are going back. You are too valuable and too dangerous to go free," Dr. Sterling said. "We've invested far too much time and research into you. It's time to come back."

I almost couldn't swallow the pill. My entire life had been dedicated to protecting humanity from the hell beasts of the Stygian, and they deliberately created one of their own. They sacrificed a broken man so they could use him, experiment on him, turn him into a weapon. Betrayal stung like a whip across my face.

The demon inside me twisted and squirmed, dying to feed off my anguish and anger. It wanted blood, vengeance, and carnage to appease the rioting feelings inside.

I'd always fought to protect the innocents, but perhaps no one was truly innocent after all.

But what also bothered me was how this tiny form of a doctor stood before me with fearless ease. As if she knew she was untouchable from any consequences.

"He won't be going with you," Betsy said, her voice a hard edge.

"Don't be ridiculous," Dr. Sterling said. "You have kept the asset under control and contained, and I'll put in a good word for you with the institute, but you will no longer be working with patient #526."

"My name is Leonidas," I growled.

With that, I couldn't keep the demon inside controlled

any longer. My coat fell off my back as I exploded at her in a torrent of wings and anger.

"No," Betsy screamed behind me. But she was too late.

Fangs elongated and talons sharpened, I was inches from digging into Dr. Sterling when a wave of exhaustion hit me.

Lifting my head, I shook the snow out of my hair and face. Dr. Sterling stood there with a tranq gun. In her other hand, she pressed her cellphone to her ear. She addressed whoever she called, saying she needed the backup.

"Betsy," Adelaide cried out, as people fled the IHOP screaming for their lives.

"Get out of here," Betsy yelled at her sister. Then she was at my side, helping me to my feet.

"We need to get out of here."

Already I could hear the thrum of engines from a pack of SUVs nearing. Sterling had called for backup.

I scrambled to my feet, grabbed Betsy around the waist, and then jettisoned up into the sky.

Betsy screamed as she clung to my neck. The cold air rushed by us as I soared away from the coming army. To help put Betsy at ease, I repositioned her, cradling her in my arms.

She buried her head into my chest, and I got the sense she wasn't a fan of heights.

The first several times I shifted, it had been confusing, overloading my senses as my body fought for order. But this time I was in control of my wings, of my wits, as I flew us away from danger.

The swirl of white, icy snowflakes filled the sky, making it difficult to see. The lack of visibility forced me to land sooner than I liked. When I set Betsy down, she was shaking like a leaf.

Her hands cupped my face, and she kissed me on the mouth. She desperately clung to me, and I wrapped her tight in my arms. It felt good. Too good. The demon raging inside me relaxed as I sunk into her softness.

"What was that for?" I asked when she pulled back.

"My nerves," she said with a watery smile. Then her expression sobered as she looked around us. "Oh, we are at that amusement park. What was it called? Lakeside. I heard they closed it a month ago because of an incident with a horde of flesh-eating pixies."

The place seemed like a ghost town, snow eerily falling on brightly colored tents and amusement rides.

She stepped away from me, examining our surroundings. "What are we going to do? Where are we going to go?"

"You have to get away from me," I said, though it killed me.

Betsy's head swiveled to give me a hard look. "They are coming for me too, Leo. They know by now that I am on your side, and based on their shady practices so far, I doubt they will just let me go knowing what I know."

My wings receded into my back. It was the first time it happened while I was conscious. Drawing them back in felt a bit as though someone had packed a backpack under my skin too tightly. I groaned as the last bit of them folded in. My hands returned to normal, and my clothes had tears but weren't destroyed from my transformation.

"All I want to do is keep you safe," I said in frustration.

"Same to you," she shot back, her hands pulling on her hair. It had fallen out of her hair tie mid-flight. "Sweet molasses monkeys. Why is everything so messed up?"

I stalked over to her and pulled her to me. "We will figure this out. I swear it."

Her eyes scanned up to mine, little snowflakes caught in

her eyelashes, cheeks bright red, and lips glistening from when she licked them. I suppressed a groan. Even after everything, I wanted Betsy like no one and nothing ever before.

Her eyes searched mine. "Leo, I—"

All my senses burst in a cacophony of alarms a moment before Betsy jerked back. The tombscream's—no, Tom's—talons wrapped around her waist. Betsy screamed as the monster pulled her back into the air.

26

BETSY

The ground disappeared from under my feet as something pulled back and up into the air. An iron grip wrapped around my waist, and sharp spikes dug into my back.

Someone yelled out, but I couldn't find my breath as my stomach jerked with the motion. The wound on my stomach flared to life with angry, burning pain. I watched the street and Leo grow smaller as I ascended in the air.

My fear doubled down as I got a clear view of the soldiers in black Kevlar creeping up on Leo from all sides.

The rat-a-tat of gunfire filled the air, and I shut my eyes. They wanted to kill the beast and didn't care if I got hit in the crossfire.

Leather wings struggled to reemerge from Leonidas. They'd only just receded, and every other time he'd transformed, he'd passed out after. He was weak. Still, he lunged at the nearest gunman, smashing his fists into them, their guns clattering to the ground to keep them from hitting me. After all, bullets did nothing to the beast currently holding me.

The tombscream hovered in the air with me, my legs dangling, as if he didn't know whether to go or stay.

The gunfire refocused on Leonidas. This time I screamed. They couldn't hurt him. He was one of the good guys. Didn't they know they were better off with him on his side? But the bullets bounced off him. He threw the soldiers this way and that, knocking them over.

Blossoms of red appeared on his arms and chest. But it wasn't blood. Tomato-red feathers stuck to him. Tranquilizer darts. At first, his fury only doubled, but then he slowed, his feet back on the ground. He staggered first right, then left, then turned and landed flat on his back.

Dr. Sterling made her way toward Leo along with a couple of the suits I'd seen clean up at the institute in the middle of the night.

The tombscream flapped its wings and launched up and off again.

Even with the distance growing between us, Leo's eyes found mine. Fear and pain filled his silver eyes, and I knew my expression mirrored his.

This time, I couldn't save him, and he couldn't save me. It would be the last time we set eyes on each other.

The creature turned left and soared away, carrying my body away but leaving my heart back with Leo on the ground.

THE KNOWING that I was moments away from a horrible death or worse closed in around me. It heightened my senses, bringing everything into crystal clarity. From the bite of the cold rushing wind around me to the sharp claws wrapped around my belly. My mind raced as the tombscream flew us far above the city where no one could reach. It searched for any way to escape the fate that wrapped around me like Saran Wrap.

I didn't even bother to struggle, not wanting to be dropped from a hundred feet. Ice pelted my face like frozen pellets until my skin was raw and chapped.

Worse yet, my fate was sealed, and I had no way of knowing what would happen to Leo. Would I die and come back as a ghost? Haunting this world for answers? Anything was possible in this new age.

The beast holding me swerved violently. Its body shuddered, and we dropped several feet. My heart caught in my throat.

The second time it happened, the tombscream cried out, and dropped again, sending my stomach up into my throat.

A flash of light blinded me momentarily, and the tombscream cried out in fury as we jerked back and forth in the air, losing height all the while.

Between the flashes of light, piercing screams, and losing ground, I wondered if this was how someone felt in the last moments of a plane crash. My legs dangled, making me feel vulnerable. I pulled them up and tried to curl into a fetal position.

I barely glimpsed snow-covered ground, when the tombscream suddenly released me. Free falling, I swallowed my scream. My body impacted into a snowbank, knocking the breath from me. Blood filled my mouth and my head rocked into pain.

I shut my eyes, but I heard the furious cries of the tombscream grow fainter as if it were traveling away.

When I finally opened my eyes, I found a pair of brown boots before me. Slowly scanning up, not sure if I was still alive, a man stood over me. The man's square jaw flexed as he regarded me with what seemed like... resentment?

"Are you hurt?" he asked, but he didn't crouch down to my level or give me a hand.

Doing an internal scan, I found, though I was terrified and battered from hitting the ground, all my limbs were present, and I didn't think I was bleeding. "No," I whispered, still trying to find my voice. It was knocked out of me when I hit the ground.

The man cast a look around as if concerned someone would see him, but then he propped a foot on a rock, in a more casual repose. "Take it slow," he advised.

With great care, I came to a sitting position. With a metal clink, the man lit a cigarette with a zippo lighter.

Blinking a few times, I scanned the air to find the tomb-scream gone. It had stopped snowing, and I lay in a field next to a road. I could see houses off a ways and a trail in the snow where my body had slid and tumbled.

The man was tall and lean, in his early or mid-twenties, but his eyes were harder, like someone who'd seen more than they cared to at his age. His dirty-blond hair hung in his eyes, giving him a roguish appearance. Or maybe that was the cigarette and the motorcycle behind him.

He didn't ask who I was, what the creature was, or how he could help. He just stood there with me, letting me get my bearings, taking drags off the cigarette, sucking in his already hollowed cheeks. As if we had all the time in the world.

When the rattling stopped in my brain, I remembered the bright lights.

"You're one of them, aren't you?"

He raised an eyebrow in question, still managing to look bored.

"A knight of the light."

His expression visibly soured, and he flicked the cigarette into the snow. Somehow that answered the question. Now I scrambled to my feet, hope blossoming in my chest. "I need your help. Your brother needs your help."

The man took a step back and gave me a look so intensely full of malice that I stopped short, my words drying up on my tongue.

My heart pounded, and I tried again in a slower, calmer manner. "Leonidas, he's one of your brother knights, right? Bad people have taken him. They want to hurt him. They made that thing you just fought off."

The man's eyes rose to where the tombscream had been, but he didn't react beyond that.

"You need to help me stop them and save Leonidas."

"No."

"They're making demons. They are going to make Leonidas into a demon," I stressed, unsure of whether he understood what was happening.

"It's not my problem." The knight turned to go.

My hand shot out, and I cried, "Wait. How can you just... not help?"

Stopping, his back to me, he said, "Because I'm not the hero in this story."

Between the hard landing and the fear and stress chewing me up from the inside, I couldn't make sense of what he said.

He swung a leg over the motorcycle and started it up with a loud rumble. "Someone will be along soon. They'll give you a ride." Then he was gone.

How could he leave? How could he not help? The disappointment he left me with rocked me. Never in my life had I ever considered not helping someone when asked or saw the need.

I wasn't left with my disillusionment for long. A car pulled over and the driver asked if I needed help. After a short explanation of being abducted by a demon, the husband and wife insisted on giving me a ride. And in the wake of one rejection, I knew exactly where I needed to go next.

27

BETSY

I bruised my knuckles from trying to break down the door until they finally let me in. The hooded monk poked a knife into my back as he escorted me down the hallway. Everything looked to be in as pristine order as when Leonidas brought me the first time.

Except this time, they led me through the large church hall to a side room full of books and a fire. Violetta stood before the fire in her purple robes. Displeasure sparked in her eye at seeing me again.

"What are you doing back here?"

The monk didn't move, keeping me under knife point.

"You need to help him," I launched into my plea.

"If you mean eliminate the demonic entity that used to be my ward, then yes, we agree," she said in a clipped tone. There was a bitterness I detected in her tone.

She didn't want to kill him any more than I wanted to be here asking this witch for her help.

"How can you say that? You are the closest thing he has to a mother. Does he really mean so little to you?"

She whipped around, her cloak swirling out around her,

fanning the flames behind her. "We aren't a family. This is an ancient order dedicated to protecting this world. He isn't my son and I'm not his mother. Leonidas is, was, a soldier in an eternal war between good and evil. And unfortunately, there are causalities in war, which are"—the lines in her face seemed to deepen—"regrettable."

"He doesn't deserve this; you know that, right?"

"But he deserves you?" She arched an imperious eyebrow.

My hands closed into fists. The monk pressed the knife into my back more firmly, making sure I knew not to do anything rash.

I pushed back all the anger inside to access the logical part of my argument. This woman wouldn't be appealed to on the basis of emotions. I had to convince her that saving Leonidas was in alignment with their mission.

My words came out with measured force. "He's still one of the good guys. So, he can sprout wings and talons. So he has demon DNA in him now. But he is still Leonidas, and he has been doing everything to protect the innocent. The institute that experimented on him is creating demons. Trying to turn people into weapons, making more of the things you are trying to stop. Leonidas told me that the order of Luxis is devoted to protecting this world from the dark. Well, it seems to me he is the only one doing any of the goddamn work trying to clean up this mess. So maybe it's time you got off your fucking ass and helped him for once."

She looked as though I slapped her.

Good. She needed a wake-up call, and if I had to hit her where it hurt, I would make sure she knew she was doing a crappy job.

My words hung in the air. Then Violetta sat in one of the high-back chairs. "I cannot."

"Are you kidding me? You have like a whole secret army of monks. I bet your sweet behind you have power you can throw around to get him out."

"He is part of a prophecy that has larger consequences."

Remembering what Travis and Krystan said about the Luxis and their outdated history with prophecies, I said, "And you have always interpreted the prophecies correctly. There have never been any unexpected outcomes because you may have not seen the bigger picture."

Her face soured, but she didn't disagree with me. I knew I'd struck a nerve, but I could feel I was alienating her by insulting her order. So, I changed tactics. "Okay then, well, either that prophecy is already in motion and you need to be on the ground floor of what's going on, or you can keep trying to push it away and let things blindside you later."

AN HOUR LATER, we drove up to a nondescript building downtown. This reminded me of a building where I imagined people slaving away in IT or software.

After some miracle, I had moved Violetta to action. She'd disappeared for ten minutes, then returned with an implacable resolve. A monk hurried out of a Bentley at the front of the church to open the back doors for us before rushing back around the front to drive.

What surprised me was, apart from the monk who drove us, rushing around to open doors, she didn't bring anyone.

The juxtaposition of the rich modernity and her purple cloak and wooden staff with a gemstone at the top made her look like an out-of-place wizard.

"Shouldn't we have brought back up?" I murmured to Violetta as the monk bowed his head, opening the door for us. I expected a posse of armed monks to accompany us. What must they think of a renegade nurse and a severe looking old woman coming to raise hell?

She didn't answer me.

The monk hurried forward to speak with the man at reception while Violetta hung back. I was painfully aware of the fact that people here wanted me locked up or, more likely, dead.

I had to hand it to the old woman; she exuded a calm power that made you straighten your spine just being nearby.

Soon we were escorted into a room empty save for a lone table and three chairs around it. I got the sense we were about to be interrogated. The monk remained in the lobby. Violetta sat down while I chose to stand.

"I thought you were going to come in, swords blazing, and we'd break him out," I said, agitated.

"Not all power is forged from violence. I'd think as a nurse, you would know that." Her biting words irritated me, but I shut my mouth. I couldn't complain, she'd come to help.

Still, I couldn't relax. I crossed my arms over my chest and paced. I didn't know where Leo was. Was he okay? Were they torturing him? Resuming treatments? At least from the way Dr. Sterling spoke, I doubted they would kill him. She spoke too much about investing in him.

After ten minutes of tense waiting and silence, Dr. Sterling entered the room with three men in suits. Two of them flanked the door, as if guarding the exit. The third man in a suit smiled widely and sat down in the seat across from Violetta. His dark hair was slicked back. In his forties, he gave the appearance of friendliness, but there was an insincerity about it. Like he was playing a part and the second he needed to drop it, he would, along with a hammer.

Dr. Sterling stood next to him, choosing not to sit as well. I sent her a scathing glare.

"You survived," she said flatly.

"Sorry to disappoint you," I said. This woman lied to me, manipulated me, and actively hurt people. I was disgusted by her, as well as my inability to see her evil designs.

"My name is Ted Garfield, and this is Dr. Sterling. I understand you have come to us with demands," the smiling man directed at Violetta. There was clear condescension in his voice. Like he was placating a child.

Violetta didn't bat an eye. "You are going to release my ward, or as you refer to him, patient #526."

Garfield laughed lightly, like she'd told an amusing joke at a party. "Violetta... Excuse me, it's Master Violetta, isn't it? The only reason we took this meeting is because it's not every day someone shows up to a top-secret institute no one should have any knowledge of, and asks for government property that doesn't technically exist."

Violetta didn't laugh.

"Maybe you can tell us how you learned of this location," he said, leaning and perching his fingers on the table.

Completely ignoring his question, she said, "You are also going to cease any and all research into the matter of making demons, or weaponizing them from this point forward."

Garfield chuckled, but a hard glint slipped into his eye this time. "If you've been listening to the conspiracy theorist who came with you"—he glanced at me—"I can assure you that no such experiments are happening. But let's round back to how you have knowledge of this institute."

"This particular branch will be closed, effective immediately. Now please bring me my ward or face the consequences of your immoral actions and poor choice of work." Violetta was downright scary when she wanted to be, and I was grateful she was on my side.

The battle of wills and superiority filled the room so that it became difficult to breathe. The guards and Sterling didn't so much as twitch a muscle. But Garfield's false buddy mode was quickly dissolving with every command Violetta gave.

Tense silence vibrated in the room until I thought he was on the verge of exploding. I'd spotted the guns tucked under the guards' jackets. If they wanted to shoot us right here, they could. And I'd no doubt as to their ability to cover up we were ever here.

Then Garfield leaned back in his seat, weaving his fingers together. "I'm curious to know why you think you could make demands on such a large scale to anyone. Is it because you work closely at Hogwarts with Dumbledore?" he asked with a smug expression.

Violetta raised her staff, then tapped it back on the floor. The purple gemstone at the top lit up and a crack of purple lightning snaked through the room with an electric buzz that made all of my hair stand on end for a moment. It felt as though I'd undergone a light electric shock.

The guards pulled their weapons, aimed at Violetta now. She remained unfazed.

"You are children playing with poisons you don't understand. You think you know power, but you can't fathom what true power is. It is something born of time, mastery, and a great deal of calculation. Not of money, petulance, and blind greed."

Dr. Sterling reacted this time, her face puffing up red.

"I'm the most cutting-edge scientist of our time, and I'm revolutionizing—"

Violetta's face snapped toward the doctor. Sterling's mouth clicked shut. At first confusion, then a volley between anger and fear danced in her eyes.

The guards cocked their guns.

The old woman turned her attention back to Garfield, who studied her with renewed intensity.

"Here is what's going to happen. You are going to receive a call. And then after that call, you are going to release my ward back into my care, along with relevant research materials. Then you will let us walk out of here with no further trouble." She glanced at me again. "Did I forget anything?"

I shook my head.

Violetta let out an impatient huff. "Do learn to be your own advocate," she chastised me, before turning back to Garfield. "And Nurse Morningstar here wishes to be placed at any hospital of her choosing with a glowing recommendation."

Before I could register my shock at her advocacy on my behalf, a phone vibrated.

Everyone's attention turned to Garfield. A line of disbelief formed between his eyebrows before he pulled out his cellphone. Recognition smoothed his features as he reviewed the screen. He answered with a clipped, "Yes."

I couldn't hear any of the other side of the conversation, but Garfield kept his eyes trained on Violetta. His expression lay somewhere between skepticism and awe.

The guns remained poised in our direction. My skin crawled from the feeling of vulnerability, knowing anything could set this room off.

Garfield hung up, staring at Violetta in open amazement. "Do as she says." His voice had a faraway sound, as if he weren't sure if he were dreaming.

No one moved. Violetta continued to stare at him with impassive, hooded eyes.

Then he jerked. "Did you hear me? Go get the subject and have the materials she wants packed up."

The guards dropped their weapons and left.

Dr. Sterling seemed to regain control of her mouth. It opened and closed like a guppy's. "Ted? What are you—"

Before she could finish, he stood and gripped her arm. He gave us a curt nod before dragging her out of the room.

When the door shut behind them, I let out a big whoosh of air. "Holy tomato skins, that was intense. And I certainly didn't expect you to do anything for me."

The master regarded me with a calculating gaze. "Don't get too excited. There is still a chance neither of you will live."

I was instantly on edge again. "What do you mean?"

The door opened and Leonidas was escorted in. Back in chains, his face was bloodied and bruised. He appeared bleary-eyed. They'd sedated him. But more than that, there was a haunted look to them. A darkness I hadn't seen before. It was as if he were a different person, changed.

Then his eyes met mine. Disbelief first, then life sparked in them and whoever that other person was melted away. Leonidas strained against the chains.

I flew at him, wrapping my arms around his neck. "Thank god you're okay," I whispered into his ear. Then I barked at the guards, "Get the chains off him, now."

They did as I ordered and Leo crushed me to him, burying his face in my hair. "I thought I lost you." There was a catch in his voice.

"I was saved by someone like you. A knight of the light."

When I pulled away, I smoothed his wild hair from his face. "Though he refused to help me come help you. Insisted it wasn't his problem."

He grunted in recognition. "Gatsby."

"Did Gatsby kill the tombscream when he saved you?" Violetta asked from behind me. She'd stood up.

Leo didn't release his grip on me, but he looked over my shoulder at his former master.

"No, he didn't. He just got the tombscream to release me and scared it off."

"What is she doing here?" Leonidas asked me.

I managed to half-turn my body. "When Gatsby wouldn't help me, I went to her. She's the reason they're releasing you."

They stared at each other for a moment, appraising each other.

"Are you here to kill me?" he asked her finally.

Violetta adjusted her grip on her staff. "No. She convinced me you still may be of use to our cause."

"Then what is the price of this savior act?" he asked, a deep scowl on his face.

Then I remembered what Violetta said.

"To prove your fealty, you will kill this tombscream." Her eyes landed on me. "And you will act as bait."

"No," he growled, muscles bunching up under my hands.

"Then perhaps I shall call them back in, tell them to chain you up again because you prefer to be experimented on. Let these people deal with the nurse."

"No," I exclaimed, stopping the fight before it got started. Then, turning to Leonidas, I cupped his face. "We need to finish this. I need to finish this. There is a man out there who has been turned into a monster, and we need to stop him." Then I turned to Violetta. "He's an innocent. He's been turned into something he's not after losing his family in a demonic attack. He needs our help."

"He's a demon now," Violetta said calmly, but her lips pursed.

"Maybe something can be done to help him. Maybe what's been done to him can be undone. Maybe it's the same for Leonidas." Before I said it wasn't possible. But I needed hope.

Silence rang out, and I had to bite my tongue to keep from pleading with her.

"Fine." She nodded. "If you can capture him, I will see about what I can do. But if he can't be captured, I expect you to do what is necessary, Leonidas."

His spine straightened at her last command. Likely a tone he'd been trained by to do her bidding. With a nod, he agreed to her terms.

"Should you succeed, we will bring you back into the fold," Violetta said.

My stomach dropped. This is what he wanted. To be back where he belonged, to be able to pursue his mission. But I wanted more for him.

For him? Or for yourself?

I swallowed over the lump in my throat. "Let's get out of here."

28

LEONIDAS

When we returned to Betsy's apartment, the sun was setting. Violetta didn't protest. If we were going to take care of the tombscream, or I guess Tom, I'd need to recover before going hunting.

The sedatives still coursed through my veins.

"No, I promise I'm fine. I can't explain, but I'm handling things. No, you don't need to fly out here."

Betsy spoke animatedly into her phone as she shed herself of her winter clothing. Jacket ripped and dirty, she still reminded me of an angel.

"I know what Adie said, and I'm telling you it would only complicate things."

She sat on a stool, her boots hitting the floor with a thud.

Leaning on an elbow, she closed her eyes. "You didn't tell Dad, did you?" She let out a sigh of relief. "Okay, yes, yes, I promise. Just please don't tell him. I'll be home soon. Give the kids my love." She hung up, covered her eyes, and sagged in her seat.

"You're going back?"

Betsy dropped her hand to look at me. "Yes. Adie told my other sisters what happened, and they are all freaking out. They're insisting I come home right away. And"—she rolled her shoulders back—"I agreed, if they let me take care of some business. I just didn't tell them that business was hunting down a demon who wants to kidnap and kill me."

"Is that what you want?"

"To be kidnapped and killed? Not particularly."

I shook my head. "To go home to Montana with your family. With Jeremy."

Her lips thinned, and I couldn't read her expression. "When we are done with the tombscream, Tom," she corrected herself, "you'll go back to the order of Luxis. Work for Violetta again."

It wasn't a question. It was a statement. And it was true. She'd brokered a deal to get me out, but I wasn't free. I didn't know what Betsy said, but the Luxis was willing to take me as I was. I could still be useful to them.

Which meant I'd go back to volleying between the temple for rest and recovery and then out hunting on whatever mission they deigned to send me on. And these days there was no shortage of need for what I could do.

I'd longed for that in the months I was captured, but now a boulder dropped in my stomach at the thought of returning to the old way.

She went on. "It's good for me to go home. I'm not cut out for this hellmouth business. And I'm needed back there. I know who I am in Montana."

"Are you sure that's who you are?"

Walking over to her dining table, my fingers sifted through the pile of soft, colorful yarns. I brushed my thumb against the pages of a book on baking pies. She turned from where she sat at the island to watch me. My heart gave a merciless squeeze.

I'd thought I knew what life was. But since meeting Betsy, I realized I'd lived in a palette of grays, and she turned my world into color. Color, warmth, and passion. It wasn't because of her apartment, or her one-eyed cat. She felt like home to me—like I belonged with her.

"You'll go home, and I'll return to my duty," I agreed. We both knew whatever this was between us wouldn't last.

She tried to smile, but it was a dull flicker compared to the bright glow of her true happiness.

Then she broke out in a laugh and brushed her hair back with her fingers. "Sweet cinnamon. From the way we're acting, someone might think we might not want to live through this."

"Nothing is going to happen to you." I wasn't laughing as I stopped in front of her. "I swear it. You will get through this, and you will be able to reclaim your life as you wish."

"I believe you." Her words came out quiet. She looked up at me from under those long lashes. Those eyes held an entire universe in them, one where nothing bad ever happened. I remembered the feeling when I first fell into her blue orbs. Instantly, I knew she was different from the rest.

The air between us heated and vibrated. I wanted her. Plain and simple. But she'd been through so much. Things she should never have endured. From her ex-beau, her job, and even me.

"What about tomorrow?" she asked.

"It will end one way or another. It won't be hard to find the tombscream. Not if I open up my mind to him, deliberately."

"When you fought him last time, you lost control. He nearly tore you to pieces." Worry tightened the corners of her eyes. She wrung her hands, as if needing to do something with them. Concern radiated off her, but I also sensed something else. Trust. Deep, unwavering trust in me.

"This is what I do," I said.

"We have to help him," she insisted.

"Betsy," I said, using her name to let her know how serious I was. "I have been in his mind. I haven't detected a trace of the person he was. I don't know if there is any Tom left."

"We have to try," she insisted. Then her shoulders slumped as if already defeated by the task before us. We needed to rest and recover. Tomorrow would come soon enough.

I reached out a hand to bury it in her hair. Then I paused when it was an inch away. "I'll understand if you don't want to."

Betsy licked her lips, then guided my hand the rest of the way to her. I leaned down and kissed her, slowly and thoroughly, silken strands sliding against my fingers.

"One for the road?" she asked against my lips.

"Better make it a good one, then," I said. I stepped into the space between her legs and bent her head back, exploring deeper with my tongue. I wanted to memorize every last inch of her. After all, I'd have to live the rest of my life off the memory I imprinted right here. I intended to do it right.

I lifted her up and set her on the island so I could get better access. After kissing until we both needed to breathe, we broke apart. I set my forehead against hers.

"I went crazy thinking you were..." I couldn't even finish.

She thought the tombscream was just a man in pain, but I knew what it planned to do to her. Break her. Tear her to pieces in the most gruesome way.

"Shhh," she said, petting my hair. "I'm okay. We're okay."

"You said my body was trying to find equilibrium. That the demon and the human were trying to find a way to function together. And with time, I'm gaining control, finding a peace between the two sides. But then when you were taken, I could feel my humanity slipping away. I'd given up, and the darkness overtook me."

She didn't interrupt me, just let me get it out.

"Even knowing you are in this world makes me want to fight. Fight to be the man I used to be."

"Leonidas." She pulled back so she could look me in the eye. "I don't know who you used to be. But I know whoever you've become is better than anyone I know."

Feeling pierced through my armor, and I welcomed it. It was the most human part of me, and sharing that with her was the most natural thing I'd ever done.

We took it slowly. Undressed each other, trailing kisses along exposed skin. Tasting and touching with such attention. I feasted on her as she lay back on the counter until she came unraveled. The swell of pride and ownership of being the only one able to do this to her filled me.

Then I carried her to the bedroom. Unable to wait any longer, we joined our bodies and rocked against each other until a matching glisten covered our bodies. I filed away each piece of her for later. The pressure of her nails in my back. The softness of her leg as I ran a hand along the length of it, up the perfect dip of her hip. The exact pitch of her mewl when I hit the spot that drove her wild.

I'd collect all these little things and take them back with me to the temple. And when I'd have a moment alone, I'd pull them out and hold their warmth to me. It would have to be enough to keep me going for the rest of my days.

When we rolled over so she could ride me, my hand fell to the curve of her back.

I should have kept quiet. Recorded the moments and sealed my mouth. But I had to ask one more time. "Why aren't you afraid of me, legs?"

At the institute, she said it was because she was more interested in helping, which left no room for fear. Part of me wondered if that's all this was. Was I a charity case? Someone else she could show up and play hero for?

Betsy stilled. She regarded me with quiet confidence. She knew the answer before it fell off her lips, and she wasn't afraid of the truth. Not here, while we were entwined.

"Because I love you," she said simply.

I couldn't say the words back. Not because I didn't feel them. My throat grew thick with emotion, so I couldn't speak. I pulled her down to me, needing to feel all of her at once.

Then we were riding a new, intense wave of motion. The love I had for her turned the fire of our already scalding passion into an inferno. I almost hoped we'd perish there.

But then Betsy shuddered in my arms, finding her release, rocketing me toward my own.

I wanted it to last longer, but I knew it would never be enough. I could come to Betsy's bed every night, yet always beg for more.

My fingers dug into her hips as I threw my head back and cried out. The monster and the man in me converged into a perfect form of worship for the woman we loved. My mouth drew even to her ear.

"I love you, too."

She sighed in some place between relief and satisfaction and held onto me for dear life. I held her right back.

If someone had told me I'd become part demon, and fall

irrevocably in love with a woman, I'm not sure which I would have thought to be more ridiculous.

But with the seconds ticking by, bringing us closer to our previous lives, nothing was funny about it.

29

LEONIDAS

"Are you sure he will come?" Betsy whispered.

We were back at what remained of the Miskatonic Institute for Deeper Insight. As soon as morning dawn broke, we drove here. The tombscream was nocturnal, but it would come out if the bait was big enough.

Sheila rested nearby, and I'd taken off my coat and shirt in preparation. I'd no doubt shift in the heat of battle.

"Yes," I said, gazing into her eyes. "I've opened my mind to the connection, and he sees you as I see you now." My vision was layered, seeing from my perspective and the tombscream's.

"Like right now?" She licked her lips nervously.

I would have kissed that beautiful mouth of hers if I weren't seeing double.

"Yes, right now."

As soon as we got into position, I relaxed my mind. I easily connected to the demon. My vision flickered red as I felt his emotions at seeing Betsy. Fierce, overwhelming violence and possessive fury consumed him. He wanted to come for her. Prove that he was the apex predator by taking my mate.

I gave him an eyeful of our surroundings. He knew exactly where we were.

"Come and get me, you sonofabitch," I muttered.

"Ahem."

"Err, I mean, son of a biscuit." Then I said, "I suppose this isn't a good time to bring up that I've heard you curse seven ways from Sunday, begging me to—"

"Are you trying to shame me?" she asked. We were bantering, covering up the tension of what was to come.

The sun streamed into the cell from the barred windows. Whatever materials they used to make this particular cell, it would hold against the tombscream. I'd tested it myself.

"No." I smirked at her. "I would never. I enjoy your idiosyncrasy. I never know what strange twist of words are going to come out of your mouth."

"Holy toodle noodles," she gasped. "The whites of your eyes have turned silver."

"See?" I said on a pained groan.

The tension of staying tethered to the tombscream became unbearable. Opening myself this much to meld our minds together, I endured an unbearable pressure of pain. It wasn't mine. The creature was in constant agony. Animal instincts were cranked up all the way until it couldn't control itself. Everything was too loud, too bright, too painful. Everything grated across my nerves with razor sharpness.

I had to cut off the connection. But I knew I'd sufficiently motivated him. It wouldn't be long.

As soon as I returned to just me, I realized my back was itching. A wing flapped in my periphery.

"Did you mean to do that?" Betsy asked, her mouth agape.

"No." I frowned. "But it's not a bad idea. If I can stay in control of my senses and meld more logic with the demon inside me, I bet I can make this quick. Maybe I can…"

She tilted her head. "What?"

"If I change now, I won't have to rely on losing control to force the rest of the shift. And you ground me." I shifted my weight. "But that's dangerous. I'm afraid I'll give into the baser part of me. When I thought I'd lost you, I reverted so quickly…"

"Try it," she said.

"Betsy, I don't want to hurt you."

"You won't. I trust you. You need to trust yourself."

I still hesitated.

"Besides, this plan won't work if you don't have a hold of your faculties."

I hated she had a point. And "plan" was a generous term. We were in a massive caged room. I'd given the tombscream a long hard look at Betsy in this setting so he would come here. But by the time the creature got here, she would be well out of harm's way. She was almost done playing bait. Though Violetta commanded the method, it was Betsy who convinced me she wouldn't be left behind.

If we captured the tombscream, we could work with Violetta and her many sources on undoing what had been done to Tom, and me as well.

But until then, I would have to use my demon side to get through this next part.

Bringing my focus inward, I connected to the darkness inside me. Every moment I worked to suppress the demon in me, like I did to shut the tombscream out. Allowing it to express itself, the change was surprisingly quick. My fingers stretched and elongated into black talons. While my bones ached and groaned with the shift, the pain was significantly less than past transformations.

Betsy eyed me with uncertainty, but she didn't run screaming. I stretched my claws out, able to take in my own form with a logical mind I hadn't retained before.

"Are you still you?" Betsy asked.

Fangs encumbered my mouth so I couldn't easily speak. I simply nodded.

Then she broke into a smile. "Okay. See? You've got this."

Her fearlessness amazed me. Even as I stood as a monster before her, I felt her love radiating for me.

I slipped a talon under her shirt, skimming it along her stomach. She shivered. Then she reached up to touch one of my fangs, before moving to delicately run a finger against my wing. It twitched at the contact, as a sound akin to a purr emerged from me.

A smile pulled at the side of her mouth.

My animalistic side wanted to sink into her, but my human brain was present this time and concerned for her safety. I let out a discontented snort.

"Right," she said, her expression sobering. She dropped her hands. "Time for step two."

I pointed out the door.

"Yes, yes, then I'll go. I'll be far away, out of harm's way. Just like we planned." Her voice softened. "And you'll be careful. Don't do anything to get yourself hurt."

Unable to make a joke or rib her, I simply ran the back of my knuckles down her soft cheek. Her eyes rounded, and she closed her hands around my monstrous one, holding it there for a moment.

After a moment, she stepped back and clapped her hands. "Okay, now for the fun part."

She stripped.

Five minutes later, Betsy had removed all of her clothes and left them in the cage. Then she dumped rubbing alcohol on a wash rag and gave herself a sponge bath.

At one point, she rose her eyebrow at me. "Looks like we had time for that sponge bath after all."

The dark, rusty sound that emerged from my throat was close enough to a laugh. I remembered requesting that very treatment when she came to my cell. But then, I'd hoped she'd put her hands on me. This worked too.

If I weren't in my demon form…

Now that my logical, human brain remained active, I knew it would help me stay in control. It would keep me from hurting anyone else. But I could tell my instincts were slowed, my brute force dullened. I would be at a disadvantage with the tombscream. But I planned to outsmart the demon, so it shouldn't matter. Before he knew what was happening, I'd have contained him again.

Still, the fact made me uneasy.

Then Betsy opened a bag of brand new, never-before-worn clothes. Before she put them on, I forced her to rub a few more spots with alcohol. There could be no trace of her scent leaving the institute, or the tombscream would know and hunt down her trail. Meanwhile, the positively delicious scent of her clung to the clothes in the cage's corner.

Once dressed, she pulled out her car keys, but lingered. She didn't want to go.

I growled. Time was running out, she needed to leave, or everything would be ruined.

"Don't die," she said, then turned and jogged down the hall.

Even as a demon, my heart twisted with pain at seeing her go. I heard the engine start up and then grow fainter as she drove away.

Keep her safe. That was all that mattered.

30

BETSY

Fear for Leonidas made it hard to breathe. My brain was crowded with scenarios where he was hurt.

He's a bulletproof, winged monster. He will hold his own.

Still, my knuckles turned white from my tight grip.

A car driving in the opposite direction swerved in front of me. I slammed on the brakes and jerked the wheel. My car slammed into the ditch and the airbag exploded open in my face. There was pain, but mostly shock. I had a strange sense of clarity. Enough to be grateful I hadn't been going faster. The claustrophobia set in. I fought with the airbag that practically crushed me. I could taste blood, but I didn't feel any serious injuries.

My car door creaked open and in moments, someone helped pull me out of the car. Pain shot through my left arm. I suspected it might be broken.

Blinking, I found myself faced with the barrel of a handgun. Dr. Sterling on the other end.

"Wh-what are you doing?" I asked, my hands lifted in surrender as much as I could.

"You think you can come in and ruin the most ground-breaking research done in maybe the history of man?" At first, she struck me as calm and implacable as ever. But under her voice was a tremor of rage. I tried to stand as still as possible, not wanting to set her off in any way.

"You think I'm going to stand for my work to be thrown away by some no-nothing nurse? Well, you got another thing coming." Her eyes tracked the road in the direction I'd just come. "He's up there, isn't he? At the institute."

The mad gleam in her eye told me exactly what she had planned. I risked saying something. "We can't go back there, the tombscream is on its way."

"Good. Then I can get back everything you tried to take from me. Now get in the car." She pointed to her vehicle with the gun. My brain raced for any idea that would keep us from going back there.

Her eyes narrowed. "I planned on using you as leverage to get subject #526 to cooperate, so I can't kill you. But I could certainly shoot you in some non-vital areas to make you more compliant."

Ice cold fear cut through the shock of the car crash. I had zero doubt she'd do what she threatened.

As she drove us back, gun trained on me all the while, I tried to think of any argument that would change her mind. But how did one reason with an armed doctor barreling straight at two demonic entities?

"Don't you want to help people? You're a doctor."

"Yes, and my research will help save billions of people. I'll give our government control over monsters to fight the worse ones. The things we've learned about these creatures from the Stygian so far are staggering. The world changed once when the gates to hell opened, and I'm going to change the world a second time."

My stomach twisted in sick knots, listening to her.

She glanced at me. "I heard your plans. You want to save them. You want to reverse what we've done to them." A harsh laugh escaped her. "There is no going back for them."

"That's not true," I said weakly.

"Don't be an idiot. Or worse, an optimist. Your *boyfriend*" —she stressed the word with mocking—"is almost nothing like the tombscream we created, though they received nearly identical treatments. The Stygian and everything in that dimension is unstable. Chaos and entropy. You think we can undo what we've done? We barely know how we achieved the results we have."

I opened my mouth, then shut it again. I didn't want to believe her.

The car came to a stop. The massive gray building looming like death itself. We shouldn't be here. Dr. Sterling poked me in my ribs with her gun. "Get out."

Guns were the great equalizer. No matter I was a foot taller than the doctor. I did as she asked.

I turned to face the building and met Leonidas's silver eyes through the barred windows of the room where we'd set the trap. The tombscream was with him in the cell. Then there was a flurry of movement. A pained roar cut through the thick walls. *Leonidas.* He rammed the bars on the windows. I watched him do it a second time. He wasn't going out the front, which told me my worst fears had just come true.

The trap had worked, but it was Leonidas locked inside. Which meant...

I clapped my hands over my ears as the tombscream's shriek pierced the air.

"We need to get out of here," I said, my panic full-blown. Sterling said something, but a buzzing in my ears kept me from catching it. It was from either the car crash or abject terror, but I knew I had to keep it together if I wanted to live.

I took two steps but stopped when I heard the cock of a gun. "Uh uh uh," Dr. Sterling warned, still standing by the open car door.

Leonidas bashed against the barred windows again. There was no chance he was getting out that way.

The tombscream streaked into the air out of a broken window from the side of the building. I trembled uncontrollably. This wasn't the plan. Not even a little bit.

The tombscream flew straight toward me. If I tried to run, Sterling would shoot me. But if I stayed rooted to the spot, I'd be taken again.

I cut right and ran. I could feel it gaining on me. I didn't stand a chance, but my legs pumped as fast as they could.

The crack of a gun reached my ears. Something slammed into me, and I went rolling. Pain exploded from my left arm again as I tumbled. Definitely broken. But I didn't have time for that. I scrambled to my feet. The tombscream lay on the ground, and Dr. Sterling quickly advanced toward us. A shotgun now nestled under one arm.

I wasn't far from the building, and glanced at the front door, wondering if I should still make a run for it. I needed to get to Leo and set him free. The entrance wasn't too far. After all, bullets hadn't proved to be effective in the past. The tombscream would be up any moment.

Then I spotted the red feather tranquilizer sticking out of the tombscream. The beast seemed to be prone, though it had taken at least five to take Leonidas down.

"Hmm," Sterling said, "it seems to have done the trick, but better safe than sorry."

Dr. Sterling stopped a couple feet away from the tombscream and took aim again. The demon shot up from the ground and the gun went flying off by the car.

It lifted Dr. Sterling in the air, clutching an arm and a leg. She dangled awkwardly from its grasp.

"Put me down, you—" Before she could finish, the tombscream yanked.

As her body gave way, tearing apart before my eyes, my stomach heaved. The tombscream let loose another shrill cry.

Tears blurring my vision, I ran into the building. All I knew was my only hope was to get Leonidas out.

Careening through the hallways, I slammed into the walls. Wings flapped behind me, closing in on me a second time. Sweat drenched my entire body, but I pushed myself harder. If I didn't, I was dead.

If I could just get to Leo and open the door. He was so close, but time moved too quickly.

Just around the corner, Betsy. Just a little farther. He's seconds away.

But I didn't have seconds. I had moments.

As I rounded the corner, I saw Leo's face in the small window in the door. He was waiting. He knew I was coming.

But I turned too fast and lost my footing. A scream ripped out of me as I went down. The second I slipped on the slick flooring, I knew I was dead.

Leo would be trapped in that cell until the tombscream went for him next. My body slammed into the far wall, and I curled into myself, bracing for the end.

Light filled the hallway.

Perhaps I'd been spared the pain of my own gruesome death and launched straight up to heaven.

I lowered my arms and found Gatsby standing in front of

me, arms outstretched. Light poured out of his hands, creating a shield between us and the tombscream.

"I can't hold it long," Gatsby said through gritted teeth. His muscles trembled from effort. The tombscream shrieked and beat against the forcefield.

I got my ass up and across to the door just as Gatsby's light extinguished. Everything happened at once, in slow motion. I unfastened the latch, and the door swung open.

The tombscream shot past Gatsby and lunged for me at the same time Leonidas emerged. A mottled, clawed hand wrapped around my neck.

I tried to swallow, but the grip was too tight. I stared into Leo's shocked silver eyes, wishing I could say I was sorry. It was too late for me.

31

LEONIDAS

H e had her in his grasp. It would take so little effort to snap her neck or worse. Still, the creature didn't make a move.

That's when I noticed Gatsby behind the tombscream. Gatsby rammed his sword through the monster's back until the front of his blade stuck out the front of the demon's split torso. With a flap of a wing, Gatsby smacked back into the wall behind him.

It wasn't a fatal blow, but the tombscream paused.

If I made any move, it could mean instant death for Betsy.

Not knowing what to do, I opened my mind, reconnecting with the demon. What I found there shocked me.

The pain of the blade was acute, but amid that agony, there was an intense sense of relief. The tombscream seemed to be on a precipice.

I sunk further into its mind and found... Tom. The physical pain was nothing compared to the emotional agony of losing his family, of knowing what the institute had turned him into. Existence was torture.

But the slice of Gatsby's sword gave him a taste of what he desired, even more than Betsy, or killing me.

Death.

He desired the relief of death, and he tasted it on Gatsby's blade.

I saw myself through his eyes as he burrowed into my mind as well. It was like viewing myself through a hundred mirrors. But in them, I found a part of me I thought was lost.

I raised a hand and connected to the well of power inside me. The everlasting light of my will surged forward like an old friend. I'd kept it suppressed, thinking it could not exist in a body tainted with a demon. But it was still there. It had always been there.

The power gathered in my hand, but instead of a bright white light, it emerged purple. The light stretched out and wrapped around the tombscream. It released Betsy, and she collapsed to the floor.

Gatsby raised his hand, trying to lend his power as well. He grimaced in frustration, nothing coming, but I didn't need his help.

I sent my divine energy into the tombscream, and it began cleansing. The skin of the demon cracked and flaked. My power burrowed in further, and I felt Tom's relief as he suddenly recognized himself. I'd freed him from the constraints of the darkness.

I was deconstructing the demon, separating the man from the monster. Though neither being could physically exist without the other anymore. In a quiet, steady stream, he turned to ash as my power unwove him.

I felt Tom's knowing that he would finally be allowed to rest. That wherever he was going, he would be reunited with his wife and two daughters.

Then the rest of him crumbled away.

Gatsby held his sword again, an all too familiar bitter expression on his face. His power had failed him yet again. Though I succeeded, I knew Gatsby would not likely forget this anytime soon.

A hand slipped around my arm. Betsy stood next to me, tears streaming down her face.

I'd done it. I'd made sure she'd be safe.

Only one thing left to do.

Let her go.

32

BETSY

I stared out the car window as Michael drove us to the airport. My arm was set in a sling from the break, and my face and body were bruised from the car wreck Dr. Sterling caused. But it could have been so much worse.

Adie sat in the passenger seat while Jeremy and I were in the back. It would be a brief trip home, but it set in motion my move back to Montana. Bubbles stayed with Martin, and he assured her they would be fine until I got back to pack everything up. Though he was sad to learn I planned on leaving.

When he asked about Leonidas, I told him we had two very different lives.

He seemed disappointed, but said he understood.

Gatsby had left on his motorcycle, not allowing me to thank him for his help. Leonidas never shifted back, though I knew he could. He ran a talon along my cheek, such longing, pain, and love in his eyes. Then he shot up into the air and flew away. We'd already agreed we'd go our separate ways after dealing with the tombscream. There was no reason to draw it out.

I took Dr. Sterling's car to get home. I grabbed my already packed bag and called Adie to pick me up in their rental car.

Adie was talking to Michael about their next doctor's appointment for the baby, and I was grateful their attention wasn't on me. I wasn't sure how I was feeling. Everything felt surreal after all I'd been through the last couple of days. Now that I was going home with my family, things seemed normal. But not.

Jeremy nudged me. "Hey, are you okay?"

I nodded and tried to smile. "Yeah, I'm just... tired."

He gave me an encouraging smile back. "Yeah, well, after all that."

Jeremy pushed, but I could feel him patiently waiting. I knew in his eyes, as well as our families', that it was only a matter of time before things returned to how they were.

"Hey Bets, you're not checking your phone," Adie said, looking at hers. "Rebecca is texting. She's asking if you can cover for her as room mom on Tuesday."

"Um, I thought Dad needed help. You said his health wasn't doing so well." My dad brushed off help, so if Adie said he needed it, I knew his house was a mess and he wasn't taking his medication.

"Well, he'll probably be too busy. He's actually seeing a woman, so they're off doing their own thing a lot. It'd be cute if it weren't disgusting."

"I thought you said he wasn't in good shape?" I asked, confused.

"Well," she paused, as if regrouping. "He said he misses your cooking a lot."

"So, he's fine," I reiterated.

"Oh yeah, they started hiking and his cholesterol has

gone down," Mike chimed in. Adie flicked his ear, and he cried out, asking why she did that.

I was still reeling from the news my father was in fine health, and also had a girlfriend.

Adie went on. "Oh, and Michael just told me he has a meeting on Wednesday, so you can take me to my doctor's appointment that day."

"Geez Adie, chill," Jeremy scoffed. "She's not going to be up for that."

I didn't realize I'd been holding my breath until he'd stood up for me. Anxiety had twisted under my breastbone as she shot orders at me.

Still, I tried to reason with myself.

I love being there for my family. Why wouldn't I be up for helping? That's who I was. The one they could rely on to make sure they were taken care of.

Are you sure that's who you are?

Leonidas's words hadn't hit me with force last night like they did now.

For the first time, I didn't feel the all-consuming guilt of my mother's absence. It was like somehow, I didn't feel responsible for every single person anymore. Like maybe I deserved to have my own life, my own needs met.

Jeremy reached over and patted my knee, continuing to speak to Adie. "She'll be busy helping me get on my feet at the hospital again. I start Tuesday. So Rebecca's going to have to figure out something else." He winked at me.

"And if you want to start nursing again, I'm sure we can find you a position easily. One without such a hard-ass like Doctor Sterling." He pulled out his phone to check it, while leaving a hand on my knee.

"What did you say?" I asked, my words barely a whisper.

"Don't tell me you're a Broncos fan now, Jeremy," Michael said. "If you do, I'll have to disown you."

"No way." Jeremy chuckled.

"How do you know my old boss's name?" I spoke loud enough to be heard over their mindless chatter.

Jeremy shrugged. "You must have told me."

I pushed his hand off my knee. "No. I didn't. I never told you anything about my job. Because we cut all ties after you left me a month before we were supposed to get married."

The memory of Leonidas taking me until I screamed his name on what was supposed to be my wedding day hit me full force. He'd been so deliberate to make sure I'd mark the day differently than I planned.

Then I gave voice to the fear bubbling in my stomach. "Did you call Dr. Sterling, Jeremy?"

He scoffed and kept scrolling on his phone, but his eyes darted in my direction.

"Oh my god, you did, didn't you? The day you guys crashed our breakfast at IHOP, you found out from Adie where I would be and told Dr. Sterling we would be there." Something new began to boil under the surface.

Michael pulled into the rental car hub and brought us to a stop.

"Okay, time to go," Adie said with a forced cheerfulness.

We exited the car, but I wasn't done talking about this.

I grabbed his shoulder. "Tell me, Jeremy. Tell me what you did."

He shrugged me off. "Hey, calm down. So what? Your boss tracked me down after that crazy demon attack on television. She saw you being loaded into the ambulance too and was looking for you. It was weird because she seemed to be surprised you were alive, though she wouldn't say why. Then when I described that Cro-Magnon guy hanging around, she said he was dangerous, and I agreed. She gave me her card, and then I called her when we came to see you the next morning. So I told your boss where you would be. What's the big deal?"

My jaw dropped.

Then, with perfect clarity, I knew what was boiling under the surface.

Anger.

My fist connected with Jeremy's cheek. Pain blossomed along my knuckles. I cradled them to me. Now I had one broken arm, and one smashed hand. Totally worth it. Jeremy cradled his face, while Michael froze in surprise.

"Sorry to disappoint you guys, but I'm not going with you. I'm staying here."

"Oh my god," Adie cried out. "What's with you? Why are you being like this? Mom would never have acted like this."

"Well, Adie, I'm not Mom. I'm your sister. And it's time I stopped mothering everyone. It's not my fault she died in a car accident. Shit happens."

With that, I grabbed the keys from Michael before he could stop me, and jumped in the driver's seat.

33

LEONIDAS

"These new powers..." She sipped her tea. "We are going to have to keep a close eye on them."

I reported back to the Luxis and monks were sent to clean up the scene at the institute.

Violetta stayed behind at the church with me. She'd been in the library room again, studying her tombs.

"Yes, master," I said, head bowed, hands folded. I'd been permitted to take tea with her when Betsy was here, but I stood off to the side now awaiting guidance. Things were back to normal.

I was Master Violetta's ward once again. A knight of the light of the order of Luxis. And my life was not my own.

Though standing here for the first time, bitterness filled me. Betsy was gone. I wouldn't see her again. I tried to console myself with the knowledge she was safe, but my insides felt hollow.

"Your nurse tried to convince me the best way to get ahead of this prophecy was to keep you close by." She regarded me over the rim of her teacup. "If indeed you herald the end of the five orders, I cannot contest the wisdom in keeping you under lock and key. Make sure you won't cause any problems."

"You can't do that." The words flew out of my mouth. "You imprison me, and my humanity will corrode away. When Betsy was taken by the tombscream, I nearly lost myself in that darkness. Lock me up, and I guarantee you will doom me."

Violetta raised an eyebrow, not saying anything for a long, heavy moment. "You speak out of turn." Then she sighed and set her saucer down. "Though I must say, I'd much rather not lock you away, Leonidas." There was a softness to her tone I was not used to. "If I were stronger, I would appoint another master and let them deal with you. Handle your situation without emotion. But I fear I cannot do so."

Something stirred inside me. Hope? She spoke with caring I'd never heard before.

"I am an old woman, used to the old ways. The world has changed, and the orders have united in a new, uncomfortable alliance. But I also see I am the only master remaining. Mistakes were made. Mistakes because our order's decision lacked... heart." A rare frailness then emerged from my master. The lines around her eyes and mouth deepened. "Your brother showed us that. That heart is the very thing we are saving."

She meant Calan. He'd risked everything for Emma. Suddenly, Krystan's words returned to me. I couldn't leave the Luxis and have a normal life with Betsy, like she suggested. But Calan and Emma didn't need a normal life, they needed each other.

Long, knobby fingers pressed into her temple. "He changed everything by challenging everything we thought we knew to be true."

"Maybe change isn't such a bad thing?" I said, my stance relaxing.

"Perhaps not…" she said slowly, coming to stand. Her hands folded behind her back. "We must protect the five orders at all costs, but perhaps we need to protect it from the inside out."

"I need her. I need Betsy," I said, suddenly.

Merely being in her presence, I was wrapped in light and love that only empowered me. I wanted to live amongst Betsy's colorful mess and take care of her so she could take care of others. I wanted long nights worshipping her under the moonlight until we both forgot our names.

"Like you said, things aren't the same anymore. We can't go back. And if I have any chance of holding onto my humanity, I need her. If you want me to work for the Luxis, things are going to be different from here on out."

Violetta's lips thinned. She reached for the hanging rope and pulled on it.

THE ENTRANCE SLAMMED open to the church as I readied myself to call forth my wings to launch into the air and speed away. But when I opened the heavy wood doors, I found Betsy racing up the stone stairs. Seeing me, she paused, her jaw slack.

"Legs," I said in surprise. "What are you doing here?"

The sun was setting, casting a brilliant play of purples and oranges in the sky behind her. Even with one arm in a sling, heavy bags under her lids, and scratches and bruises marring her face, there was a brightness in her eyes.

"I—" she faltered, then seemed to gather her courage. "You were right. I'm not the person I used to be. I don't want to go back to Montana." Her words came out in a flood. "I need to build better boundaries between me and my family. Because of you, I've stopped heaping blame for every little thing onto myself. Things may be messed up here near the hellmouth, but I like who I'm becoming here. I'm strong enough to survive, I think maybe even thrive, in this place."

I didn't know what to say. She barreled on. "And I think you need better boundaries with Violetta and this order. You can do so much good, and even with your new abilities, you can continue to be the hero you were before, if not better."

"Thank you," I said, though it almost came out a question. I still towered over her, two stairs above her.

"In the spirit of the new Betsy, I'm learning not to be afraid to ask for what I want too. I want you and I will not apologize for it. I want to stay here. And I want you. No matter what that looks like, I will do whatever it takes. Help patch you up after missions. Even if that means begging Violetta some more. Camping out on the doorstep here until they let me in to see you. I'll visit you as much as they'll let me. I'll make a truckload of casseroles and pies to bribe your monks." She'd become frenetic, words rushing over one another, gesticulating madly.

I grabbed her one flailing hand, letting the doors slam behind me. "That's not going to work, legs," I said, stopping her speech in its tracks.

She shook her head. "I don't accept that. I want to try." Her eyes turned glassy. "For the first time, I know what I want, and I won't accept less. You stupidly taught me to have standards for my life. And this is a non-negotiable for me."

I pulled her up another stair, not loosening my hold on her wrist. "It's not going to work," I repeated, calmly, "because I won't be here at the church."

"They're moving you?" she asked, panic skating along her tone.

"I won't be here because I told Violetta where I would complete missions and continue my duties. Things have to be different now. I won't be sequestered in the temples anymore. So, you can't feed the whole temple to be with me, because I won't be here."

"Where will you go?" she asked, sucking in a breath. Hope and fear warred in her eyes.

I pulled her up until she stood next to me on the landing. "Well, I was hoping to see a girl about an apartment with a one-eyed cat. But if I'm presuming too much here—"

Before I could finish, Betsy launched herself at me. She threw her one free arm around me, kissing me enthusiastically. I'd take that as a yes. I kissed her back and held her tight to me, but still careful not to hurt her.

Knowing I could be with this woman every day filled me with a magic that surpassed the powers I'd discovered to release Tom from his demonic prison. It was the true magic that would change this world, sappy as that sounded. Suddenly, I understood my brother Calan more than ever before.

"Wait, is Violetta going to allow this?" She peeked over my shoulder as if expecting armed monks to burst out the doors to attack us.

One side of my mouth curved up. "Yeah, she agrees you add... heart to the situation."

I almost wondered if my master hadn't known things would end up like this before I did.

"I need you, legs," I rumbled, nuzzling into her neck.

"I need you too," she said, clinging to me, her voice scratchy with emotion.

"There is still a chance what Violetta says is true. That

I'll turn dark. That my brother knights will turn dark, and we'll be the downfall of the five orders meant to protect this world from the Stygian."

Betsy pulled back slightly, a look of resolve settling on her face. "Well then, you definitely need me. I'll whip your rear into shape if I think you've stepped out of line. Even if that means I need to buy a bigger spray bottle or roll up more newspapers."

I couldn't help the wolfish grin that spread across my face. "You're not afraid of the big bad monster?"

She shrugged with a sly smirk of her own. "Turns out I like a little monster in my man."

EPILOGUE

Betsy

"Oh god," I screamed, legs twitching as I neared the edge.

A matching groan emerged from Leo as he pounded into me. With my hands wrapped around the bars of my bed frame behind me, I hung on for dear life. I was so happy to be rid of that sling.

Buzz buzz.

I turned to look at the ringing phone on the bedside table.

Leo gripped my chin to bring my focus back to him. "Stay with me."

"It's probably important," I said, torn between the sweet friction he generated between my legs and the need to help.

"This is important," he growled.

"She's going to make you move back into the church if you don't answer," I argued.

"I'd kill them all," he said. He dropped a hand between us to play with me. Sensation rocketed through me, but I held off release, attention still torn between the beast hovering over me and the still-buzzing phone.

"Liar," I gasped.

"Want to bet?" he asked, doubling the speed of his hips.

The next words in my throat died as heat engulfed me. Leo followed me into bliss that left us both shaking and panting.

Buzz buzz.

I reached over and picked up the phone, accepting the call before handing it to Leo, who'd collapsed on me.

"Yes?" he grunted into the phone. After listening a moment, he said, "Okay, I'm on my way," then hung up.

"Demons or spirits?" I asked.

"Both. Apparently, the entities are working as a team. Pretty rare." He dropped kisses along my neck. Goosebumps prickled up on my skin. I felt boneless and utterly amazing, but I stayed focused.

Leo got up and stretched, muscles expanding in the most enticing way. But we didn't have time for a round two.

"Good gravy babies. That sounds like a handful. Should I text Travis and Krystan and tell them we can't come to dinner?"

"Actually, that was them calling. They are already on their way, but they need someone to take care of baby Tristan while we go monster hunting."

I was up like a shot then. "Oh, baby time? I'm so ready! I just finished this cute little hat with elephant ears for him."

Leo smirked as he pulled on his pants. "Should I be concerned you are going to steal their child?"

I pretended to think about it. "Yes. The best idea here would be to make one of our own to keep me out of prison for baby snatching."

Though we were half dressed, Leo grabbed me, pulling me flush against him. "Now there's an idea." His large hand lay against my flat stomach.

I was only half kidding, but the idea of making a family with this man made my toes positively curl. When his fingers dipped lower, I grabbed his hand. "Best to do some research before we start making babies with wings."

"Sounds like an excellent project to get rolling," he agreed.

With Violetta's help and some other powerful characters from some of the other orders, I was helping develop a real research division dedicated to helping people affected by the Stygian. What the Miskatonic Institute should have been.

They agreed it could help us monitor Leo's situation as well, help keep him in control of the demon inside him.

This time, my phone dinged. Five more subsequent dings followed.

"Adie?" Leonidas guessed.

"Probably," I said. She'd had her baby last month, and I'd even gone out for a couple of days to help. While she still resented my staying in Colorado, my sisters and I were building a new kind of relationship. They didn't love that I wasn't at their beck and call, but I knew with time, we'd be all the better for it. And to feel free of the weight I carried, blaming myself for my mom's accident, was utterly life-changing.

As much as I still desired to control the world around me, help those who needed it, I realized it didn't require punishing myself for how things were.

Oddly enough, my dad was the one faring the best. His new girlfriend really breathed life into him. They went hiking and hunting together. He said he agreed that I needed to do what was right for me, and they'd be there if I ever needed a soft place to land. It was my turn to be supported. I cried like a baby when I repeated what he said to Leonidas, the reality of it finally penetrating years of responsibility and duty that nearly crushed me.

Jeremy would always be a part of the family since he was Michael's brother, but he was already on the receiving end of karma. Turned out he wanted me back because he was terrible at his job and got fired.

He also had grand designs to play the field, but none of the women cared to get into the game with him. I found out from one of the nurses back at the hospital in Colorado Springs. After hooking up with one of the other doctors, Jeremy expected her to do his laundry and make him breakfast the next morning. That story spread like wildfire, burning all his prospects in a hurry.

As if sensing my train of thought, Leo asked, "She still trying to get you back with Jeremy?" Bubbles now lay across his right shoulder, purring loudly as he petted her.

"No," I said. "Thankfully, she's over that phase. And she got the memo. I really didn't care about his situation anymore. Even though I'd been the one to supposedly create those expectations for him. I had to tell her, yet again, I have a new set of standards for myself."

Leo dipped down to kiss me. "Good, and I only have the two expectations of you."

"Two?" I asked, raising an eyebrow.

"One"—he raised a finger—"keep breathing."

I laughed. "I think I can do that."

"Two." He raised another finger, then trailed them both down my neck to the swell of my breasts. He leaned in closer. "Sometimes, I need you to breathe faster." His voice was husky with desire again, letting me know exactly what he meant.

Oh yeah. I think I could do that.

Want a bonus epilogue featuring Gatsby?

Visit hollyroberds.com to read it now!

ONE BAD KNIGHT
CHAPTER 1

KAT

Never had I experienced so many sleepless nights. Excitement bubbled in my tummy like pop rocks. I slipped out of bed in the middle of the night because I couldn't sleep again. I would turn eleven in only seven days.

Moonlight filtered in through the French doors, drawing me toward it. I stepped out onto my balcony into the crisp night. Everything was bright from the full moon, so when I looked to the left, the expanse of lawn and gardens stretched out behind the house.

The moon's twin shimmered in the pond out back. Soon, my dad would be throwing parties outside again. His serious, old friends weren't very fun, but I loved how they decorated everything in twinkle lights and brought out the chocolate fountain.

My arms crossed on the railing as I listened to the whisper of palm-sized leaves. A massive sycamore tree shot up past my third-floor balcony and was always active with birds and squirrels, but not a single animal chittered right now.

I'd barely seen my dad the last couple months. Nanny Maureen reminded me this morning, as she braided my hair, that my dad was a very important man and working very hard right now.

He was up for re-election, which meant he was almost never in the house, and when he was, he was in his office and not to be disturbed. I needed to be on my best behavior. If I was a good girl, it would help him focus on what was important.

The wind picked up my hair and whipped it around my face, causing goosebumps from the cold and anticipation to rise along my skin.

But my birthday? The whole day was going to be just my dad and me. None of his campaign people, absolutely no work, and I got to decide what we did the entire day. I chose ice cream and a painting class. I almost picked the museum, but people always bothered him, and I'd end up wandering around the exhibit on my own while people took pictures and asked my dad questions.

But on Saturday we would get messy with paints, and make big, beautiful sunflowers I planned on hanging in my room.

As I inhaled a deep breath of spring night air, I found myself locking eyes with a strange boy sitting in my tree.

I reared back, but the two sharp gray eyes remained fixed on me. A scream froze in my throat.

He seemed about my age, but his eyes held the weight and intensity of someone far older. They pierced me like blades and rooted to the spot.

I scrounged up my voice. "What are you doing up here?" I asked.

He didn't speak, didn't move, just stared at me.

"I'm Kat. What's your name? And how did you get up

here?" With a quick look down, I confirmed there wasn't a ladder. I could climb from my balcony into the tree, but the limbs were far too high to get to it from the ground.

Another beat passed before I suppressed the urge to roll my eyes and said, "You aren't a T-Rex. Just because you aren't moving, it doesn't mean I can't see you."

His brows furrowed.

I didn't know how I knew, but I read his expression. "You don't know what a T-Rex is? You know? Like a dinosaur?"

One of his eyebrows dipped as he frowned. I held my hands out to show size. "You know, massive lizards that roamed the earth before humans? Didn't you learn this stuff in school?"

At that, he looked away and his muscles tensed. Suddenly I was afraid he would leave. Strange as it seemed, I didn't want the boy in my tree to leave.

My cheeks grew hot. "I'm sorry, I didn't mean to make you feel bad. I go to a special private school. I don't know what they teach in other schools. That was rude of me." My mom told me when I was little that we were privileged, and I had to be sensitive to that.

He didn't respond, but he didn't leave like I thought he would. The boy continued to stare at me as if trying to figure out all my secrets.

I didn't have many. Only the ones in a shoebox under my bed. It held the diary I kept safe with a small key, the half-empty bottle of my mom's perfume, and one of my dad's special cigars that I told myself I was borrowing. I didn't want to smoke it or anything. I just wanted something grown-up and important in the box.

Something in his intense gaze made me feel... special. Like I was the most interesting thing he'd ever seen in his life. I weirdly felt the same way about the boy with sharp eyes in the tree outside my bedroom window who didn't know about dinosaurs.

A breeze swept through my thin nightgown, and the chill of the bright spring night bit into my me.

Good girls don't let strange boys sit in their trees in the dead of night. And they certainly don't invite them into their house.

What was I doing? I wasn't supposed to talk to strangers. But... kids didn't count. It wasn't dangerous even if the kid was strange.

"Are you cold?" I asked, unable to help myself.

The boy's sandy hair was windblown, and he wore dark clothes under a beat-up jacket. I'd spent my fair share of time hiding in this tree, drawing in my sketchbook so my cousins couldn't bother me. I'd stay up there reading until my fingers turned numb from the cold and it was hard to turn the pages. My dad didn't mind as long as I was at dinner when he told me to be.

The boy didn't answer, but a forward tilt of his head told me everything I needed to know. My mom used to say I was extra good at seeing into people's hearts. Mine told me his was cold.

That bothered me, a lot.

"If you come in, we can make hot chocolate. Since you're taller, I won't have to climb up on the kitchen counter to reach the box." I knew people liked to feel useful.

A thick tree limb stretched over my balcony. I held out a hand. The boy looked down at my hand and then back at my face, as if calculating something.

I could be patient. I'd once been so patient and still, I'd gotten a squirrel to come over and grab a peanut out of my hand. It took hours, but was so worth it.

Just when I was about to curl my arms around myself to keep what little warmth was left near my body, he moved.

The boy easily crept from limb to limb without even having to look. In the last bit of distance between us, he regarded my hand as if still considering leaving.

Then his frozen hand slipped into mine and I closed my fingers around his bigger hand and smiled. For some reason, my heart wanted to burst. This was far better than the squirrel.

I was right. Standing next to him, he was taller than me by almost a head. He smelled like pine, and his face was thin and serious. Most of the boys in my class still had round, ruddy cheeks and obnoxious laughs when they did something stupid or teased each other.

Suddenly, I would have given anything to hear this boy laugh. But I didn't know any jokes, so I just gave him another reassuring smile, and led him inside.

We paused inside my room, as he looked around with a perplexed expression. It felt like bugs were crawling inside my stomach as he examined my special place.

The last time I let someone see my room, it was a girl, Devin, who didn't go to my school, but we met at one of my parents' work parties. She lived in a different town, but I wanted to be friends, so my parents let me have her over for a play date. But after she saw my room, her mouth turned into an "o" and she looked sad. Like I'd done something to hurt her.

I loved my bedroom. Toys, paint sets, and books covered nearly every inch. The big doll house filled one corner of the room and the other side had a comfy purple chair next to my bookcase. I spent hours there. But the ceiling was my favorite. My mom painted it for me. On the side where my bed was, it looked like a starry night before it morphed into pinks and oranges to a sunny day with fluffy clouds on the other side.

Devin told me I had too many toys and that I was a spoiled brat. I hurriedly offered her my favorite doll to play with to prove I wasn't. She took it, and said she got to play with two more while I could only use one since I had them all the time.

I didn't mind. She came over a few more times, but after a while she only wanted to play with my toys and didn't want to talk to me. The last time I saw her, she grabbed the scissors and started to cut and tear off the heads of some of my stuffed animals. I begged her to stop, but she screamed that I didn't deserve it. Why did I deserve good things, and she didn't? I tried to tell her she deserved good things too, but she didn't listen. My mom found us screaming and sobbing, fluff covering my entire room.

After calling Devin's mom for pickup, my mom tried to console me by saying the girl was very poor and didn't have a lot of toys. That it made her hurt inside and do things to try and fix the hurt, but that Devin's hurt also wasn't my fault. But I knew my room was something to be ashamed of. I loved it, but I never invited anyone over from school. The girls in my class were all interested in makeup and clothes now, but I still liked making up stories and playing by myself.

Suddenly petrified that the boy would tell me I was a spoiled brat and leave, I froze. As if sensing my fear, he turned toward me, his face softening for the first time. It wasn't a smile, more thoughtful and almost... protective. Then he stepped in closer to me and I knew he was telling me he wasn't going to leave.

I swallowed the lump in my throat and led him out to the hallway. I didn't turn on the lights, so we crept in the dark, down the big winding staircase, past the sitting room, library, and my dad's office until we got to the kitchen at the back of the house.

With the boy's help, we got down some hot chocolate packets. I was careful to boil water but not let the kettle scream and wake anyone up. Though I tried to get the boy to sit, he refused. He just stood at the edge of the big island, casting glances at the door as if someone might come in any moment.

I dumped extra marshmallows into his and slid the mug toward him with a smile. He looked at me, then back at the mug. Leaning over, he sniffed at it. I tried to suppress my giggle, not wanting him to feel weird, but it came out anyway. He shot me an uncertain look before his lips gave me a lopsided imitation of a return smile. My heart fluttered in response.

He bent over, his nose dipping in the whipped cream. Then he jerked up. Though he looked silly with white fluff on his face, his eyes turned sharp and focused. Steps approached down the hall.

My dad entered the kitchen, still wearing his work clothes, which were rumpled. Though it was past midnight, he'd just gotten home from work. My head snapped back to the boy, but he was gone. He'd disappeared, like magic.

"Kat. What are you doing up late?" my dad asked with a frown. I was about to explain when he caught sight of the second mug. "Is that for me?"

Deep lines creased under his tired eyes, and his thick hair was messy. His usually pale skin neared orange because one of his advisors told him a spray tan would look better on TV. But it made his skin smell weird.

I heard tense whispers in the hallways of our house for weeks that the election wasn't going well.

I nodded mutely, looking back at the spot where my new

friend disappeared. The boy didn't want to be seen. He'd been scared. And I worried if I told anyone about him, he'd be mad I didn't keep his secret. So I said, "Yes, Daddy. You can have the one with extra marshmallows."

"Thanks sweetie," he said, then he paused. "You look more like your mother every day."

My dad and I looked almost nothing alike, but we had the same upturned eye shape and thin nose. My medium brown skin, dark hair, and full lips made me look more my mom.

I smiled at first, but then I let it slide off my face. My dad hadn't looked up from the marshmallows as he said it. Something about the way he said it made me feel he didn't like that I resembled my mother. He seemed... unhappy. My fingers picked at my nightgown. Maybe if I were like the other girls and put makeup on, it would make me look different from my mom. Would he want that?

Then my dad picked up the mug, ruffled my hair, and made me promise to go back to bed once I finished my hot chocolate.

When he left, I sighed and my shoulders relaxed. I didn't realize they'd gotten all scrunched up. Then I raced to the kitchen door leading to the outside. No sign of the boy. He wasn't in the tree, either.

I couldn't fit the boy in the shoebox under my bed, but he was my biggest and best secret.

....

THE NEXT NIGHT, he was there again. Waiting, watching from the tree. It took less convincing to get him to join me this time. I got him to try hot chocolate finally, and he immediately wanted three more cups. By the third one he looked positively green in the face, and I had to keep my giggles quiet.

It went on that way the entire week. I'd wake up in the middle of the night, too excited for both my birthday and my new secret friend. Every night, I'd find him there in the tree and he'd leave before dawn.

I showed him all my toys, but he seemed particularly drawn to the picture of me and my parents by my bed. I picked it up and kissed it, explaining my mom died four years ago and I missed her so much it hurt. But she was an angel in heaven now. From his serious expression, I guessed his mommy was in heaven too, though I didn't know for sure.

Another night I took him into the living room to show him our new kittens. While petting one of the little tabbies, I explained we had to give them all away but weren't they cute?

He regarded the small fluff balls with a serious expression. When I handed him a kitten, panic crossed his face.

"You'll be okay. Just pet them gently, like this." I took his hand and showed him how.

"What do you use them for?" he asked. It was the first time I heard him speak. My stomach somersaulted, and I instantly wanted to hear his voice again.

"Use them for?" I asked. Wasn't it obvious? "You love them."

Something I said must have upset him because his face closed off from me. He bent over the kitten he held and continued to pet it the way I showed him.

I leaned in and dropped a kiss on the kitten's head. It let out a tiny mewl.

Mimicking me, the boy kissed the kitten's head and it mewled again. I got another one of those lopsided, "almost" smiles. My heart fluttered again. We took turns leaning over and kissing the kitten's head, until our faces bumped into each other.

Rubbing my forehead, I laughed too loud. I clapped my hand over my mouth and his eyes followed the movement. When I eventually dropped my hand, he continued to stare. Then he leaned forward and pressed his lips against mine.

My heart nearly jumped out of my chest. It was quick and warm. I'd seen people kiss on TV, but it felt different from what I thought it would. It was squishier. But I liked it. I couldn't stop grinning at him, and he gave me an even more lopsided smile. In the morning, I wrote three whole pages in my diary about it. It had been the best week ever.

* * *

The night before my birthday I practically sprung out of bed. I made the boy promise to come back at midnight when it was officially my birthday. We could celebrate together. I was going to show him my secret shoebox. Maybe even let him read a couple pages out of my diary if he wanted, but I would choose which ones.

I tied on my pink robe and tried to do everything I could to distract myself, but time moved impossibly slow. Not even my sketchbook could hold my attention, so I went around the room, rearranging my toys.

Five minutes before midnight, I heard something boom. The sound had come from all the way downstairs.

Maybe my dad had come home. He hadn't been home most nights, making it easier to sneak around with my big secret.

I didn't bother being quiet as I went down the stairs. Another crash, and I broke into a run, wanting to catch what was happening. Light spilled out from under my dad's office doors, so I pushed them open.

I froze, eyes widening as I tried to take everything in. Papers and books were strewn everywhere. Broken statues from the shelves were scattered on the throw rug. The double doors leading to the back terrace were wide open, the sheer curtains flapping almost violently as the breeze swept through.

My father lay slumped over his desk and the boy stood next to him, covered in my father's blood.

No. No, this wasn't right. Everything was all wrong.

There was so much blood.

My father wasn't moving. He should be moving. I didn't like how still he was.

The curtains slapped against the doors even harder and a dark, monstrous shadow swelled from them. It floated into the office.

My skin turned to ice, and I couldn't take a breath.

The dark mass twisted and turned over my father, as if inspecting him. The boy turned to look at the darkness, his lips thin and eyes hard. He wasn't afraid.

But I was terrified. I clutched my robe, feet glued to the floor, afraid if I moved, the darkness would notice me.

A strange half groan escaped my throat despite myself. I grabbed my own neck, but it was too late. The shadow jerked up. My heart pounded against my ribs. It saw me. It started toward me, and a scream got caught in my throat. I still couldn't force myself to move.

Part of me prayed I would wake up from this nightmare.

The boy stepped in between us and lifted a hand up at the monstrous being. Light shot out of his hand as he said some strange words I didn't recognize.

With a screech the shadow twisted up into the air and blew back out the doors, like a furious tornado.

I was left shaking like a leaf, still clutching at my robe. The boy turned around to face me. He set his hands on my shoulders as if he wanted to help but didn't know how.

The boy wore a pained expression as he looked back at me. Was it regret or pity I saw in his eyes?

I desperately wanted him to say something. Anything. The pressure in my chest felt like it would explode at any second as warm drops hit my face. I was crying. I tried to look past the boy to where my dad lay, still unmoving.

The boy put a hand on my face to guide me to look back at him instead. He searched my eyes and visibly swallowed. Then he lifted his hand and gently swept his palm down my forehead until it forced me to close my eyes.

I continued to shake, but he removed his hands from my shoulder and eyes. A tear slid onto my lips. Then I felt the soft pressure of his mouth on mine for the second time. The saltiness of my tears mingled with the kiss.

Then the air around me turned cold. I opened my eyes. The boy was gone.

The grandfather clock in the hall struck midnight, announcing my eleventh birthday and the death of my father.

Get your copy now!

THE FIVE ORDERS SERIES

Read the rest of The Five Orders Series to see Leonidas in his first appearance, and find out how the hellmouth opened up.

The action-packed, steamy, slow-burn, paranormal romance is now a complete series.

Read on for a preview of Book One: Prophecy Girl.

A LETTER FROM THE AUTHOR

Dear Reader,

Thank you for reading!

I loved revisiting the Five Orders series, and finally giving Leonidas his own story. There are so many of the characters in that series that are begging for their own story. So let me know if there is anyone you want to read more about!

Loved this book? Consider leaving a review as it helps other readers discover my books.

Want to make sure you never miss a release or any bonus content I have coming down the pipeline?

Make sure to join Holly's Hotspot, my newsletter, and I'll send you a FREE ebook right away!

You can also find me on my website www.hollyroberds.com and I hang out on social media.

Instagram: http://instagram.com/authorhollyroberds

Facebook: www.facebook.com/hollyroberdsauthorpage/

And closest to my black heart is my reader fan group, Holly's Hellions. Become a Hellion. Raise Hell. www.facebook.com/groups/hollyshellions/

Cheers!
Holly Roberds

WANT A FREE BOOK?

J oin Holly's Newsletter Holly's Hot Spot at www.
hollyroberds.com and get the Five Orders Prequel
Novella, The Knight Watcher, for FREE!

Plus you'll get exclusive sneak peaks, giveaways, fun lil' nuggets, and notifications when new books come out. Woot!

ACKNOWLEDGMENTS

Thank you to my editors Jo and Christie who find all kinds of jewels like "viral" when I meant to write "virile." Thank you to my friend and beta reader, Sarah Urquhart, are the best emotional support Canadian. Even when you are yelling at me about removing the smutty language. (*hands up* I put it back!)

Also thank you to Erin Cameron Poletti for casting a critical medical eye over this baby, so I stop sticking needles in arteries where they don't belong.

This was a tough one to write and I so appreciate my friends and family who reminded me this is my true joy, even though I have to get through the tough parts.

And thank you to l'husbun for acting as a mirror for me and helping illuminate my toxic writing patterns so I don't torture myself and you. Way to make me a better, more self-aware human being! *fist pump*

Last but not least, thank you to the readers who started with me in The Five Orders series to come full circle to this. I hope you enjoyed it.

ABOUT THE AUTHOR

Holly started out writing Buffy the Vampire Slayer and Terminator romantic fanfiction before spinning off into her own fantastic worlds with apocalyptic stakes.

Recently relocated to New Hampshire from Colorado, Holly is exploring the possibilities of become a witch (as one must consider when living in New England) and is hard at work implementing the word "wicked" into her vernacular.

She lives with her husband whose handsome looks are only out done by his charming and wicked supportive personality.

Two surly house rabbits supervise this writer, to make sure she doesn't spend all of her time watching Buffy reruns.

For more sample chapters, news, and more, visit www.
hollyroberds.com